© 2024 Robyn Singer

**Robyn Singer**
The True Adventurer

All rights reserved. No part of this publication may be reproduced, stored in a retrieval system or transmitted in any form or by any means, electronic, mechanical, photocopying, recording or otherwise without the prior permission of the copyright holder.

**Published by:** Cinnabar Moth Publishing LLC
Santa Fe, New Mexico

**Cover Design by:** Ira Geneve

**ISBN-13:** 978-1-962308-22-9

Library of Congress Control Number: 2024936860

# The True Adventurer

ROBYN SINGER

Dedicated to my Goblin Gal

# CHAPTER 1: LAYLA

*Good morning, human!*

I yawned as I sat up in my bed and stretched my arms out, reaching for the sun. "Good morning, Juri."

Leaping out of bed and greeting the day, I pulled my curtains open to reveal the beautiful sky. It was a perfect, light shade of magenta that made the stunning cobalt sun stand out even more than it usually did as it rose.

Proquenna was a beautiful world, with fabulous flora and adorable fauna, and Fexxa University's campus was the prettiest spot on the whole planet. Every student here was an elite artist, and we were all permitted to put up our pieces wherever we wanted. The shelves in my own dorm room were, of course, filled exclusively with some of my awesome creations, but once I stepped out into the dormitory halls, and especially once I stepped outside the building, I couldn't turn around without seeing a masterpiece of a painting or sculpture created by one of my peers or instructors.

It had been the perfect environment for me to study and truly hone my craft. Thanks to the instruction of Ms. Bunny, the reading assignments others might have skimmed through, and the vast resources offered by the school, I wasn't the same glassblower I'd been a year ago.

This school was everything I'd always dreamed of. By the time I graduated in three years, I was going to be renowned as one of the best glassblowers in the universe. I may have valued the craft over gidgits, but if I did get super rich off of my work, I'd be able to rub it in g-gma's face. Hopefully, she'd gotten over the whole blackmail thing and wasn't plotting to kill me.

*What are you standing around for?* Juri asked. *Get dressed and go get us some foooooood!*

I sighed with a smile, continuing to look out my window. Even if she'd taken some getting used to, I was even more grateful for Juri than I was for my education. If Aarif hadn't put her machine parts inside me, the wounds I'd sustained from the fight with Kaya would have killed me.

I still had no idea why I was able to talk to her. I'd done some research into robotics and cybernetics, but I hadn't found any leads. I'd also tried calling Aarif a few times, but he never picked up. He wasn't himself anymore. Still, the thing I was probably most grateful for was that Juri was a girl. I could only imagine how badly my dysphoria would strike back if I had to share a brain with a boy.

"Don't worry, I'm craving cafeteria veggie sausages as much as you. I'm just appreciating the day."

*The day will be here… well, all day. Food! Now!*

Giggling, I took off my pajamas and changed into one of my flowy, tie-dyed dresses. I washed my face, put on a small layer of organic, cruelty-free makeup, took my estrogen, and grabbed my bag before heading out the door.

Living in Sculpture Dorm-C, the cafeteria was about a seven-minute walk away.

Compared to the laps Yael used to have me run around the old school, that was nothing. Plus, I never got tired of admiring pieces positioned between my starting point and my destination, like Yeray's "Journey into the Volcano" and Tea's "Gigantess". The craftsmanship involved in the latter, especially, was something I could admire for years.

While I walked, I listened to my EZ Street playlist. It mostly consisted of their latest album, but I'd also stuck in a few of my personal favorite songs. I would never get tired of "Always Like a Bridge."

Arriving at the cafeteria, Pena and Rachel ran up to me, waiting for me like usual. My besties had big grins spread across their faces and were dressed similarly to me, though Pena wore a tie-dyed crop top and bell bottoms instead of a dress.

"Layla!"

I was enrolled at the school under my real name, and my real name was how my friends knew me. I used to think I'd have to disguise myself and enroll myself in art school under a fake identity, but after everything that went down, my bounty was removed. If Molina had meant that as a "Sorry I turned my back on you and became an evil overlord" gift, she really should have just sent a card.

"Morning, ladies!" I cheered, hugging them both. "You ready for the protest later?"

"Totally!" Pena replied. "This awful war needs to end, and we're gonna do our part."

"I totally get why the Utozin Authority and independent worlds don't want to surrender, but they have to see that they can't win," Rachel followed. "All fighting back is doing at this point is causing more innocents to die."

I nodded. Under different circumstances, I might have agreed with them. But unlike them, I intimately knew the people who were responsible for all this violence and death. On both sides. Whether the universe wound up a totalitarian fascist state or a capitalist oligarchy, the suffering wouldn't end when the war did.

Of course, I'd kept my mouth shut about my connections with the current empress and chancellor. I loved Rachel and Pena, but they were safer not knowing more than they needed to about my past.

*War schmore!* Juri shouted. *Get us the goods!*

Juri had a very predictable pattern. She'd ask for food and then once we were fed, she'd ask for belly rubs. It was a damn good thing I liked getting belly rubs too, and that my besties with benefits were happy to provide them.

After grabbing our food and sitting down at our usual table in the middle of the cafeteria, we got to talking about our current projects. A few of the only students who hadn't already gotten one came up to me while we were talking so they could get an autograph. I was used to being admired from my years as a cheerleader, but I still blushed at how confident everyone was that I was going to be a superstar. After my Freshman Final Showcase, I'd had to sign over two hundred autographs in a day.

Once I was finished eating, I couldn't stay long. I only had one class today, Art History 102, but it was scheduled bright and early. I was one of the only students who regularly signed up for morning classes since most everyone else usually had hangovers or drug trips to sleep off. Artists loved to party. I did too, but I also never wanted to miss the sunrise.

After class, I had an hour to kill before the protest on the quad. I thought about heading to the workshop to get some work done on my secret project, but I decided that could wait till tonight. Instead, I went back to my room. Rachel had starred in a play a couple of weeks ago and she'd been begging me to check it out. She was an abstract painter first and foremost, but she also enjoyed acting as a hobby and wanted to make sure she'd done a good job.

"What do you think, Juri?" I asked, fifteen minutes into the play as I munched on hazelnut chocolate-covered popcorn. "A story about a blind woman, a deaf woman, and a mute woman who all love each other but don't know how to tell the others? Pretty romantic."

Needs more cute boy dogs!

"You say that about everything we watch."

Because you never show me anything with cute boy dogs! I was never able to get the Foodgivers to show me them, and now that I have someone I can talk to, I can't even get you to show me them. A girl could swear you're being discriminatory against DRRRRRRRRRRR.

"Uh, everything okay?"

Juri barked at the top of her lungs. *Sorry about that. We just got a message. An encrypted one.*

I fell back over onto my bed, tossing my tablet to the side as I let out a groan. "Shun. I told her to stop contacting me."

Juri growled with hate. *She took away the Foodgivers. I want to eat her face.*

"I know, girl. I know."

Emperor Kaybell may have started the war, but that never would have happened if not for Shun. Kaya was our friend. She'd changed. And then in an instant, Shun undid all the progress she'd made. I wasn't sure if Molina became a dictator because of Yael's death or if that was who she'd been on the inside all along, but either way, she and her new wife wouldn't have been able to maintain their reign without Kaya.

I hated Shun. From lying to us for years about who she really was, to pretending to be my friend, to enabling all these atrocities, she was despicable. But in her mind, she'd done nothing wrong. She'd only done what she felt was best for the Authority. An Authority where she'd been raised in secret as their greatest prodigy. An Authority she'd never stopped serving. An Authority that she'd been given command over in wartime.

In her sick mind, she had a chance in Hell of getting me to work for her. Shun may have been far smarter than she'd let on, her entire "brawn over brains" thing having always been an act, but she knew my aid would still be invaluable in winning the war.

Neither Molina nor Kaya had ever reached out to me for help. Again, I didn't have a clue what was going through Molina's head, but in the months following Yael's death, I kept waiting for Kaya to call me. Maybe if I'd joined her when she'd given me the chance, I could have saved her and prevented all the death.

*Let's get back to the play,* Juri said. *There are no cute dog boys, but it's better than thinking about herrrrrrrr.*

I nodded, sat back up, and grabbed my tablet. With the rest of the free time at my disposal, I finished watching the first act of the play. It wasn't the best, but Rachel's performance in her small role was fantastic. I had full confidence in her ability to make it as a painter, but acting would be a realistic fallback for her.

The quad was already packed when I got there. Hundreds of students, and at least a few professors, in colorful outfits were standing underneath the blazing sun. Some held computer-generated signs with the word "War" with an "X" through it, while others held hand-painted signs that depicted people from different worlds holding hands as they all bowed before Molina and Kaybell, the empire's motto of "All Worlds Under Cykeb" written underneath. Still others had brought their guitars to sing anti-war songs. It sucked that none of the guitar-playing guys here were boy-band-level cute, because they had some real talent.

"Here you are," Pena said, handing me a sign. "Great turnout, right?"

"Totally," I said.

"I wonder if we'll get as much attention as that protest on Flownon-7 last month," Rachel said. "They were directly acknowledged by Chancellor Shun."

I clicked my tongue. "I mean, yeah, but she shut down the university where the protest took place."

"A necessary sacrifice," my friends said in unison. "Jinx!"

I shook my head, continuing to smile. From a certain point of view, they weren't wrong. Once the war was over, the number of immediate casualties would drop significantly. Their only mistake was thinking that one party or the other needed to win this war.

"Rachel!"

Spinning around, my smile faded as Rachel's ex-boyfriend Gadthorp stomped into our personal space. Wearing a minimalist white blazer with thin streaks of color etched across it and matching pants, his outfit gave off a much different aura than his tense face and stiff body language.

*Uggggh!* Juri groaned. *This motherfucker.*

Rachel pouted and crossed her arms at the sight of her ex, Pena and I mimicking her in solidarity. "What do you want, Gadthorp?"

Gadthorp cracked his knuckles, unable to keep his eyes focused on us and moving his head around. "I've been doing a lot of thinking, and I've realized you had every right to dump me. I fucked up so bad. But I've been doing a lot of self-reflection and growth, and I just… it would mean a lot if you'd take me back. Please. Give me another chance."

Pena and I turned our heads to Rachel, anticipating her response. I'd never particularly liked Gadthorp, but I'd never see Rachel happier than when they were together. Of course, I'd also never seen her more sad and angry than when she caught Gadthorp cheating on her.

"He's stupid rich," Pena whispered. "And hot as ever."

"He also turned out to be a huge jerk," I whispered.

Rachel looked at each of us before looking back at Gadthorp. She then turned her nose up at him. "For the sake of every other girl on this campus, I hope you really have learned to be better. But I'm not interested in moving backward." Gadthorp's face crumpled. "I'm sorry, but I can't risk getting my heart broken again."

Gadthorp grit his teeth and clenched his fists as he shook his head. "No. Please. Just give me one more chance. I need you. I love you."

Pena was clearly won over by the declaration, a wide grin spreading across her face as she pulled her hands to her heart, but Rachel's expression and posture didn't change.

"If that's true, then you'll leave me alone. Please."

Gadthorp's whole body shook as he lunged his arm out and grabbed Rachel's wrist.

"Hey!" Rachel cried. "Let go of me!"

"Not until you take me back!"

"You just said you learned to be better!" Pena said, her own infatuation having finally been obliterated. "Listen to her!"

"Stay out of this!"

"Please! You're hurting me!"

Screams continued to fly back and forth. There was likely something I could have said to defuse the situation, but my mind turned to what Yael would do. There was no situation she couldn't talk her way out of, but at the same time, there was often a much quicker, more effective method of solving a problem.

First, to get this creep away from my friend, I threw my sign down and elbowed him in the heart, knocking him back and stunning him as my girls gasped. Then, to make sure he got the message, I sped behind him, grabbed him underneath his arms, and threw him down into the ground with a German suplex.

*Yeah!* Juri cheered. *That was awesome!*

I dusted my hands off as I stared down at the now unconscious jackass. "I doubt he'll be putting his hands on you again. You okay Rachel?"

Rachel and Pena looked at me in horror, as if I'd killed the guy. "Layla, what the Hell was that?"

"Yeah. Was that some weird move your creepy grandma taught you?"

"Um, yeah," I lied. "No need to look so freaked out, guys. It's just self-defense."

Rachel shook her head. "Violence is never the answer."

"He was hurting you!"

"Ever heard the old expression about an eye for an eye?"

I had. Yael thought it was bullshit.

"I'm sorry I scared you," I said, picking up my sign. "You know I'm not proud of my heritage or what I know because of it. Can we move on and forget about this?"

Pena's jaw dropped. "Girl, his unconscious body is still two feet away from us."

Shit. Right.

I smiled brightly. "I'll call a nurse."

The rest of the protest didn't go great, with no media attention and my friends icing me out the entire time. Rachel could have at least said, "thank you". If they disapproved of what I'd done to Gadthorp, they definitely weren't gonna like what I was planning. What was already in motion.

That night, I went to my personal workshop. I had a lot of projects due for classes I needed to finish, but I wasn't here to work on any of them. I was here to work on the special project I'd been developing for a while.

On the surface, it looked like a normal silver blowpipe with gold highlights. However, on the inside, there was microtechnology the likes of which the universe had never seen. Which was exactly why I'd been stuck building the thing for so long. I had no training as an engineer, but I was a quick study, and by my estimation, I'd be done in a month.

Maybe it would have been nice to continue to live as a normal artist. It was all I'd ever wanted, and I truly loved the campus that had become my home. But I couldn't ignore my past, or everything going on around me in the present. Not when I had the power to do something about it.

Molina, Aarif, P'Ken, Shun, Griffin, Marcos, and Kaya. They were my friends and my professors. They were my family. Now, we were all separated, and, in their own ways, each of them had fallen.

Yael Pavnick wasn't a good person, but she wouldn't have just stood back and done nothing about this.

"Holy shit," I said in awe. "Juri, I think I've got it."

What?! Really?!

"Yeah, I'm shocked too. I guess I underestimated myself."

I picked up my pipe and swung it around. "Say hello to the Glass Striker Model 1. Potentially the most dangerous handheld weapon ever invented."

I wasn't Yael. I was better. I had different ideas for each member of my old family than she would have had. We had different priorities. But my heart was in the same place as hers would have been.

I was going to protect the universe from the empire, I was going to punish those who'd caused so much pain and suffering, and I was going to save Kaya.

Yael Pavnick hadn't been a hero, but I would be.

"Come on, Juri," I said, strapping the Glass Striker to my back. "Let's get to work."

# CHAPTER 2: KAYA

"What's our ETA, General?"

"We should be reaching Caldey-Cocoon's atmosphere in twenty-five minutes, Princess."

I twirled my hair around my finger. "Splendid."

The voyage from Cykeb had been peaceful. I'd had ample time to listen to music and shop for art in my room, torture the prisoners I'd brought along with me in the brig, and take advantage of the other amenities my ship offered.

The *Winjolla*, named after my departed, beloved aunts, was second only to my mothers' flagship, *Ricochet Supreme*, in terms of grandeur. 2400 meters in diameter, it was crewed by a staff of 15,000, all of whom I was free to terrorize to my heart's content, with 30,000 ground troops also living on board.

I'd gotten to design every aspect of my ship, from its weaponry, which was capable of leveling small continents, to its torture chamber, which I prided myself on being the most nightmarish chamber of horrors ever devised—putting even Mother's past works to shame—to its spa, swimming pool, light squash court, juice bar, and karaoke studio.

The only thing my ship lacked was someone to enjoy all of this with, but my mothers rarely ever left the palace, and there was no one else worthy of my time. I'd tried forcing some of my lessers to have fun with me in the past, but the only enjoyable parts of those experiences had been when I'd blown their brains out. Being better than and above everyone else could really suck.

On the bright side, I was almost 14. In just over one year, I'd be allowed to make the members of EZ Street my personal concubines. Then I'd never be lonely again.

Plus, the highlight of these trips was always the destination, not the journey. As the crown princess of The Holy Cykebian Empire, and the most advanced cyborg in existence, I had the honor of serving as my mothers' ultimate sword. If a rebellion took place that our soldiers couldn't quash themselves, or if initial conquest was met with more resistance than initially anticipated, I was deployed to handle it. I never failed my mothers. I never would.

"Princess, we've arrived."

Grinning from ear to ear, I rose from my chair in the center of the bridge. "Beam me down. I'll let you know when to deploy the troops across the planet's surface."

"Yes, Princess. Understood, Princess."

My helmsman did as he was told and a moment later, I was standing in the middle of Caldey-Cocoon's capital city: Jeradoth.

The blood-red sky matched the dirt beneath my boots. Their architecture was cylindrical, all of their buildings the same sickening shade of green. The air stank of cold macaroni and cheese. From what I'd read, their only major export was middle- quality feathers.

I'd only been here five seconds, but I couldn't fathom what about this pathetic world its people treasured so much that they wouldn't want to be a part of the empire. It wasn't as if I was complaining, though. If every world submitted immediately, I'd never get to have any fun.

These people couldn't even fight for themselves. All their hope was in a single warrior. A cyborg who believed himself my better, fighting for Cocoon independence. What a joke. If we didn't want this rock, the Utozins would just be snatching it up for themselves.

Floating up above the city, I charged up energy blasts in my hands. When I was looking down at the population of 20,000 like the ants they were, I fired my lasers. In an instant, the largest skyscrapers in the city were completely annihilated alongside everyone inside them.

I couldn't help but laugh as I breathed in the ashes of the dead, impertinent vermin, and listened to the haunted screams of the populace.

Now, I just had to wait. With this much death and destruction on display, the planet's "hero" would be showing up at any minute.

Any minute.

Any minute.

*Any min*--fuck I hated this part.

"You!"

I exhaled, glad that my target had finally shown up. Didn't he know how rude it was to keep a princess waiting?

"Hi there," I giggled. "Like what I've done with the place?"

During my first tour of the universe, when there was killing to be done, I'd worn the special combat suit I'd had made. It was efficient, it hid my identity, and most importantly, it looked super cool and intimidating. When I wore it, it was almost like I was a different person. Like I was trying to be someone else.

Not anymore. Dressed in my spotless and pressed military uniform, I proudly showed off my identity to all who earned my wrath. Above all else, my time with Yael had taught me to be true to myself. No matter how awful that truth was.

"You monster," my target said, floating in the sky a dozen yards away from me. He was dressed in a white cloak with black tridents plastered all over it, and while his face was obscured by his hood, I could see that it was covered in scars. "You just murdered thousands of innocent people. How can you be so casual?"

"Because I'm a god, duh," I told the fool. "I'm free to do whatever I want with filth like you and your people." I pursed my lips together. "Honestly, you should be blaming yourself. If you hadn't killed all the troops we had stationed on this world, I wouldn't even be here."

The cloaked man growled. "You're no god. You're a demon." The cybernetics in his arms and eyes glowed green. "Caldey-Cocoon has maintained its independence for over 1,000 years! It will not fall to the empire now!"

"You wouldn't believe how many times I've heard that line," I laughed.

"Quit your guffawing," he growled. "The innocents you just murdered will be the last lives you ever take. Today, for my friends and family, I break the empire's ultimate sword!"

"Heard that one, too. You're not very original, huh?" I shrugged. "Go ahead and take a free shot."

One other thing I'd learned from my time with Yael? A good fight could be as satisfying as the bloodiest kill.

The cloaked man flew at me, layer after layer of metal growing around his arms. Pulling his arm back, a flash from it momentarily blinded me, and in that instant, I was punched across the face and sent crashing down into the rubble I'd created.

I moaned as I hit the ground, the people cheering for their

hero. My flawless uniform had been tarnished, and blood had been drawn from my face. Oh yeah, this was gonna be fun.

I stood up as the cloaked man met me on the ground. "That actually hurt a little. Impressive. What's your name?"

"Horatio Hagidashie," he answered, pounding his mechanized fists together. "And I'm just getting started."

I brushed my hair back into place. It was proof of the empire's superiority over all other cultures how we'd progressed technology over the past six years. Where once genetic enhancements and cybernetics had been outlawed, now, if you weren't a genetically engineered cyborg, you were worth less than nothing in a real fight. Our enemies had only become so advanced because of our own advancements. Of course, no one in the empire was made as strong as me, and none of our enemies were even close to building a warrior who could pose a real threat.

I was the only one who could be trusted with this much power. I was the only one Mother trusted.

Horatio charged at me, the poor fool thinking he'd actually be able to land a hit without me letting him. While he fired off a flurry of lightning-fast punches, I popped out my katars and danced around his attacks, humming "Always Like a Bridge" as I did so.

"Are you singing?!" the muscular rodent asked in an outrage. "I am the hope of the universe! Do not underestimate me!"

Not halting his attack for a second, two more robotic arms popped out of his back; blood, flesh, and skin flying off of him. With four fists now swinging at me, it was a blast dodging all of them, not being able to waste an attosecond of thought or movement. Of course, the best part was how Horatio growled in irritation at his inability to hit me.

Still, I had no information on what other tricks he had up his sleeve. If he pulled out anything else while I was playing with him like this, the tide could turn in his favor. I couldn't have that.

I leaped up into the air. Horatio chased after me, but he was too damn slow. While he was racing upward, I flew around and behind him and sliced off his extra limbs. His screams of agony were music to my ears.

"I would have cut off your real arms too, but we haven't gotten to that part yet," I said before kicking him into the dirt. "After all, we need an audience."

The civilians who hadn't yet fled the scene ran away as quickly as their normal legs would carry them. They were like scurrying little rats.

I pressed down on my earpiece. "General, send the camera crew and make sure they're broadcasting to the entire planet."

"*At once, Princess.*"

"Camera crew?" Horatio panted. "What are you up to?"

I shook my lowered head as the camera crew appeared all around us. "So stupid. So, so stupid." I looked back up with a smirk. "Your people look to you as a hero. You even put on this whole, over-dramatic heroic performance. It wouldn't just be enough for them to hear about your death. They need to see it. Hope must be extinguished."

I smiled and gave a giggle for the cameras. "Hello, people of Caldey-Cocoon! I am Princess Kaya Langstone Bythora, and as of this moment, myself, as well as Emperor Kaybell Kose Bythora and Empress Molina Bythora Langstone are your gods. Your savage world will return to having the privilege of being a part of The Holy Cykebian Empire, and worship of my mothers and me is once again mandatory. While your planet will become a better, happier place, you will be punished for your previous rebellion, and as such—"

"Silence!" Horatio rose to his feet and wrapped his remaining arms around me. "You're faster than me, but my grip can crush anything. Die, demon!"

This was too perfect. It was good for the cameras to catch one last struggle on the hero's part. I barely felt his grip. No one's grip was stronger than the empire's.

Releasing a blast of electricity, I sent Horatio flying off of me. As I walked over to him, he shook on the ground.

"This is your hero, Caldey-Cocoon! The man who was supposed to protect you! But as you can now see, the empire's strength is absolute! We are the only ones who can protect you!"

"I'm not... finished," Horatio said, coughing up blood.

"Yes. You are." I stomped my boot down on his face, crushing his jaw. "Lick my boots."

"N... never. You can kill me... but I'll never submit."

I pressed down harder on his chin. "Let me rephrase my demand as a threat then. Lick my boots, or I'll finish what I started and raze the rest of this city.

Moments like this were exactly why I'd had to kill Yael. No matter how much it hurt to do so, I knew she'd only ever be disgusted by me. I liked to think that, if nothing else, she'd have at least appreciated what a badass I was.

Horatio trembled. He now faced not only the inevitable writhing pain that faced all who opposed me but also the question of whether his personal morals or convictions were worth more than the lives of thousands. There had been a few strange souls who had indeed refused to break under pressure, but I'd been able to see from the start that while he may have been pretty strong, there was nothing special about Horatio himself.

His head quivering, he licked my boot. The camera crew snickered along with me. "You know, I don't think you're cleaning the scum off my boot fast enough."

Gripping Horatio's wrist, I ripped his right arm off, blood splattering all over me. Horatio screamed in anguish, the cybernetics and enhancements that had gotten him so far now betraying him by keeping him conscious and forcing him to endure unimaginable pain.

"Keep licking!" I screamed through gritted teeth, tossing his severed arm aside. "This is what's coming for all of you who do not submit, people of Caldey-Cocoon! Your lives will be made better than ever as you serve the empire, but first, you must be punished for your insubordination! All worlds under Cykeb!"

"All worlds under Cykeb!" my camera crew cheered.

I licked the blood off my lips as the light left Horatio's eyes.

———

Seated in what would soon be the new magistrate's office, I sipped some of the special black bean tea I'd brought with me. Shows of force were fun, but they could get my blood pumping a little too much. The tea helped calm my nerves. Here and at home.

"Update?"

General Fraizer bowed his head. "The planet has been nearly entirely retaken, Princess. Officers, general infantry, death squads, and members of the protectorate legion have occupied all sixteen major cities and all forty-eight villages with populations over 1,000."

"Excellent," I said, setting my teacup down on a saucer. "My mothers will be most pleased with such a rapid pacification. Well done, General."

"You honor me with your words, Princess."

I did.

"Are the remainder of our troops gathered outside?"

"As requested."

Picking up my fork, I took a bite of blackberry cheesecake. Conquering worlds also worked up an appetite, which was why I never left home without the best chefs Cykeb had to offer. They were perhaps the most valuable vermin of all.

Wiping my face, I uncrossed my legs, stood up, and strutted out of the office, General Fraizer following behind me. It was customary for me to give a speech after a successful conquest, and while no one should have had any problem waiting for me, the sooner I got off this piece of shit planet, the better.

Stepping out onto the balcony, standing underneath the maroon night sky, I folded my hands behind my back, hardened my face, and looked down at thousands of my armored soldiers. At the sight of me, each and every one of them dropped to one knee.

"For thousands of years, The Holy Cykebian Empire has displayed its superiority over all other cultures! We are smarter! We are stronger! We are elite! Only once all worlds are in our grip will perfection in the universe be achieved! For each world we conquer, we bring safety, security, and certainty. In exchange, all we take is their unquestioning loyalty. A generous deal! After all, only we know what's best for them. And yet, there continue to be worlds, worlds like this, that resist our benevolence! For that, there must come punishments."

I reached out my arms to the sides. "Punishments which you, my loyal soldiers, must carry out. We shall give Caldey-Cocoon our usual treatment! For 24 hours, pillage and kill to your heart's content! This shall be a day this world will never forget!"

I jutted out my elbows to the sides. "All worlds under Cykeb!"

"All worlds under Cykeb!" my soldiers chanted in unison, saluting back at me. "All worlds under Cykeb! All worlds under Cykeb!"

Turning around on my heels, I walked back into the quaint office. I didn't like telling the soldiers they were more than they were, but it was good for morale. And while I had my own ideas for how worlds like this should be punished, I couldn't question Mother's instructions.

"Princess, won't you be leading the massacre?" General Fraizer asked, continuing to act as my lapdog.

I sat back down at the desk and took another sip of tea, putting my legs up on the desk.

"I'd love to, but I really must be getting home. I have a birthday party to attend."

# CHAPTER 3: LAYLA

After Yael was killed, Aarif, P'Ken, and I split up her belongings. I told the others it all should have gone to them, but P'Ken assured me Yael wouldn't have wanted me to go empty-handed. That had left me with a small fortune, a healthy amount of wrestling merchandise, some dresses, and my own personal ship: *Cascade*.

The gargantuan ship used to belong to P'Ken, but she told me where she was going, she wouldn't need it. If I'd known what she'd meant at the time, I would have stopped her. I hadn't been taking very good care of the ship, so there was dust and cobwebs all over the place, but the weapons systems seemed to be functioning perfectly. *Cascade* was primarily built for combat, and it could do toe to toe with nearly anyone.

*But they never taught you how to operate the weapons?* Juri asked, not long after we left Proquenna. *Really?!*

"It never seemed like there'd be any point," I said, leaning back in my chair with my feet up on the command console, munching on a piece of celery. "Don't worry, it's not like anyone knows we're plotting treason. We shouldn't even have a reason to use the weapons."

*I hope you're right.* Juri howled repeatedly before panting. *I don't want anything stopping us from seeing Foodgiver!*

I nodded. "We need Aarif if we're gonna make this work. Just remember he may not be like he used to."

Juri practically laughed at that. *Foodgiver never changed. Not really. He just has moods.*

The poor girl was in denial. After Aarif had screened one too many of my calls, I'd tracked him down to make sure he was okay. I was fully expecting to find him now in the same state I'd found him then. I hadn't spoken to him at that point. There'd have been no point. Even now, while I was fairly confident in my ability to convince him to help me, I wasn't sure there was any hope of bringing back my old professor.

Before leaving the planet, I'd called his watch. Like always, he didn't pick up, but I was able to trace the signal to Toz. It wasn't Aarif's home world, but it was where he'd lived on the streets after he got out of jail. It was where he'd met Yael.

*You should really let me do the talking when we get there.*

"Juri, I love you, but I have no way of knowing if I give you control of the body that you won't keep it for yourself to chase cute dog girls."

*It does sound fun… but no! You can trust me, human! Juri promises!*

I sighed. "We'll see."

As we neared the planet, which was 99% sand, I received a call on my watch. It was Pena.

I'd left without saying goodbye, and even though they'd been mad at me, she and Rachel were probably worried sick that I hadn't shown up for breakfast. I wanted to tell them I was okay, but I couldn't. I had to keep them safe and out of this business. If all went well, I'd be back to sipping asparagus milkshakes with them in no time, but if things went south, I couldn't have them going down with me.

I landed *Cascade* on the outskirts of a small town called Fif. Consisting of only about two dozen or so buildings, there wouldn't have even been room for me to land within the town itself.

Getting off my ship and entering the town, I stuck out like a sore thumb. A hot girl in a bright, tie-dyed, organic silk dress with a blowpipe strapped to her back who smelled like a rose didn't exactly mesh with a drab, brown, and weary environment inhabited by dirt-covered, smelly outcasts who dressed in the cheapest clothes they could afford to make, and many who, from what I could tell, suffered from one form of physical deformity or another.

As I walked down the street, sand getting in my boots, I kept an eye out for the tavern, as all of the town's residents who were hanging out outside had their eyes squarely on me.

Especially the men. God, men were gross.

*Not all men!* Juri shouted. *Foodgiver is a man!*

"One, never say "not all men". Two, you'd know what I mean if guy dogs had always been weird around you."

*Girl dogs hit on me lots. I liked the attention!*

"Yeah, that sounds about right."

It didn't take long to find the tavern. Pinching my nose, I went right in. The place wasn't packed, relative to its small size, with seven patrons present. One of them, seated at the far end of the bar, caught my eye instantly. He may have grown out long, poofy hair that looked as greasy as a meat burger, he may have grown a beard that was even less well kept, and he may have developed wrinkles, put on thirty pounds, and smelled like piss, but I'd recognize Aarif and all his tattoos anywhere.

"Professor!"

Foodgiver!

Every guy present who was sober enough to be aware of their surroundings turned their attention to me, just like the guys outside had. The sooner I could get Aarif out of here, the better.

As I ran up to the disheveled mess of a man I'd once known as the best engineer in the universe, he chugged back the remaining contents of his mug and slammed it down.

"Another." While the bartender refilled his glass, Aarif turned to me, looking me up and down. "You get a bad case of stupid or something?"

Not the greeting I'd expected.

I smiled, looking into his tired, bag-adjacent eyes. "Aarif, it's me. Layla."

Aarif gave a thumbs-up as the refill was finished. "I'm not so wasted I don't recognize you, kid. I'm just surprised you'd ever come here."

What's wrong with him? Why isn't he happy to see us?

"Shh, girl," I whispered. "I'm not sure I understand."

Sipping his drink, Aarif narrowed his eyes and glared at me. "You think I can't recognize that look in your eyes?"

"My eyes?"

He took a much longer sip of his drink, a foam mustache forming above his lip. "If you were here to pay your old pal a friendly visit, I'd tell you to have a seat so we could catch up and share a drink. But whatever you're planning, I don't want any part of it."

How does he know why we're here?!

It had taken me a second, but I had an idea.

Not about to take no for an answer, I dropped the smile and then dropped my butt into a seat next to Aarif's. The stool was stickier than any part of *Ricochet*.

"I've missed you," I said. "And you know I don't drink."

Aarif licked up the foam dripping down his baggy face. "Missed you, too." He sighed. "I'm guessing you're not going to take no for an answer so you can give me your sales pitch to, I dunno, break Marcos out of prison, get revenge on the bitches who betrayed us, or something equally ridiculous."

It hurt. It fucking hurt seeing a man who I'd respected so much and who'd been a daily part of my life reduced to this. Juri's whimpers were making it clear she felt the same way. If Yael were here, she would have slapped the shit out of him for thinking anything was impossible or that leaving members of the family behind was an option.

No matter how flattered I was that he saw Yael in me, though, I wasn't her.

I leaned in closer. "I want you to help me bring down the entire Cykebian Empire."

That wasn't even the entirety of what I had in mind, but it was enough to get the intoxicated Aarif to laugh hysterically, fall off his stool, and roll around in the filth.

I don't… I don't want to see this, human.

"Bear with it, girl," I whispered.

It took a minute, but Aarif was able to stop laughing and regain enough of his senses to stand up and sit back down, now with a mocking grin on his face.

"Please. Continue."

I sneered back at him. "Millions of innocent people have died in this war. Millions more will die before it's over. And it's all our fault this is happening."

"I'd be more inclined to blame the tyrannical warlords, but go on."

"I set the precedent for Yael having students. If it wasn't for me, Griffin and Marcos wouldn't have gotten wrapped up in all of this, and Shun wouldn't have gotten the opportunity to infiltrate Yael's operation. And if she'd never met Yael, or if any of us supposed geniuses had been able to pick up on her deception, Kaya wouldn't have—"

"Don't." Aarif cut me off, sneering back at me. "Don't you dare put what that little monster did on me."

"She's not a monster. She's a kid with too much power who got overwhelmed and scared and made a big mistake."

"Right. Say, those millions of dead innocents you're so concerned about? How many has she personally butchered?"

"She's 13."

"And with more blood on her hands than warlords ten times her age." "She's only doing her mothers' bidding. And she's the spitting image of both of them."

"She needs our help!"

"She took everything from me!" Aarif's face shook with the rest of his body as tears formed in his eyes and streamed down his cheeks. "She took everything from me."

As in sync as ever, Juri was crying too.

With a deep breath, I reached out and softly held Aarif's leg, dropping the sneer. I couldn't blame him for being angry. Not only had he been the least close to Kaya out of all of us, but while I'd had a new life to start, a new life I'd been eager to start for years, he'd been left with nothing. Kaya killed Yael, and injured Juri and me to the point that putting us together was the only way to keep us alive. With Molina's betrayal, P'Ken heading back to her mom to recover on her own, and my own departure following suit, he'd lost his career, his entire family, and everything important to him in a matter of days.

I squeezed his leg, holding back my own tears. "I miss her, too."

Aarif nodded rapidly, wiping his tears and snot on his arm. "Yeah. Yeah, I know."

"You said it yourself. I have a plan. A pretty good fucking plan if I say so myself. I promise you, we can take out Emperor Kaybell, we can take out Molina and Shun, we can rescue Marcos, we can end the war, and, yes, we can save Kaya. But I can't do any of that without you."

Aarif looked into my eyes as he hugged himself, ceasing his shaking. Was he trying to read how genuine I was in my confidence, or was he just trying to see Yael?

He cast his head down with an all-too-quick laugh. "It's still burned into my eyes, you know? *Ricochet* landed outside the school. P'Ken and I were crying over losing Juri, but hey, at least Yael had made it back okay. Just like she'd promised me she would. We ran outside to greet her, and instead found the little princess, covered in blood, holding her lifeless corpse, and telling us just how sorry she was."

The timing couldn't have been worse. I'd spent the past year hoping Kaya would contact me, but if I'd just woken up a little faster, I could have been with Aarif and P'Ken that day. I could have talked to her and been the friend she needed at that moment.

"If Yael couldn't convince her what she was doing was wrong, no one can. Especially now that she's listening to her moms and not just her aunts." He looked up at me. "Go back to school, Layla. Keep your head down, graduate, and become a famous artist. Or, you know, go and give fascism a blowjob like everyone else. Doesn't matter to me. I just don't want you getting yourself killed. And sorry, but I'm not in the mood for dying either." Aarif stood up, turned around, and walked toward the entrance in the furthest thing from a straight line. "Be a pal and cover my tab, kid."

*Stop him!* Juri hysterically cried out. *Make him stay, human!*

Without Aarif, I had no way of finding Jellz. And without Jellz, my plan had no hope of succeeding. I wasn't sure I could even mentally handle what I was up against if I didn't have a part of my family at my side, and Aarif was the only one left.

I didn't want to do this. It would hurt him even more than he'd already been hurt. It was an even bigger risk to myself. But it needed to be done.

"Aarif, wait." My professor halted with one foot already out the door. He looked back at me. I wasn't going to get a second chance if I backed down now. I allowed my tears to flow down my face as I curled my lips. "Juri is alive."

Aarif shut the door, and, leering at me, stomped over to where he'd been seated. "The Hell did you just say?"

"It's true," I said, bobbing my head. "She's in here with me. Constantly talking. I can actually understand her. She's the best companion a girl could ask for."

It's true, Foodgiver! I'm here! I'm here!

Disbelief, horror, and relief were equally spread across Aarif's face as he took heavy breaths.

"That… that's not possible. That doesn't even make sense! We put her robotic parts in you to keep you alive, but there shouldn't have been any way for her mind to carry over."

"I don't get it either. Believe me, I've looked into it. Whatever happened, it's beyond anything anyone understands. But it's true."

His face still damp from earlier, more tears ran down Aarif's face. "I swear to the gods, Layla, if you're bullshitting me, you're dead."

I shook my head. "She misses you. She loves you as much as

ever. But don't take my word for it. Juri... come on out."

What? Really? But you said...

"I said I didn't want to risk you not giving it back. I also don't want you licking him in my body, so just come out for a second, okay? Promise me you'll follow these rules?"

Yes! Yes! Yes!

I exhaled. "Okay, Aarif. Here's something I'm sure you've wanted for years." Shunting myself to the back of my brain, I allowed Juri to take the driver's seat. "F... f ...Foodgiver?"

Aarif's eyes widened. The voice Juri spoke with wasn't any different from my own, and, outside of my recently acquired claws and fangs popping out, my appearance hadn't changed.

And yet, he could see who he was now speaking to instantly. "Juri."

"Foodgiver!"

Juri drew even more attention than I had when I'd come in, as she tackled Aarif to the floor. I could feel how much effort it was taking her to do as I'd said and not lick him.

"It's you. It's really you." Aarif's tears were now of joy. "Oh, my gods. I thought I'd lost you."

"Nothing can stop the greatest dog in all of history!" she cheered. "And if you come with us, we never have to be apart again!"

Aarif laughed as held her, me, tight. "I have so many questions right now, but... shit. We're all gonna die. But I'm not about to let either of you die without me. Tell Layla I'm in, provided you and I get to talk, really talk, for an hour every day."

Deal!

"She says yes!"

Juri crawled off of Aarif and stood up, bouncing on our feet.

For all my concern that Juri might try to steal the body, she handed control right back over to me.

*Hope you trust me more now, human.*

I giggled. "With my life."

I turned my attention to Aarif and offered him a hand up. He took it, firmly clasping his hand around mine and rising to his feet, looking just a little bit more like the man I used to know.

"Okay, Captain. Tell me what you have in mind."

# CHAPTER 4: KAYA

In a way, shopping was a lot like killing: it never got old.

Unlike the gross, salty, and buttery peasant snack that shared its name, Popcorn the corporation was a girl's best friend. For a small fee, it let you browse through all the most trendy, need-to-have products and purchase them, all from one location, and have them shipped to you anywhere in the universe in under 24 hours. My mothers had commandeered many of their ships to support the war effort, but Popcorn had managed to mostly stay on schedule. So long as my clothes got to me in under 48 hours, the delivery boys got to keep their hands.

Scrolling through their platform and buying whatever caught my fancy, laid back on a plush sofa and with my headphones on, blasting music at volumes my mothers would never permit in the palace, was a relaxing way to spend the voyage home. It was a lot of work squashing a rebellion, and I needed to be properly rested before my birthday party.

I hadn't gotten to spend a great deal of time with Molina since she and Kaybell's wedding day. Or, well, a lot of time that wasn't about work. It had been a beautiful, wondrous day, and the following morning, war was declared on the Utozin Authority. Despite still not really knowing her, I loved her. And I knew she felt the same way. Why else would she have promised to take a whole day off to celebrate with me? She'd also mentioned having a big surprise for my present, but I didn't really care what she gave me; I only wanted to spend real time with her.

It wasn't like I was angry with her or anything. Sure, I'd waited my whole life to meet her, and now all our time together was formal or professional, but that had nothing to do with me. She was putting the empire first and prioritizing conquest, which would be over with before long, and she always complimented me on my excellent performance in the field. It wasn't like she didn't want to hang out. She'd told me she wanted to the first time we spoke. That didn't change because of what I'd done to Yael. She'd promised.

And then there was Kaybell. The mother who'd given me life. The fearsome, unstoppable leader of the empire who'd raised me. I didn't know how, but Molina had helped her regain her sense of Cykebian pride. She wouldn't have declared war otherwise. Kaybell should have been happier than ever, but now she always looked so sad. Was it because of the loss of her sisters? Or was it my fault?

I flipped myself over and shouted into a newly delivered, freshly stuffed pillow. No matter how much fun my excursions were, the last year had sucked. This had to all be worth it.

---

When we arrived back at the palace, I was barely keeping my eyes open. I had fallen asleep at some point, but I hadn't been able to stay that way. In and out, in and out. For hours. Gave a girl a nasty headache.

Since the war started, a wall had been constructed outside my grand, beautiful home, expanding our security beyond the palace's gates to deter potential protestors. Touching the wall with a bare hand would result in third-degree burns, and twenty snipers were positioned atop it at any given time. Additionally, measures had been taken to prevent beaming down from a ship directly into the palace, and a ship would need clearance to even beam someone down to the courtyard. My mommies were taking zero chances.

Before heading down, I got washed and changed. I didn't just feel gross; I looked gross. Unacceptable for the crown princess. I had myself bathed, my hair done, and put on a sleeveless yellow top with pink pantaloons. Hoping it would put a smile on Molina's face, I also strapped a new sword I'd purchased from Popcorn on my waist. She had a similar one in her own collection, so when she saw it, she'd have to be pleased I'd gotten one just like it for myself.

I finally beamed down into the courtyard, where the usual greeting party awaited underneath a bright blue sky. Soldiers, servants (redundant, I know), and bannermen dropped to one knee and welcomed me home.

"Welcome, Princess Kaya! All worlds under Cykeb!"

Honestly? It was getting a little old. Traditions were traditions, but I could go for some fresher material. Maybe I could get Mother to allow me to blast EZ Street on the city's speakers every time I came home. That would probably need to wait for the war to be over, though.

The only member of the welcome party to remain standing was the man in charge of it. Despite being just another ant, he was the only person left who had the confidence to speak to me as a human being, and not just his princess. While I'd usually consider such an attitude to be disrespectful arrogance deserving of immediate execution, it was understandable given he possessed the favor and protection of the empress.

"Princess Kaya," Griffin said with a polite smile and his hands behind his back as he stepped forward. "I hope your mission went well."

I held my head high as I pumped my shoulders. "I never fail."

Griffin politely chuckled. "I know. But it's still important that you're taking care of yourself while you're away."

I rolled my eyes as I started toward the palace, Griffin following behind. After being cooped up in the ship for so long, I didn't want the palanquin.

"Are my mothers in the throne room?"

"Are they ever anywhere else?"

"Is that a tone?"

"Am I wrong?"

While he could be annoying, having Griffin around was actually nice. Like Layla, he'd been one of Yael's students. When everything was changing last year, he'd been on Cykeb with Molina and had attempted to romance Aunt Jolla, but as he was such an insignificant noble, she'd merely played with him. He'd been the one to survive, though, and after Molina rose to power, despite an initial impulsive reaction, he'd fallen in line with her.

I giggled to myself. The same couldn't be said for the other, poor, common student who'd been on Cykeb at the time.

Still, Griffin's noble upbringing and loyalty to the crown mixed with being a student of Yael and a former part of that family made for a combination that was easier to talk to than anyone else. Plus, Molina didn't like talking about Yael. He did. And he could also tell me things about Layla. It was fun listening and thinking about what could have been.

I took a breath as I stepped forward into the palace's main hall. I was about to speak with my mothers in front of the court. I couldn't think about any of that right now. Only we mattered. Only the empire mattered.

---

Horns blared to announce my presence as I entered the throne room. The court was packed today. Dozens of the most powerful, influential, and unfortunately old people in the empire were gathered and dressed in spotless, flowing robes and jewelry. Every last one bowed their head in respect as I walked past them. It was rare that so many were present; the crown's focus was on the war, and Molina trusted no one but herself when it came to military matters, but I doubted it had anything to do with me.

"Kaya," Kaybell said, sipping her wine. "Welcome home."

Mother's tone was warm and gentle. It was nice, but even with how sweet and loving she'd always been with me, there'd still persisted a strict authority. That was gone. Perhaps I was being paranoid, but it sometimes seemed like her voice lacked confidence at all. Coupled with how she'd allowed Molina to take complete control of the war effort, I feared she could be sick and unwilling to tell me. There was no real reason to worry. If she was sick, she'd be receiving the best treatment possible for whatever ailment she had. I just really, really didn't like secrets.

"The report you sent was flawless," Molina said. "Well done."

Unlike Kaybell at the moment, Molina was flawless. Her tone, like the expression on her face and body language, was as hard and cold as she was. I knew from Mother's stories that there was a soft side in there, but right now she had the attitude a war-time empress and general needed. There was no time for weakness.

"Thank you, Mothers," I said, walking with my back arched and my head held high as I took my seat next to them.

Traditionally, princes and princesses stood adjacent to the

emperor's grand throne and the empress's slightly less impressive throne, but Molina had insisted on a new custom being formed in celebration of the empire's sword. This did have the unfortunate side effect of Molina's throne being centered as it sat between the other two, centering her, but Kaybell hadn't minded.

I wanted to hug my mommies, as I'd been gone a few days. I'd need to wait till we had some privacy to hug Kaybell, though. Public physical affection was not appropriate at all, and Molina didn't like being hugged

"What matters were so important that attendance of this size was necessary?" I asked.

Molina folded her hands in front of her. "There was a series of bombings. Several of our most vital manufacturing facilities have been wiped out. Thousands were killed and after only a few hours, we're already weeks behind on production of everything from domestic supplies to Cykerdroids."

Those damn Utozins were animals. If Mother would just let me, I'd kill every last one. "Why did I not see any word of this reported?" I questioned, keeping a lid on my bloodlust.

"Do not be foolish, Kaya," Molina said. "This is the largest hit against us Chancellor Shun has succeeded in landing since the war began. If I allowed this to be reported, it would be a sign of weakness on our part. Weakness on our part breeds hope in the people of the worlds we conquer. And with hope, there is rebellion."

She turned to me. "You may enjoy your work, but that doesn't make it any less distasteful, or make the Empire seem any more appealing toward the independent worlds currently aligned with the Authority." She looked forward once more. "The people want a hero like the champion of Caldey-Coccoon. Not a monster."

A monster. Why would Mother call me that? I enjoyed playing

one, certainly, but I didn't want either Molina or Kaybell calling me that. At least not in a non-cutesy way. To kill and destroy to our heart's content was simply our birthright. In her own words, we were goddesses.

I shook the thought from my mind as I faced forward. I was being paranoid. Mother was just stressed in the face of the Authority's latest attack. That was all. Oh, if I'd known all the trouble Shun would go on to cause, I would have made sure to kill her when I had the chance.

And I knew Molina felt the same.

I didn't speak for the remainder of court. Kaybell hardly said a word either, and even Molina largely just sat back and listened to reports. This was why I wasn't ready to be emperor.

Yet. Especially not in wartime. Much as I wanted to kill every Utozin, I knew that wasn't practical. My mothers were the smartest women in the world, and they knew how to listen and wait.

No matter how boring that could be.

"Mothers, have either of you eaten?" I asked as the noblemen and women filed out of the throne room. I positioned my hand on the hilt of my new sword to draw attention to it. "I'm starving."

Molina stood from her throne and walked down the staircase. "I have private meetings. You two enjoy."

She didn't even notice my sword.

I looked directly at Kaybell. "Mother?"

Kaybell smiled at me before getting up from her own throne.

"The emperor requires a little nap, my angel. You should go and take one, too."

She strutted off just as quickly, beckoning for a servant to refill her wine. Without another glance sent my way, I was left alone in the throne room, save for a handful of guards.

I banged my head against the back of my throne. "Home sweet home."

---

Upon slipping under the canopy and colliding with my bed, I tore open one pillow after another, before tossing the final one into the air and blasting it to dust.

My room was awesome. It was bigger than most people's homes, Hell, my closet was bigger than most people's homes, and filled with the finest art and furniture from all across the empire. The walls were lined with posters and albums from all my favorite boy bands, and my soft-as-a-baby's-butt mattress was framed with the same type of metal I was partially made of.

If only I felt half as awesome as my room looked.

Things weren't fair. Everything was supposed to be perfect when I returned home from my adventure with Yael. To my shock, Kaybell and Molina had already gotten engaged. With how joyous the reunion was between the three of us, I could hardly even care about Aunt Wink and Aunt Jolla's deaths. Just as Molina was more excited to meet me than she was somber over Yael's death.

There had been the wedding of the century, we'd declared war on the final obstacle toward total Cykebian domination of the universe, and we were going to achieve that together—as a family.

But no matter how I tried to distract myself through music or shopping or blowing away rebels, I couldn't change that everything sucked. Molina was 100% focused on the war and nothing else, and she barely ever acknowledged me. Kaybell wasn't the same woman who'd raised me, never having time for me, but always time for a drink, and the closest thing I had to anyone who gave a shit about what I was ever doing on my own was fucking Griffin.

I'd stood at a crossroads and been given a chance most never get. The chance to choose exactly who I wanted to be. When I struck Yael down, it closed off a path for me forever. I wasn't sure I was making the right choice, but I felt like I'd made the only one I could. Now? Now, I didn't know.

But my birthday party was coming up. All of these thoughts and fears would go away then. Another spectacle to brighten my soul until the war came to an end, and things could be just as I'd imagined them.

That was still a couple of nights away.

Holding back the tears I was only ever supposed to make others shed, I reached for my tablet. I scrolled through the last year's worth of pictures on it before I found what I was looking for: the last picture I'd taken with Yael and Layla.

Yael had the biggest, dumbest grin on her face, one that hid the mind of the universe's greatest genius behind it. Her arm was wrapped around the shoulders of Layla, the kindest and sweetest girl I'd ever known, my best friend and EZ Sister, whose smile shined like the brightest sun. And between them was me, grinning with juvenile excitement over winning a board game, and making peace signs with my hands that Yael had taught me.

It was a different life. A different path I could have taken. I'd wanted to call Layla so badly for so long, but after what I'd done, I couldn't. She wasn't Molina, she wasn't really family. She'd never forgive me. She'd have come here by now if she could.

I slowly and carefully dragged my finger down the screen as I stared myself in the eyes.

Looking up, my eyes landed on the beautiful sculptures Layla had made that I'd purchased second-hand, each one screaming at me.

"I'm sorry."

# CHAPTER 5: LAYLA

I was a smart gal with a half-robot body, a dog in my brain, and a blowpipe capable of mass destruction strapped to my back. All pretty cool, but not enough to take on two warring empires. For my plan to work, I needed to be able to hit the Cykebian Empire and the Utozin Authority where it hurt. And for that, I needed Jellz.

I'd never met the old, old man, but I'd heard all about him. He'd been Yael's manager/agent before she'd joined the Banshees, and he'd gotten rich enough to retire. Yael had built her own career as a thief, but it was Jellz who would get her the gigs that allowed her to do so. He was able to do that because, after spending over six decades in the criminal underworld, he had connections everywhere. To say nothing of how he was the best hacker she'd ever met besides Marcos. He was also, apparently, an odd fellow, but I could work with that.

"He's lasted so long because he's paranoid beyond reason," Yael had once told me. "Trick to getting what you want out of him is letting him think he's in control of the situation."

It was almost overly simple how many of Yael's tricks boiled down to rules like that, but it made sense. If people could never get over themselves and their own egos, they'd always fall for it.

Finding Jellz, I imagined, would be more difficult than winning him over to my cause would be had I not gotten Aarif on board. The man knew how to stay hidden, to the point I doubted even g-gma could find him. He was like a ghost. Maybe there were others, potentially other former clients, he trusted, but as far I knew, Aarif and P'Ken were the only living people who'd spoken to him in person in years. P'Ken hadn't been an option, but with Aarif serving as my navigator, I was able to fly from Toz to Jellz's last known location, Migdhilt.

The voyage had lasted two days and gone about as well as I could have expected. Aarif spent his time getting drunk, rambling, and waiting for his allotted hour with Juri, Juri constantly begged for "just a little" more time with him, and I hadn't been able to get a good night's sleep because of Aarif screaming from his night terrors. I couldn't blame him, but the bags under my eyes were becoming a problem, my brain wasn't working as quickly as I needed it to, and I didn't have enough organic skin cream or veggie booster shakes to mitigate this.

Once I'd gotten what I needed from Jellz, a pit stop and a one-night stay in a hotel were mandatory. Maybe I'd even have time to sculpt something. Would certainly help soothe the nerves.

"Jellz never could just pick a hospitable world to hide out on," Aarif groaned, before sneezing, as we got off *Cascade* and stepped out onto the planet's surface. "Always had to make it difficult. Have I told you about the birds of prey?"

"Several times."

In the past, Migdhilt's wide-trunked, thick-barked, gargantuan trees had been a goldmine for lumber distributors and corporations that required the material for their products. At least two small wars had been fought over the land rights. There may have been a third, but with the entire native population having either been killed or moved far away by the time the second one was over, there was some debate.

These days, with the world having been completely deforested by evil, greedy corporations, the wondrous trees I would have loved to see in person were long gone. The height of the trees and the width and density of their leaves had previously made air travel difficult, but now, it was traversing the ground that was hazardous. The suits had only been focused on the lumber as they ravaged this world and had paid little or no attention to its flowers. Either as a result of radiation, or potentially a symbiotic effect of losing the trees, the flowers across the surface had begun emitting gelatin-like pollen all over the planet. The pollen hid the ground, it needed to be waited through like a pool, it made it almost impossible not to sneeze, and it had mutated the wildlife.

I violently sneezed into my elbow, already congested all the way down to my stomach.

Tactically, Jellz couldn't have picked a better place to hide. The pollen made it easy to hide sensors and alarms, no known filtration systems had been developed that were capable of blocking it out, Cykerdroids had proven to get stuck in it, and if someone found him and was slowly trudging through the pollen, they'd have to contend with the mutated wildlife.

We hadn't been able to reach Jellz on the way here, so I trusted that Aarif had his coordinates straight. Otherwise, we could be here for a while.

*Bleh, I don't want to even be here for a little,* Juri bemoaned. "You can't even smell or feel it."

*Yeah, but I know you're smelling or feeling it and I know it's gross.*

"Is she okay?!" Aarif asked. "You'd tell me if she wasn't, right?"

I held in a moan and held back an eye roll. I got being overprotective after losing her, but he had to trust me.

"Yes, everything is fine. Juri's just a drama queen."

Hmph!

Aarif sighed, before sneezing. "Sorry. I just… life's been hard. You, well, saw that. Kinda funny when you think about it. I had to get dragged out of that bar kicking and screaming, while you left your picture-perfect, hippie-dippy, college life without a second thought."

"It wasn't 'without a second thought'," I clarified. "I took my time on the Glass Striker specifically because I was scared. I didn't even mean to finish it when I did. Hell, I didn't even start working on the thing till six months ago. I tried ignoring the war and just being a good student and friend, but it wasn't long before I became glued to the news. I couldn't avoid my responsibilities."

Aarif laughed. "Your 'duty to protect the universe'? How very Sunriser."

The Sunrisers. They'd be a problem down the line. They'd been formed originally by The Cykebian Empire but had served as an independent entity, servicing all corners of the cosmos.

No more. One of Molina's first acts after starting the war was to get her sister Morphea, the Sunrisers' acting Supreme General, on her side. Together, they worked to have the Sunrisers as an organization fully absorbed into the Empire's military. Besides Kaya, they were the crown's most dangerous tool.

"Don't even," I said. "This isn't about some vague idea of right or wrong. Or even the blame we carry. Yael did everything for us. We were her family. We owe it to her to do what we can for the rest of her family."

Aarif clicked his tongue. "You know I'm not much of a fighter, but I hope I can at least knock out some of Griffin's teeth while you're knocking sense into him."

"If you don't, I will." Aarif seemed surprised by that, so I shot him a smirk. "I know we're not all just going to hold hands and make flower crowns. Molina, Griffin, Kaya, and everyone who is responsible for this war needs to pay. I just believe there's room for life after that's done." My smirk weakened. "Well, probably not for Molina. But I can try."

Aarif laughed. A refreshing sound. Unfortunately, it was cut off by the sound of multiple growls in the distance. The wildlife had noticed us.

"How sure were you about those coordinates again?" I sneezed.

"More sure now than before. Jellz would want his safehouse somewhere where the hostile fauna gathered."

"Right."

Reaching my arm over my shoulder, I took hold of the Glass Striker and unsheathed it. "I still can't believe you made your secret weapon a glassblowing pipe," Aarif said. "It's a little much, don't you think?"

I spun my pipe around my head and under my leg, getting warmed up. "It's called a blowpipe. And would you have preferred a sword? It makes more sense than mixing wrestling moves with krav maga, and Yael made that work."

"You're not Yael." Actually reassuring to hear him say that. "So what can that thing do, anyway?"

More growls echoed, at least one new animal's cry mixed in. "I'll show you."

I took hold of my pipe with both hands and wrapped my lips around the mouthpiece. I wouldn't actually be showing off what the Glass Striker would do here, but that sounded like the right thing to say. There was no way I was actually going to hurt some innocent animals, but I'd designed this weapon with one purpose above all else: beating Kaya. And that meant it had some non-lethal tricks.

My heart was racing. I'd never been in a real fight. I'd trained plenty in school, and I'd done what I could during Yael's second fight with Kaya, but I'd never really been in one. I should have been scared, but how was I supposed to be afraid of some animals when I was taking on the whole universe? No...

I was excited.

From the pollen, a silver wolf with a blue-tipped mane and yellow feathers pounced at me. I almost froze, but even with the break I'd taken, my three years of training were ready to kick in. Concentrating on my target, blowing into my pipe with carefully controlled breaths, being extra sure not to sneeze while I was doing this, and rotating with finesse the blowpipe with the only part of my body I regularly worked out—my fingers—I formed a bright yellow glass sphere around the wolf, trapping it inside, and dropping it at my feet.

Human! That was so cool!

The wolf growled at me again, and even though she knew it couldn't hear her, Juri growled back.

"I'm sorry... what was that?!"

I knew there were more predators coming, so I kept the pipe close to my lips. "Pretty cool, right? I'll show you how it works, later."

Another of the same breed of wolf, as well as a bear with striped fur and spines like a stegosaurus on its back, rushed toward us in opposite directions. No time to trap them both, which meant trick #2.

Blowing into the pipe once again, I gave it a single harsh turn. Sealing someone or something in a bubble was something I needed to be careful with, but the rest of the Glass Striker's abilities were each triggered by a single, specific command.

A giant glass net stuck out of the other end of the pipe, made up of a rainbow of various shards. Spinning around, I scooped up both the wolf and the bear. If they tried to get out, they'd be cut by the glass shards, but animals were smarter than humans gave them credit for. With them both safely in the net, I blew and spun just as before, trapping each animal in their own sphere. Once that was done, with my lips still around the mouthpiece, I took a deep breath in, deactivating the net and dropping the two new spheres to the ground.

Yeeeeeees, human! So. Awesome!

"Woah," I panted. "Okay. Ha ha ha."

"What's so funny?" Aarif said, still in disbelief at what he was seeing.

"Oh, nothing. I'm just realizing I never actually tested this thing."

While I had a good laugh over my little mistake, Aarif looked like he was about to claw his own eyes out. Or maybe my eyes. Either way. It took more energy just to do that little than I'd expected. I'd need to keep that in mind.

"I think we're good," I said, sheathing my weapon. "The spheres will dissolve in an hour. We should be long gone by then."

"Okay, okay, okay," Aarif breathed. "So yes, I absolutely need to know what's going on there, it seems both fascinating and impossible, but is this really all you've got?"

I giggled as I sneezed over and over and over again. Preventing myself from doing so while I'd been blowing hadn't been easy.

"Weren't you listening? Those were just a couple of the nonviolent things it can do."

Aarif weakly smiled. "This isn't some weird, Banshee magic like, 'The True Adventurer', right?"

"Not... entirely? Questions for later. Let's find Jellz's safehouse before any more animals notice us."

Aarif did as I said, shutting up outside of one more sneeze, and led us through the pollen for about another two minutes. At that point, we arrived at what almost looked like an oversized coconut but could only be our destination.

"Let me handle this," Aarif said, approaching the front door. "Jellz no doubt already knows we're here, but he's probably still gonna stick a shotgun in the face of whoever knocks."

Aarif knocked on the round, wooden front door, not once, not twice, not even three times, but eight times, specifically at a rapid speed.

"What did my mom tell my dad?" a gravelly voice I presumed belonged to Jellz asked from inside.

"You're adopted," Aarif answered. "Now pay me child support."

From the other side of the door, Jellz cackled. He opened it and, continuing to laugh, slapped Aarif's arm. No shotgun was present. I questioned momentarily if he'd gotten less paranoid than I'd heard, but then I remembered what I was standing in.

Jellz had shaved his head bald, his cheeks bore burn scars poorly covered up with makeup, his peach skin was covered in pimples, and he was nearly as filthy as the people of Toz, dressed in a stained white tank top, jean-shorts, and a gray trench coat.

"I thought you were dead," Jellz spoke, allowing me to see his metal tongue. "Only on the inside," Aarif cheekily replied as the two men shook hands.

Jellz glared at me. "Layla N'gwa. Interesting." He gestured with his head to the door. "Get inside. I don't like being outdoors this long." He pointed at me. "That's how they get you."

And there was the over-the-top paranoia I'd been waiting for. Poor guy. I couldn't imagine being scared of the beautiful outdoors.

"It's nice to meet you," I said.

He gestured with his head again. "Inside."

Mildly annoyed by his rudeness, I did as he asked and followed him and Aarif inside, Jellz slamming the door behind us.

From the looks of it, Jellz had packed an entire living space into a singular circular room. There was a couch with a stack of books next to it, a refrigerator and stove adjacent to a shelf of canned food, a dissolving toilet, and a sophisticated computer set-up, all crammed together.

*Cozy.*

"One word for it," I replied to Juri, coughing at the scent from the clearly incomplete job Jellz's dissolving toilet had been doing.

Jellz plopped down on his couch with his arms stretched out. There were no chairs, so we were left standing.

"So, what's this about?" the old man questioned. "Not a single former client has ever paid a social call, especially one who looks like he's been taking dystopia especially hard, which makes me think we're gathered here because of you, great-granddaughter of Madame N'gwa."

I couldn't wait for the day people stopped calling me that. When I saved the universe, she'd be known as my great-grandmother, not the other way around.

"You're correct," I said. "About why we're here and about the state of the universe. And those things are actually connected. I want your help to save it."

I was completely expecting him to laugh, but he didn't. Despite how ridiculous I knew it sounded, he just nodded along.

"I'm listening."

"Really?" Aarif questioned. "Just like that?"

"She's the descendant of the second-best thief the universe has ever known, and she was the star pupil of my girl." He kissed his fingertips and raised them up towards the sky. "She says she can get us out of this hellhole, I'll give her a chance."

My smile widened with relief. This part would be easier than I thought.

"Okay, so basically, I–"

I was cut off as the front door was blown in by explosives. Before I could question what was happening, how it was happening, or how either Aarif or Jellz were reacting, each of us was taken out with a taser round, electrocuting and stunning us, and leaving us shaking on the floor.

"J... Juri?" I barely was able to speak.

All... all good, hu-human.

This couldn't be happening. Of all the places I'd expected to run into human enemies, this had been the last. No one else should have known we, or Jellz, was here, and if they did, Jellz's alarms should have picked up on them. There was only one other person who could have known where Jellz was, but for them to have come now of all times would mean...

As I finished that thought, jackbooted soldiers flooded the tiny house, some armed with the stun guns that had taken us down, while others packed laser rifles or machine guns. The troops stepped out of the way so the only Sunriser captain who could have found us could strut on in.

"Laya. Aarif." P'Ken grinned, cane-whip in hand. "How nice to see you both again."

# CHAPTER 6: KAYA

I hated secrets. Secrets were how people hurt you. They were how you let yourself get hurt. But not all secrets were terrible. Some secrets were really just surprises. Surprises adding a little bit of shock to a fun time. Surprises like my birthday party's venue not being the palace but my mothers' flagship; my present, and the next surprise for me, were far, far away.

The imperial flagship, *Ricochet Supreme*, took its name from the smelly old ship Molina had once called home. I'd come up with it, and it was one of the few things I'd ever said that had made Molina truly smile. It only felt right. With how much Molina had loved her, and how much she'd tried to do for me, Yael deserved a tribute.

RS wasn't too much larger than the *Winjolla*, only 100 meters greater in diameter, but size wasn't everything. I was still under five feet tall, but I was the hottest and most deadly girl in existence, and some of the cutest boys were barely any taller. It featured many of the same amenities, although it tragically lacked either a karaoke studio or torture chamber, instead possessing the ballroom I now stood in alongside the empire's elite. What truly set it apart were its weapons. Oh, how I almost wanted to give this unmatched artillery a hug and sleep on it.

Forty cannons, each capable of sinking even the largest of continents from orbit, self-replicating mines and bombs, and long-distance missiles that could hit a target with near flawless accuracy from half a million miles away. The operation and maintenance weren't cheap and required an additional 400 men, but while most of it was rarely used, the weaponry made for a more efficient deterrent to some than a "little girl".

The party had been going on for a little over an hour and, so far, it had been splendid.

While I wasn't permitted to have all of my favorite bands perform, my mommies had gotten all of the ones they'd deemed "respectable", on the condition I did not speak to them. That worked for me. I was still a little nervous around boys. The last thing I'd want would be to trip over my words and drool over their beautiful faces.

There was a buffet of all my favorite foods, to eat in moderation of course, the black and silver lighting created a wholly unique atmosphere, there was not one, not two, but three ice sculptures of me, and all of the fashion on display was positively peak, with my own highly detailed, diamond-studded golden gown of course stealing the show, the greatest seamstresses in the empire having spent four months on it. I was even allowed to have some wine! The only annoying parts were having to talk to the nobles and act like I gave half a crap about them or anything they had to say or think, and being unable to take my mind off what surprise was in store for me.

Carrying on a mindless conversation with a simpleton my own age, I sipped some juice. I'd already burned through the amount of wine I'd been permitted to have. It was delicious, but, while I wouldn't admit it, I didn't even want it anymore. My head was so woozy. It made no sense that adults held important conversations while drinking the stuff. Wouldn't they want to be clear-minded when making big decisions?

Once the idiot daughter of a dutchy or something walked away in her cheap-ass heels, I scanned the ballroom for my mommies. Today was supposed to be about us. It was supposed to be about me! But so far, it had been like any other day. And there was no sign of either of them.

I cracked the glass in my hand, only catching myself an instant before it was completely shattered. Not that it stopped juice from dribbling out onto my hand and shoes. Yuck.

Obviously, they were here. We'd all gotten ready and gotten onto the ship together, we'd all made our entrance together, and Molina told me it would just be a little bit before she could get back to me. Everything was still going to be splendid. So long as Molina and I spent the day together, everything would be perfect. But...

Had Molina lied to me? It wouldn't have been the first time she'd broken a promise. If she had, what else could she have been lying about? And what did that mean for my surprise? Why would she be lying? Why would she do that? Why could no one just ever be straight with me?!

This was nothing new. A mother who loved me but paid no attention. Kaybell may have always been nothing but sweet to me, I may have been her perfect little angel before I'd found myself and Molina had embraced me as I am, but I wouldn't have even become the way I was if she'd ever paid attention. If she'd ever noticed what her sisters were doing. Did she really care? Yael had said she did, but Yael was dead! Yael was dead because I couldn't change what Kaybell had let them make me! Yael was dead, Kaybell and Molina didn't care, I was all alone in the crowd, and I just wanted to—

My glass shattered in my hand. Splinters of glass went flying in every direction as the remaining juice stained my dress and even got in my hair. Like it even mattered. Everyone was looking at me, wondering what their princess, the empire's sword, had done. I couldn't care less what any of them were thinking. No matter how sharp their stares were. I just wanted to kill them all.

"L'chaim!"

Griffin approached me, clapping his hands, dressed in likely the finest tunic he'd ever worn, and wearing a stupid grin on his face.

"Our glorious princess is having the time of her life!" he cheered. "Thank you all once again for coming!"

There was an awkward applause. I didn't understand what had just happened, and I doubted most of the nobles did either, but no one wanted to appear ignorant of a potential tradition. They readily resumed their previous conversations and took their eyes off me.

"Picked that one up from our old friend," Griffin said. "Is there anything I can do for you, Princess? Are you okay?"

No. I'm not okay. Duh! I have no one, I have no idea what winning the war I'm fighting will even mean, I have no idea who's telling me the truth about anything, I betrayed the people who loved me, and mindless hedonism, the euphoric sensation of spreading death, and drugged-up tea are the only things keeping me from constantly breaking down crying!

Obviously, I couldn't say any of that, so I just shoved him aside and stomped off. I appreciated the help, he was too sweet for his own good, but I couldn't deal with this right now. I needed to get out of here.

With each step I took and each clack of my heels, my head took another spin. Why had I wanted to drink wine? And why did I have so much, so fast?

Exiting the ballroom into one of the ship's cold corridors, I leaned against a wall and panted. The cybernetics inside me could adapt to anything. Anything life-threatening, that was. If I got alcohol poisoning, they would flush the alcohol out of my system or simply make me immune. But just a splitting headache? They weren't designed to do anything about that.

I needed water, but I couldn't return to the ballroom. Not yet. I needed to find my mothers. A task made much easier, but more concerning, as laughter echoed from down the hall and around the corner. It wasn't a laugh I'd heard before, but the voice behind it was unmistakable.

"Mother?"

Forcing my way down the hallway, struggling to walk straight and only keeping my heels on because I knew I'd have to return to the party soon, I followed the off-putting sound.

Rounding the corner, I found Kaybell, the emperor of the Holy Cykebian Empire and the most powerful woman in the universe, dressed in the finest robes and jewelry, sitting on the floor, unattended and unguarded, with a glass of wine in her hand.

"Mother?"

She laughed to herself for a moment more, before turning her head and noticing me. She grinned, but there was no warmth behind it. Like she wasn't even there. I wasn't stupid. I knew how alcohol worked. I just hadn't expected it to hit me so hard. And never in a million years would I have expected to see my mommy be as piss drunk as Yael and her crew would get.

"Kaya," she said. "Are you enjoying the party?" She frowned. "What happened to your hair?"

I shook my head and forced a weak smile back. "It's wonderful, thank you. I just made a little bit of a mess I need to clean up."

"Not words a mother ever expects to hear from her princess."

I tried to giggle, but it just didn't leave my mouth.

"Mother, how much have you had to drink?"

"Oh, not too much. Nothing to worry about. I'm simply indulging myself for the special occasion."

I narrowed my eyes. "You're always drinking."

"As empresses have for centuries."

"You're the emperor. Not the empress."

"Yes. I am."

Mother reached out open arms, grinning wide. It took me a second to realize she wanted me to come down onto the floor to be hugged. I really didn't want to degrade myself, but the floor was at least clean and polished, and I'd been dying to be held by one of my mothers again; I couldn't pass this up.

As I accepted the warm embrace of her arms, Mother hugged me tight and stroked my hair. It was wonderful. It was everything. It was love. Why did she have to be drunk for this?

"Mother?"

"Hm?"

I didn't want to ruin this moment, but it was already wrong. I'd been worried about her for months, and I felt more justified in my concerns than ever. I had to ask.

"Are you ok? Are you sick? You can tell me if you are. I won't be worried. I know Cykebian medicine will help you. I just want to know… so I can help you, too."

Mother hummed as she eased up on her grip but continued stroking my hair.

"Do you know why empresses have long been found with wine

in hand?"

I shook my head.

"It's a stressful life. Blessed, but stressful. It's a burden. To have everything, to have the greatest empire ever known serving you while you live in service to your emperor, ensuring their happiness, comfort, and sense of ease. And that isn't always an easy job. Emperors can get stressed. Angry. Other things."

My eyes widened in horror. "Are you saying... Molina is sick?"

Mother laughed. She stopped stroking my hair and rested her hands on my face.

"No one is sick, my angel." She kissed my forehead. "Everything will be okay. Just remember that I love you."

Her soothing words only further confused and concerned me.

"What are you talking about?" I asked. "Is the war not going as well as I thought? Did I do something wrong?"

"Oh, baby." She pulled my face into her chest. "Of course you did."

My eyes jolted wide open and my mind was cleared as a wave crashed against its muddied shores.

"Wh... what did you just say?"

I pulled back, looking up at my still smiling mother in horror. I needed an answer, but she didn't have time to give me one.

"What is going on here?"

Kaybell and I turned our heads as Molina approached us, dressed head to toe in black, with a splash of Sunriser orange, silver jewelry, and flanked by guards. Being dressed for a party didn't make her any less imposing or her presence any less overwhelming.

"Why are you not in the ballroom enjoying yourselves?"

I stood up, only shaking a little as I did so. Kaybell remained on the floor, chugging back the remaining contents of her glass.

Standing as tall and straight as I could and keeping my head high, I smiled brightly at my mommy. "I spilled some juice on myself and came outside to clean up before I embarrassed myself or the crown. Kaybell was already out here."

Molina nodded and looked down at Kaybell. "What's wrong, my love? Too much to drink?"

Kaybell groaned as she set her empty glass down, her eyes now weary and showing weakness.

Lips pressed together, Molina smiled as she reached out her gloved hands to take Kaybell's and help her stand. She could have so easily had a guard do that, but she loved Kaybell too much to allow anyone else the honor. They'd been through everything together, and Molina had given up everything for her, just as I'd given up so much. Maybe she could get a more clear answer about what was wrong with her, or maybe she already knew. Regardless, now wasn't the time. Now was the time to be her perfect princess.

"Do you need to lie down?" Molina asked, the two looking into each other's eyes. "You don't seem well."

"No. No, I'm… I'm okay."

Molina's smile exposed her whitened teeth. "Good. I'm happy to hear it." Molina planted a kiss on Kaybell's lips. Gods, I couldn't wait until I found my husband. I wanted to be kissed like that. "Let's stop drinking though, shall we?"

"I think that's a good idea as well," I said. "This stuff is poison."

Kaybell's eyes were pained by our request, but it was for her own good. Whatever was wrong, alcohol was clearly just making the pain worse. Mother reluctantly nodded.

She'd thank us soon. This was unacceptable behavior from an emperor. I just wanted her to be okay, even if she didn't seem to care if I was.

Molina turned to me, continuing to smile. "I apologize for being kept away. I'd hoped to take a single day off from the war, but these incompetent fools cannot seem to function without me. It's all settled for now, though. I'm all yours.'

Was this another lie? She could so easily have been lying. She could have just been avoiding me because I was… no, no she wasn't lying. Of course she wasn't lying! I was just being paranoid. Again. She wouldn't be here now, telling me this, if she didn't wish to be with me on my special day.

"I understand completely," I said, smiling back at her.

"Good. Now, go do as you wished to and clean yourself up. Take the emperor as well. She could use some help."

"Yes, Mother."

"I actually think I'd rather go lie down," Kaybell groaned. "You were right about the wine being a mistake. I'm fine, really, but I would be embarrassing myself."

"Nonsense," Molina said. "I know you can hide this just fine. And you don't want to miss the main event."

I bounced on my feet. "Is it almost time for my surprise?"

Molina laughed under her breath as she nodded.

"I hope this present will make up for my common absences." She bent her head down and kissed Kaybell's shaking hands. "It's going to be a blast."

# CHAPTER 7: LAYLA

There was a time when I'd considered P'Ken Amatyn one of the coolest women I'd ever met. As Yael's original apprentice and right-hand woman, she'd been a role model to all of us studying under her. Along with being the only one of our professors remotely qualified to be an educator, she was Yael's superior on the softer sides of being a thief. She wasn't as strong or as smart, but she could blend into any crowd and charm anyone. She was strict, if kinda terrifying, but she was beautiful, never looking anything less than fabulous in her elaborate dresses, and she cared so much about helping each of us reach our full potential, whether that meant staying up late training with me or sharing fashion tips. She was the big sister I'd never had.

Needless to say, I wasn't nearly as enamored or impressed with the fascist standing over me.

While Aarif, Jellz, and I were paralyzed on the ground, she stood tall, surrounded by her armed men with guns aimed at us. She was dressed all-nice in her pressed, mostly black uniform, her dark-skinned face elegantly made up with the same finesse she'd once shared with me.

I didn't know what she was doing here, or how she was even here, but I couldn't be stopped here, and not by her. If I could reach the Glass Striker on my back, I could take her down no problem, but I could barely even wiggle my arms.

The obvious strategy was to get her talking. Keep her talking long enough for the paralysis to wear off so I could blow P'Ken and her goons away. But P'Ken had to know anything I'd try. She was the one who'd taught me after all.

"It's so nice to see you both again," P'Ken said, to my relief, doing the talking for me. "Although I can't say these are the circumstances under which I imagined a reunion."

*Bad Foodgiver,* Juri said.

"And whose fault is that, you traitor?!" Aarif screeched back.

P'Ken rolled her eyes. "Really? We're doing this?"

"You somehow think I'd be happy to see you?"

P'Ken's practiced, polite smile faded as she glared at Aarif, then at me, before turning to Jellz. Jellz's face had gone red, like it was about to burst. For all I knew, there were explosives in there that would make that happen.

"Jellicimo Horzinski," she spat at him in the same tone she'd used toward me when she wanted to make me feel like a little girl about to get spanked. "You are under arrest for more crimes than I have time to list, but thankfully doing so isn't part of the job."

Jellz shook his puffy head, flashing P'Ken with his messed up and broken, grit teeth. "I'm suddenly glad the kid is dead. She'd cry if she saw you now."

"I'm sure she would. Take him away."

Two of the soldiers picked the old man up off the floor, forcing his arms behind his back and cuffing him as they dragged him off. As long as he could, he kept his fiery eyes on me. He probably wanted to scream some passionate, inspiring words, but he said nothing at all. We didn't know what P'Ken knew, and even though he didn't know any details about my plan, we couldn't give the game away.

P'Ken cracked her knuckles as her attention returned to me. "You haven't said a word, Layla. Are you not happy to see me either?"

"Can you blame me given the circumstances?" I finally spoke up.

P'Ken giggled before hardening her face once more. "Leave us. Return to the ship with the others."

"Ma'am?" one of her men questioned.

"I'll handle these two myself. Horzinski is a slippery snake who must be handled firmly." Her men nodded in affirmation and filed out of the cozy house. "Shut the door."

With that final command given, the last of the soldiers left.

"There," P'Ken said, stepping forward toward the couch and taking a seat, and crossing her legs like she owned the place. "Now, then..." Her face lit up. "How are you two?"

I took a breath. P'Ken wasn't interested in arresting us. When the three of us had split up, P'Ken had gone to mourn with her mother at St. Shiala's School for Girls. Four months later, she was the Sunrisers' newest captain and the face of much of the Cykebian military's propaganda. I didn't have the faintest idea what had happened there, and initially, I'd hoped she was undercover, but it had become clear over time she was now a true believer in the empire's mission. Captain P'Ken Amatyn had left multiple worlds devastated, without a shred of mercy.

All of this hurt. But it also meant Jellz was smart to keep his mouth shut. If P'Ken so much as suspected Aarif and me of what we were planning, she wouldn't have been making a family reunion out of this. She still cared about us and believed us to be normal civilians.

Aarif, meanwhile, clearly wanted to kill her. His rage toward the monster his old friend had become was, understandably, palpable. In his current mental state, everything he had to say was going to come out.

I could work with this.

"How do I fucking look?" Aarif growled.

"As depressing to see as I'm sure it is to appear," P'Ken said. "Layla! Dear! Talk to me, please. How's college been?"

I licked my lips, visualizing what I wanted to make happen here. "As wonderful as I always dreamed. How's being the empire's bitch?"

Aarif snickered.

P'Ken nodded in frustration. "So you two aren't even interested in hearing my side of the story? Would you be giving Griffin this treatment?"

"Nah," Aarif said. "That noble little sellout, I think I could take."

P'Ken repeated, "Okay", under her breath multiple times. She hadn't even been prepared for us, had she?

"You wanna tell us what you're even doing here?" I asked. "No way us all coming here at the same time was a coincidence."

"That is correct," P'Ken said. "Before I took this job, I thought of Jellz. He's never been either a fan or a direct enemy of the empire. Still, in light of what happened, I advised Empress Molina to keep an eye on him. With this being before I was officially a documented Sunriser, Jellz had no way of knowing that I'd given up his location. He of course changed locations after my hiring was put on the record, but by then it was too late." She looked around the house. "Living this disgusting life out of paranoia for nothing."

"He hardly could have guessed that you of all people would turn."

"I didn't want it to come to this! I'd hoped he'd keep his damn head down and stay in retirement. Just as I hoped, Aarif, that if you wouldn't accept my offer, you'd keep yours down. But you couldn't even do that."

It was difficult, but I was able to turn my head to look at Aarif. "An offer?"

Aarif snorted. "Yeah. She came by the bar once or twice. Wanted to clean me up and make me her chief engineer. I told her I'd rather be ripped apart by a Cykerdroid."

"Sounds right." I cracked my neck looking back at P'Ken. "What exactly do you think we're doing? Or are doing?"

'That's what I want you to tell me," P'Ken said. "My spies reported *Cascade* moving toward this awful world. I left my ship to you, and Aarif was the only other person who'd know where to find Jellz, so odds were it was the two of you aboard. I had as little idea now as I did then, but I felt it was safest to shoot first, arrest Jellz second, and ask questions later." P'Ken leaned forward on the couch. "What is going on?"

I wanted to smack myself for not considering the self-inflicted blow that was coming here in *Cascade*, but it really wouldn't have mattered. I'd failed to foresee P'Ken precautions, and even if Aarif and I had come in a cruiser, we still would have been reported. We may just have shocked P'Ken a little more the moment she stepped in was all. As things stood, even if P'Ken hadn't prepared properly for this conversation, she had control. I needed to change that.

"My question first: Would you kill us if you were ordered to?"

"A ridiculous question with an obvious answer. Whatever's going on, you haven't done anything yet. And it would take a lot to push Empress Molina that far. Difficult as it may be to believe, she still cares for you both."

"And what about the emperor?" Aarif asked. "I know Kaybell's the same as ever."

P'Ken looked at Aarif with wry amusement. For a couple seconds, her jaw lowered bit by bit. Then she burst out laughing.

"What's so funny?" I asked, her voice grating against my ears.

P'Ken shook her head as she composed herself. "You two. You don't have the faintest idea what's really going on, do you?"

"The second Yael was dead, Molina married Emperor Kaybell. The Cykebian Empire, led by Emperor Kaybell and Molina, declared war on The Utozin Authority, led by Shun, and all of them are evil," I said. "What am I missing?"

P'Ken looked down at the floor as she tapped her cane against her hand.

"Emperor Kaybell hasn't held any real power for longer than I've been a Sunriser."

Aarif and I looked at each other in confusion. Surprised as I was by P'Ken's statement, I took note of how loose my body was already feeling, and how quick both Aarif and I were to react. P'Ken must not have had us hit with serious voltage. I'd be ready to move soon.

"What are you talking about?" Aarif asked.

"It's a mess, honestly," P'Ken said, eyes on the floor. "Not one I can say I support." She held her head up. "Molina didn't get together with Emperor Kaybell after Yael was murdered. She'd already made her choice to leave her beforehand and was sleeping with the emperor."

GRRRRRRRRR!

*Same, girl*, I thought, incensed. *Same*.

"Didn't think I could hate her any more," Aarif said. "How could she?!"

P'Ken shrugged. "I don't know. This was something she confessed to me in private, and she was stingy with details. What I do know is that sometime between Kaya returning to Cykeb and revealing what she'd done, and my own arrival at the palace, Molina had changed. She'd pushed Kaybell toward making a pre-emptive strike against the Utozins, and while Kaybell was horrified by Kaya's renewed and now open giddiness for death and destruction, Molina used it, as well as Kaya's desperation to win her approval, to make her a loyal weapon. With Kaya firmly on her side, as well as the majority of the Cykebian nobles who cared nothing for civilian casualties, she consolidated power, labeled Kaybell overly weak and gentle, and rendered the emperor nothing more than a pretty face for the public with a ubiquitous glass of wine. Oh, sure, there were those who didn't like the idea of following a ruler not of noble birth, but they believed they could be the ones to exploit her. She made sure that they didn't last long."

My whole body shook as my jaw hit the floor. What. The Fuck?!

"What the fuck?!" Aarif shrieked.

"Yeah!" I followed. "That!"

P'Ken sighed. "I wish I could tell you more. Molina and I aren't exactly friends these days. We've shared maybe four conversations that weren't about the war over the last eight months. I don't know why she's done all this. My best guess is that, when Yael died, so did something inside Molina. Maybe more than one thing."

This… this changed everything, and yet nothing. Most of my plan could still work just fine, but there was also a tradeoff. If Kaya was being directly strung along and manipulated, then saving her could potentially be easier than I thought. But if Molina was the one behind it, then I'd need to apologize to Yael when I got to Hell; I had to kill her.

"Okay," I said, wiggling my foot and feeling like I could jump up. "If that's all true, and you know all of it to be true, then what the Hell are you doing working for her?"

"The little lady asks a damn good question," Aarif said.

P'Ken stood up from the couch, pressing her cane down against the floor to help her, and dusting herself off. There was an unease to how her face and body moved in these few seconds.

"We had a good thing going," she started. "A very good thing. For five years. The best years of my life. And then, in just a few days, it all fell apart. Yael was killed, Molina took the throne, we lost Juri, Shun betrayed us, and Griffin and Marcos were imprisoned. It was just the three of us left. Maybe we should have stayed together, a family and all that, but that was never really an option. Layla, you deserved to go to school. Aarif, you were already coming apart at the seams, and at the moment I wasn't strong enough to handle that. I was hurt too, but I couldn't put that on either of you. So I went to see my mother. It was always going to be temporary. I was happy to see her, she was happy to see me. Happy to see that, even as a thief, I was the fine young woman she'd raised. And that is who I was. A thief. I had every intention of going back to that life eventually, with or without the rest of you, but the longer I stayed, and rested and contemplated, the more I realized that being a thief was never really what I lived for. I was damn good at it and I loved it, but... what kept me going *was* all of you. It was Yael. And so, a new thought occurred. "What would Yael be doing right now?" And when I answered that question, even if I had my doubts, it was the right thing to do, there was only one path forward I could push myself to take."

A chill passed through the house, and I felt the last of my body's numbness fade away.

Whenever I was ready, I could act.

"How could you think this is what Yael would have wanted?" Aarif snarled. "Being a Sunriser, stripping away people's rights and freedoms… it's everything she stood against!"

"You think I don't know that?!" P'Ken shouted back, losing her cool. "Of course it was! But do you know what was more important to her than anything? Molina. And by the end? Kaya, too. If Shun hadn't ruined everything, I guarantee you, Yael would have given Kaya what she wanted: the two of them and her biological mothers all one big happy family ruling the universe together. Yes, if Yael was here, and if Shun hadn't traumatized Kaya, the empire wouldn't be doing what it has been. But regardless, I know in my heart that, no matter how evil their acts may be, Yael would want me to support her wife and child. As the closest thing she had to an heir, it's my duty." She stared down at the floor, despondently. "We were never the good guys."

"We were never the bad guys, either."

I got where she was coming from. I did. It didn't excuse anything she'd done, or all the pain she'd wrought, but at least this made sense. Since she was younger than I was, she'd devoted her life to a woman and her teachings. And with her gone, she'd decided the woman herself was more important than anything she'd ever imparted. Personally? I thought Yael would be kicking Molina's ass and saving Kaya.

I still wanna claw her face.

"Yeah. I get that."

"What was that?" P'Ken asked weakly, squeezing her forehead.

"Nothing," I said, wanting to hold onto as many of my secrets as I could. "I'm sorry."

"Don't be," P'Ken said. "Now then…" P'Ken slammed her cane

on the floor. "No more distractions. What are you two doing here?"

I tilted my head, staring into P'Ken's big, brown, cold, wet eyes. Just as I'd hoped, her casual approach and Aarif's rage had kept us all talking long enough for the paralysis to wear off. At least for me. A part of me had hoped I could talk P'Ken down here, but that wasn't going to happen. So now, there was only one choice.

"Okay, okay, I'll talk. It's really not that big a deal."

"I'm listening."

"Right. Well, the thing is, you aren't the closest thing to Yael's heir." Leaping off the floor and drawing the Glass Striker, I swung the most advanced handheld weapon ever designed like a big damn stick and knocked P'Ken's cane-whip out of her hands. "I am."

I was sure she'd been given genetic enhancements and maybe even some cybernetic upgrades giving her a firm grip, but I'd inherited more than just Juri's brain, claws, and fangs.

While P'Ken was off guard, I stuck my lips around the mouthpiece, rapidly twirled, and–

HUMAN!

I didn't even see her coming. I didn't even notice P'Ken closing the distance between us and chopping my throat, knocking the air right out of me and leaving me gasping. Aarif tried jumping her, but she just tossed him aside.

"Let me guess, some special glassblowing-themed weapon," P'Ken said as she took the Glass Striker from me. "If you thought you could fight me, or whoever else in the empire, with it, it must be pretty powerful." She smacked me across the face with my own weapon, knocking me back down. "But only Yael could have made something so ridiculous and impractical actually work."

P'Ken turned around to retrieve her own weapon, but like Hell was I just going to let her. This wouldn't end here. I couldn't breathe, but I wasn't the only one in this body. And Juri didn't need to breathe.

Transferring control over to the best girl ever, Juri didn't hesitate to pop out her claws and fangs and rush P'Ken, roaring as she did so. Unfortunately, that gave P'Ken the notice she needed to be aware of the incoming attack, even if she didn't know who was behind it.

"Positively beastly," P'Ken said as she dodged strike after strike, even blocking one with the Glass Striker. "I'd ask if this is a result of putting pieces of Juri inside you but—"

Juri, look out!

Juri was ferocious. She could fight even when I was compromised. But she wasn't the smartest girl. She wasn't even paying attention as P'Ken got her hands on her cane-whip and struck us with the tip to electrocute us with a much higher voltage than earlier.

Control of the body returned to me as we fell over, completely immobile. "Layla! Juri!" Aarif cried.

P'Ken glared at him with disdain. "That wasn't very nice. And very confusing." Swinging her cane-whip, Aarif was electrocuted once again as well. "You will both answer my questions. Even if you need to do so in the brig."

# CHAPTER 8: KAYA

G36-B was just large enough to be classified as a planet instead of a moon. It had been an independent world for a few years, with a name that would be lost to time, before it had been claimed by the Utozin Authority. Hidden among various other independent worlds and away from Utozex territory, the previous Chancellor had thought it would be an opportune location for secret military bases and research facilities. Striking a deal with their former president, the chancellor moved the planet's measly population of 50,000 to a variety of Utozin colonies and set up shop.

Naturally, no one could really hide from the Cykebian Empire. Aunt Morphea's men had found it a month into the war, and subsequently bombed their bases and deployed Cykerdroids to wipe away the rabble and arrest their leaders. That was the last I'd heard, but as it turned out, Mother had kept a few hundred scientists and soldiers behind, to perform research in the name of the empire, and to perform experiments on.

And now? Now this world would be my birthday present. "I get to blow it up?!" I squealed with excitement.

Molina nodded with a pleased smile. "*Ricochet Supreme*'s weaponry has received a variety of upgrades. Targeting the molten core of a world directly, its cannons can now destroy worlds in an instant. To date, I have only had the weapons tested on uninhabited rocks. But I know you relish new thrills, and our research here has run its course, so yes…" Molina's smile widened. "Happy Birthday, Kaya."

My heart raced. Or did it flutter? I wasn't sure, but my hand was over my heart feeling it as my face lit up like an inferno. I also wasn't sure if it was because of how amazing this surprise was and how fun it sounded, or if it was because it was thought up and given to me by Molina.

Either way, I could have jumped up and screamed with exuberance. She cared. She understood me. She loved me.

"Thank you so much, Mother," I said, hugging her. "I couldn't have asked for more."

Molina hugged me back. It wasn't very tight, but it was nice. "I really do hope you can forgive me for missing much of the party. Unrelated to the war, this has taken much preparation."

Oh gods! Of course! That made so much sense!

Pulling away, I grinned at Kaybell. "I'm so sorry, Mother. Thank you, too."

"Of… course, my angel."

I reached out a hand and gently took hers. We'd gotten freshened up together, but while I felt better than ever, Mother was clearly still under the weather. I'd almost agreed with her that she should go lie down, but now that I knew what the climax of my party would be, she couldn't go anywhere. If anything could help her mood, it would be an all-new demonstration of the empire's power—her empire's power.

Escorted by guards, the three of us returned to the ballroom, naturally to thunderous applause, and took center stage. The ship was positioned right outside G36-B's atmosphere, the curtains had been raised to reveal the largely barren world, and Molina had given me a remote. The rest of the preparations had already been taken care of. When signaled, all I'd need to do is press a button... and boom.

But she wasn't the only one who'd made preparations. It was my special day, so I'd written a speech for the occasion. It had only taken a few minutes to adjust to work in the glory of what was about to happen.

The lights went out, a spotlight came down on my mommies and I, the Cykebian anthem played, gathering the crowd's attention. My subjects gave small bows and a quiet applause. The applause only lasted a few seconds, but with how excited I was, it felt like an eternity.

"Loyal Cykebian nobles," I began. "Thank you all for joining my family and I on this most holy of occasions. As the future emperor of the Cykebian Empire, every year of my growth is more important than the last. And I am proud to say that I have grown more this past year than any before... although, obviously not physically." Pause for faux laughter over joke about my permanently petite stature. Aaaand, proceed. "I have learned so much about myself, about what it means to rule, and about our culture. The greatest culture the universe has ever known!" Pause again for light clapping. Aaaand... "Today, I am 14. By Cykebian law, as originally dictated by my ancestor, Emperor Leon, in one year, I will be a young adult—eligible to sit upon the throne in the event Emperor Kaybell cannot. This is not something any of you need worry over, however—the crown is as strong as ever, and with myself as its ultimate sword, it is invincible!" Another applause... "You all know what an honor it is to be able to celebrate this day with me. You are the elite of the elite. But it is just as much an honor for me to be able to spend this day with you. It is for that reason that I share the incredible sight which is about to behold us live. The ship you all stand on now has been upgraded in ways only Cykebian science could achieve. It is now capable of destroying entire planets! And, to celebrate this day, I shall be displaying this new weaponry for the universe! In 60 seconds, I will destroy G36-B, and kill everyone still there, with the press of a button!"

The cheers and applause were thunderous. Individually, it meant nothing. I would kill any of them in an instant if necessary. But as a whole? These were truly my people. Bloodthirsty elites who knew their place, and knew it was their right to punch down until every ant was squashed. Horrible monsters without compassion. Just like me.

THUMP THUMP! THUMP THUMP!

My flawless smile cracked a little. My senses were as far beyond other people's as my strength. My hearing, I generally moderated to keep from driving me crazy, but with her standing right behind me, I couldn't not hear Kaybell's heart beating hard and fast.

"Mother, are you okay?" I whispered through my grin as a holographic countdown clock appeared above us.

"Are you?" Molina echoed with equal concern.

"I…" Kaybell started. "I didn't realize there were still people on the surface."

"Why does that matter?" I asked. "It's just soldiers and prisoners."

"Exactly," Molina said, taking Kaybell's hand. "Did you send someone important down there without telling me? I can't think of any other reason you'd take issue. They're just peasants and Utozins."

Kaybell opened her mouth to speak, but again, no words came out. With her lips together, she weakly nodded.

Why was she doing this? Why was she being so weird? Why was she making me worry so much? Now of all times?!

The countdown clock hit ten. In a few seconds, it wouldn't matter what her problem was. And for the next few seconds, I had to not care. This was about me. This was about what I was born to do. This was my gift from my Mother.

"3! 2! 1!"

My thumb slammed down on the remote. As the clack sounded, *Ricochet Supreme*'s cannons fired. Holy white light raced toward the surface of G36-B. In the blink of an eye, Ragnarok devastated the planet. It was blown apart like a crumbling cookie, most of the world reduced to dust, while fires visible from the comfort of my party consumed the larger chunks.

My heart raced, my heart fluttered, like it never had before. Yes! This was everything!

This was my destiny!"

"A HA HA HA HA!" I laughed in amazement as the crowd cheered and applauded once more. I squeezed Molina tight. "Thank you, Mother! I have never felt more alive!"

Molina stroked my hair. "Anything for my princess."

I could have cried. Not out of sadness or anxiety like earlier, but from pure joy. I was loved. I was understood. I could see my true future right in front of me. And I would walk the path in the comfort and support of my mothers' arms.

"AHHHHHHHHHHH!"

All of those feelings were ripped away as I was sucked back into the reality of something being horribly wrong with Kaybell. Shrieking like a banshee, she fell over on her knees. My heart sank as the crowd gasped.

"Mommy," I muttered without any strength behind my voice.

I meekly reached out to her, but Molina pushed my hand away. Looking up, I couldn't tell what she was feeling or thinking. Only that her eyes were empty.

"You animals!" Kaybell wailed. Tears and mucus streamed down her face, ruining layer upon layer of makeup and distorting her image. "You monsters!"

"My love, let's take this elsewhere," Molina said. "You're spoiling the mood and embarrassing the crown."

Kaybell looked up at Molina. While Molina's eyes were the cold ones she wore while discussing military matters, Kaybell's showed a look I'd never seen in them before: hatred.

SLAP!

There were murmurings in the crowd. Those came to an end as, in a single motion, Kaybell stood up and slapped Molina across the face. The silence was deafening. Saying the moment after felt like it lasted an eternity would have been an understatement.

"Embarrassing the crown." Kaybell laughed. "What is there to embarrass?! The crown *is* an embarrassment!" She bulged her eyes and held out her arms. "This empire is an embarrassment! The greatest culture the universe has ever known? We are barbarians draped in silk and velvet! Our technology is stolen, our so-called equality a lie! We 'civilize' worlds while committing wholesale slaughter! And we laugh! We laugh and laugh and toast!"

She paused as her tears momentarily made it too difficult to speak. What was happening? Mother had stopped being soft when the war began. Even if she was still that weak, she wouldn't have been saying this.

"I am Emperor Kaybell Kose Bythora, daughter of Stephen and descendent of Leon, first emperor of Cykeb and founder of the Sunrisers, ruler of The Holy Cykebian Empire. No one believed the lies we tell ourselves more than me. I was a creature of nightmares whom all of you would have celebrated when I took the throne. But I changed. I changed, and many of you turned against me." She narrowed her eyes at Molina. "I changed for you." Her head turned to me. "For both of you." She looked back at Molina. "I knew I could be better, I believed the empire could be better, and you both deserved better. I was wrong."

I was frozen. I couldn't move, I couldn't think, I couldn't speak. This was a nightmare.

This had to be a nightmare. I'd only felt so helpless once before. When Shun had nearly murdered me in my bed. I could see the tears running down my own face, but I couldn't feel them. I could see and hear the crowd. Rage and disgust on their faces and in their voices. And then there was Molina. Silent with a dry, unreadable face.

Then, finally, an expression emerged. She smiled. Not politely or warmly, but like a different person. Like the person I'd briefly known before she was empress.

"Kay... I love you."

Kaybell's breath got heavier as her body shook. Her knees trembled while her hands remained ready to strike again.

"No matter how much you hurt us, no matter how much pain and suffering you spread, no matter how many worlds you conquer... it won't bring Yael back. And you will never be anything but an average commoner longing to be special."

Molina's smile disappeared as quickly as it came. "Do not say her name."

"Why not? Look at yourself. Look at everything you've done! Is this what you think Yael would have wanted? Do you think she'd still love you like this?!"

I wasn't sure what any of this had to do with Yael, but I hadn't even thought of that. For as much as I was sure Yael would never be able to accept me as I was, I'd neglected to realize that would mean she wouldn't love the same Molina I did.

"Yael was my weakness," Molina spoke. "She was weak. Just like you. You always have been. You had all the power and you couldn't even stop me from leaving you behind for her."

"Because I respected you! Because I loved you! That isn't weakness!"

"No, love isn't a weakness. Not being willing to do anything for it is."

I had to say something. I had to do something. I couldn't just stand here and watch this nightmare unfold. I didn't understand any of this, I didn't get it, I couldn't help. All I could ask was…

"Is this my fault?"

I practically squeaked the words out. Like a little mouse. But it was better than staying silent.

Kaybell didn't even look at me, not taking her eyes off of Molina. Molina, meanwhile, turned my way.

"Of course not, Kaya," Molina said.

"But… but this sounds like it's about Yael. And I killed her."

"You are a child. You cannot blame yourself for how you were raised. You did not kill Yael. You are not responsible." She looked back at Kaybell. "She is. But I forgive her."

"Bullshit!" Kaybell screeched. "Yes, it is my fault. All of this is my fault. The result of my mistakes! But don't you dare lie to her that you want anything more than to hurt me. And her."

I gripped onto Kaybell's arm. My body had moved on its own. My brain wasn't working, but it knew it had to do something more.

"Mother," I said, trying my best to smile through my tears. "Please stop this. I don't know what's going on, or what's wrong with you, or how much of this is from the alcohol, but please stop. We can talk about this later. Everything will be okay. We're a fami—"

Kaybell struck again. This time, she struck me. I couldn't even feel it as she shattered my world.

"I'm sorry."

We both fell to our knees in tears. Whatever Kaybell felt couldn't possibly compare to what she'd just done to me. She'd hit me. My mommy had hit me. Looking at me with complete disgust. Like I was the monster I knew I was.

Guards and more guards rushed up to and surrounded us. Molina must have gestured a command, but all I could see was darkness.

"Lords and ladies," Molina said, no longer speaking to us. "I apologize for this embarrassing display. Personal issues should never be allowed to interfere with the needs of the empire. Clearly, your emperor is in no condition to rule. She is compromised; she is mentally unfit. By Cykebian law, and by my right as empress, I hereby assume temporary control of The Holy Cykebian Empire until such time arrives that my wife is fit to rule once more. Should that time ever arise."

The cheers and bellows from the crowd all sounded like static. They wanted this. They supported this.

And so did I.

"No!" Kaybell roared as she attempted to strike Molina again, but I stopped her, restraining her arms behind her back. She wouldn't get to hurt us anymore.

"I am sorry it has come to this, my love," Molina said. "Escort the emperor to a free room. When we return to the palace, she will be confined to her chambers until further notice."

Kaybell tried to scream again as guards took her off my hands, but she failed. She didn't have any fight left in her. The nobility applauded as she was dragged away.

I didn't understand. I couldn't understand. I wanted to keep screaming and crying and I wanted to vomit. I wanted to kill everyone around me. I wanted the truth! All I wanted was the truth!

But the truth wasn't being told to me. The only truths I knew were that Kaybell had spoken against everything I believed in, that she'd hit me, and that she'd said I'd done something wrong. The only truths I knew were that Molina believed in what I did, and that she was the one with her arms now wrapped around me.

"She will always blame you for what you did," Molina said, stroking my hair. "But I never will… my sword."

I hugged her back. What else could I have done?

# CHAPTER 9: LAYLA

I told you so.

I moaned/yawned as I banged the back of my head against the wall of my holding… quarters? Captain Amatyn was still playing with kid's gloves. That was the only explanation for why I'd been put in a spare lieutenant's bedroom, not even in the barracks, as opposed to a holding cell. It wasn't much, being smaller than my dorm room, but it beat the alternative. In what had to be close to three days since she'd arrested me, P'Ken had also been making sure I was delivered real, vegan food, as well as my hormones.

She'd still been making sure I knew I was a prisoner. I wasn't allowed to leave these four cramped, drab, and colorless walls. There were four security guards right outside my door, and she'd equipped me with an anklet that would alert half the total security personnel who served on the *Mangalarga* if I took a step outside. My cage was a comfortable one, but a cage nonetheless. She'd left me with no tech, she'd strip searched me for and removed from the room anything that could even hypothetically be used as a tool to escape, and she hadn't left with me any forms of entertainment or means of communication.

The idea of P'Ken committing torture at all was difficult to stomach, but it was a realistic one. That wasn't how she was going to play this here, though. She saw me as no threat, saw no rush to get the answers she wanted out of me, and was intending to wait me out. The accommodations were a carrot to make me docile, while the isolation and stimulation deprivation were the stick meant to break me. Still a form of torture, really, but a less direct approach than the empire typically utilized.

P'Ken wasn't just playing nice; she was underestimating me. She was toying around and doing as she pleased because she felt in total control of the situation. Three guesses where she learned to do that.

"Yes, you did," I said. "I still don't think it was a bad idea."

*You lost so bad!* Juri hammered in. *The Glass Striker is cool, but it's really stupid, human.*

"You didn't even get to really see it in action!"

*Because of how impractical it is!*

I sighed, running my hands through my disgusting, greasy hair. It wasn't worth trying to explain to Juri why I'd designed it the way I had. I knew what the most top-of-the-line schematics for the empire's genetically enhanced cyborgs looked like, and I knew Kaya was multitudes more powerful than them. The strength boost and enhanced senses I'd gotten from Juri were nice, but I needed a weapon, specifically, for the purpose of being able to match her in a fight. And that meant tapping into a power source no one else had. One that almost no one else could. Impracticality wasn't a design flaw; it was a necessity. My only mistake had been jumping the gun and leaving school before I'd had time to train with it. But how could I have waited with how many people were dying?

*Mmmm,* Juri grumbled. *I hope Foodgiver is okay.*

"Don't you worry your non-existent head about that, girl. Aarif's been through way tougher scrapes than this. He always got through them and was home in time to feed you."

Juri smiled. At least, I figured it was a smile. It was really more like a ray of sunshine in my brain. I'd pulled some real nonsense assembling the Glass Striker, but I really didn't have any idea how any of this was working.

The doors to my room slid open and I practically jumped off the floor. I'd already gotten lunch, and it definitely wasn't dinner time yet. This was something new.

A security officer entered, accompanied by two security guards. He was a short, round man with broad shoulders and an unfortunate shaved-in-the-front-but-not-in-the-back haircut. He also desperately needed to rejuvenate his skin.

"Hi there!" I exclaimed cheerfully, aiming to get them off-center. "What's up?"

The officer sniffed. "Captain Amatyn has requested you be brought to her office." One of the guards cuffed me. "If you attempt to run or resist, we have authorization to shoot." I was walked past him and out of the room. "Do not mistake your position."

"Be easier if you weren't sending mixed messages," I mumbled, not believing they'd actually shoot.

The *Mangalarga* was easily the largest ship I'd ever been on. *Cascade* could fit in it at least seven or eight times. It was as empty as it was massive. Not in physical space, but emotionally. The atmosphere as I walked down the corridor, the looks I saw on crew members' faces, and the glances they shot me, it was all devoid of heart.

And how could it not have been? P'Ken may have gotten the golden parachute into being a captain for Molina, but common ground troops came from around the universe. Hell, this was a Sunriser ship. A lot of these people had genuinely enlisted in the hopes of making the universe a better place. Of course they were miserable fighting this pointless bloodbath of a war.

As the doors to P'Ken's office opened up, the guards shoved me forward. This was still a military ship, so it wasn't anything too lavish, but even this corrupt version of my old professor couldn't deal with just endless black and silver. There was a colorful rug underneath my feet; her desk, which clearly cost a fortune, had mists of purple mixed into the black; there were a few tasteful paintings hung up; an ancient tea seat was set to the side, and...

"You bitch."

"That's not a very positive customer service attitude to have," P'Ken joked, seated at her desk and playing with one of my sculptures. She carefully set it down on the desk before looking back at me. "Leave us."

The Sunrisers' saluted and did as they were told, leaving me alone with their captain.

"I was only trying to support you in your creative endeavors," P'Ken said. "And I wasn't the only one."

"Why am I here?" I asked. "Three of us going for a picnic?"

"Now how could we do that when we don't have any pear honey?"

A genuine laugh escaped my lips. Fuck. Guilt bubbled up in my stomach. I knew what P'Ken had become, I knew how many people's deaths she was responsible for, and I was still laughing at our old, stupid inside jokes.

"I guess we'll never picnic again," I said flatly. "I'm still not talking."

"To me? I assumed as much." She slid a tablet on her desk forward. From the decals on it, my tablet. "But your princess would like to speak with you."

"Kaya!"

I rushed forward to grab the tablet, but Captain Amatyn stuck her cane in my face before I could reach it. Not that it mattered much with me still cuffed.

Kaya had tried calling me. Finally, after all this time. I didn't know why, and I didn't care.

This would have been so much easier if she'd called a week ago, but I didn't care about that either. She wanted to talk to me. And that made me more confident than ever that I could save her.

"Get me out of these things and let me talk to her! You have to do whatever she says, don't you?!"

P'Ken circled her cane around my face. "I allowed it to ring. As far as she knows, you were unavailable. I will allow you to call her back and discuss whatever you girls would like. I know you still care for her, as she still cares for you. But, in exchange, you will tell us both what you are up to. No room for negotiation."

Dammit.

"Okay," I said with a heavy breath. "You win."

"I know. Be sure to wish her a happy birthday; she just turned 14. And please, do not lie to the poor girl. She despises liars."

For good reasons.

"You have a deal. Please. Just let me talk to her."

My legs almost gave out underneath me as P'Ken remotely deactivated my cuffs. This was the best chance I was going to get. The right combination of words could end the war right here, right now. Yael could have done this. I had to be able to as well.

While I thought hard to silently ask that Juri stay quiet during this, P'Ken tapped on the tablet a couple of times, calling back Princess Kaya.

My stomach bubbled with anxiety as it rang, but it didn't get much of a chance. She picked up almost immediately, a hologram of Kaya appearing above the tablet. My heart pounded; she looked like she'd been crying for hours.

"Layla!" she wailed.

My heart thumped as I pushed the first words out of my mouth. "There's my EZ Sister."

She giggled. I laughed with her. I initiated our old handshake, and she did the same. We flipped our hair, bumped our fists together, wrapped our pinkies around one another's, clapped our hands three times each, and flipped our hair again. I'd come up with the handshake on the spot as I'd been thinking of ways to make Kaya feel at ease on *Ricochet*. There was no special meaning to any of it, but it made her happy. And that was special enough.

I didn't know where to start. I should have but I didn't. I had to let her take the lead and build off whatever she said. I couldn't take a chance on a poor approach.

"I've missed you. How are you?!" she asked, grinning through her otherwise tired face. "I know you have been attending art school. Is it everything you hoped for?"

Got it.

"I've missed you, too. And it is," I answered truthfully. "And more. I'd love to show you around my campus. What about you? Have things gone like you hoped?"

It was targeted. And cruel. But I had to go straight for the heart. Playing totally nice last time had gotten me shot in mine.

Kaya's smile fractured as she forcibly held it together. "Of course! Have you not been watching the news? My mothers and I are finalizing the empire's conquest of the universe and no one can stop us! It's magnificent, and my mothers and I couldn't be happier."

I'd heard Kaya spout plenty of the elitist, megalomaniacal, sadistic crap her aunts had drilled into her head. There'd been no hesitation and no doubt. I could already hear the difference now. Her voice was shaky, and she tripped on certain words.

What the Hell did you do to her, Molina?

"It's good to hear that. You deserve only the best from my old professor, the empress."

Kaya's chest pumped as she nodded. "I am so happy you picked up. Besides my mothers, I have been surrounded by nothing but boring, noble fools. Or, in Griffin's case, just a noble fool."

I forced a laugh. "I've missed you too. How is Posh Boy?"

"Fine. I'd rather it was you living in the palace, though."

I'd have rathered it was me as well. If I'd been her lady-in-waiting, if I'd constantly had her ear, things wouldn't be the way they were.

"That would be something," I hummed. "Oh yeah, I almost forgot, happy belated!"

Kaya weakly giggled and grinned. "Thank you. Um. You know I'm not fond of apologizing. Generally speaking, it is beneath me."

I raised an eyebrow curiously. "But?"

"But, most people, nobles, commoners, and foreigners alike, are beneath you as well. I am sorry I shot you. You were supporting me and I… overreacted to you not completely submitting."

Music to my ears. The urge to bring up who else she'd hurt that day was strong, but that wasn't the right way to play this. The instant I dropped the Y-word, this became about her. It needed to be about us.

"I wasn't even mad," I half-lied. "Thank you. But I understand what you were going through."

Kaya held her head down, casting her eyes toward the floor.

"Kaya?"

She sniffled. "Then why did you never respond to my message?" Out of the corner of my eye, I noticed P'Ken cringe.

"What message?" I asked with suspicion, keeping an eye on the captain.

Kaya tilted her head up, eyes wide. "The one I left for you with you the engineer and Captain Amatyn! When I… when I dropped off the body. I told them to tell you when you woke up that my invitation was still open! If you wanted to study, fine, but you could have called me! I've been thinking you hated me!"

"What?!" I cast a stink eye toward P'Ken. All the finishing and military training in the world couldn't hide her shame. "Kaya, I never received that—"

"Princess Kaya…" P'Ken pushed through whatever she was feeling and circled around her desk, taking a spot next to me and entering Kaya's field of vision. "Wonderful to see you as always. I trust your birthday party was as enjoyable as you'd hoped?"

What game was she playing? There was nothing she could say that could turn this around for herself in Kaya's eyes outside denial, and from the formal way P'Ken was speaking, there was no way she cared about her more than she clearly still did about me. There was no way she'd trust her more. Unless…

Crap.

"Captain?" A seething Kaya asked in confusion. "What's going on here? Why are the two of you together? And why did you not deliver my message?! Not that it really matters. You're dead no matter what!"

Her voice was just like it had been in her last moments on *Ricochet*. Pained and full of rage and confusion.

P'Ken smiled like nothing was wrong. "Please, calm yourself,

Princess. Have some tea. I assure you, I did forward your invitation to Layla as soon as she was recovered. It is unfortunately possible that either the injury, the treatment, or the painkillers she was given made her forget."

Fuck you.

"As for why my old student and I have reunited, I've been wondering the same thing. We are presently aboard the *Mangalarga*. My spies informed me that the ship I'd given Layla was heading toward the location of retired career criminal Jellicimo Horzinski. I moved in to intercept, fearing she was getting herself wrapped up in something unfortunate. I discovered not only she but also Aarif had gone to speak with him, and with neither of them willing to cooperate and tell me what they were doing, I had no choice but to take them all into custody."

I forced myself to stay calm. Or at least to keep the appearance that I was. P'Ken didn't need to have a close bond to pin the blame on me if Kaya knew what I was up to. I couldn't lie to her. That would only make things worse. Not to mention P'Ken would no doubt put me in an actual cell for crossing her. I had to spin this. P'Ken wanted to redirect blame? Two could play at that game.

"Layla?" Kaya questioned, her voice trembling.

I donned my own smile. "P'Ken could hypothetically be right about your message. The rest of what she's said is fact. The truth is..." I paused to shoot my confidence-full grin at P'Ken. "I've been worried sick about you."

"Worried?" Kaya whimpered and laughed, as I could see the wheels turning in P'Ken's head; she knew what I was doing, but she couldn't stop me without putting the onus back on herself. "Why would you ever be worried? About me fighting the war? Hello! I'm killing everything that stands in my way!" She pursed her lips and pouted. "Or are you worried because that's what I'm doing?"

"Kinda. You know me. You know I'm not going to support the murders of countless innocent people." Kaya crossed her arms. "But I also still believe in people being able to live their lives however they wish. I don't like seeing reports of the cities you've razed, but I'm more personally concerned about *you* razing them."

Some may have considered half-truth and lies by omission to be lies, but I wasn't in a position to question that. Too much was riding on this.

"I don't understand."

"Sorry. It's just that when you were with us, you realized this wasn't what you wanted. It was only after Shun attempted to assassinate you that you went backward. I could be totally wrong, but that… has never stricken me as a realization, so much as a trauma response. I've learned all about that kinda thing at school. And I know Molina has gotten pretty bloodthirsty and cruel since I saw her. I just wanted to make sure you were doing this because you wanted to, and not because she was making you."

There was something in Kaya's eyes. A pain. A hurt. A desperation. It only lasted for a moment before she looked at me like I was crazy and burst out laughing, but I knew what I saw.

"Don't be stupid, Layla. You're better than that. Of course I want this! No one can make me do anything. I do appreciate the concern, though." She narrowed her eyes. "What does this have to do with Horizinski? Or the smelly engineer?"

"I didn't know we were still on speaking terms. I believed that if I wanted to speak with you, I'd need to come see you in person. And that would require some assistance, so I picked up Aarif and sought out the best hacker I know who isn't being held prisoner by your mom."

"That's not Mother's fault; they chose not to bend the knee." Kaya snickered. "Or, well, I suppose they didn't." P'Ken gave a polite chuckle. "In any case... is that it? Why wouldn't you just tell Captain Amatyn that?"

"A very good question," P'Ken echoed, clearly not buying it.

"I'm sorry," I said again. "I am aware of the reputation that now precedes her, and I wasn't sure if I could trust her. For all I knew, she'd arrest me for plotting to infiltrate the palace. You guys are pretty ruthless. It hurts not being able to trust the people you love, but...I'm no soldier."

Deflect, deflect, attack Molina. Deflect, deflect, attack Molina. Kaya was in denial, and with P'Ken hovering over me especially, I wasn't changing that now. But I could plant as many seeds of doubt as possible.

"Then we should go straight to the palace." My eyes widened as P'Ken spoke, her face beaming with sickening sweetness. "I will take Layla and Aarif directly there. They won't be able to have the honor of meeting the emperor at this time, but we can all have a little reunion, and her highness can decide what to do about Horizinski. ETA 49 hours. Does that sound nice, Princess?"

"Yes," Kaya whispered. "Yes!" she exclaimed. "Bring them immediately." She turned to me. "We are going to have so much fun! Who knows? You may even wish to stay."

"Maybe," I said, nodding along. There was nothing I could do to fight this. Right now, I had to play along, or Kaya would turn her rage back toward me. That was the last thing I could let happen. "I'm happy this was all just a big misunderstanding. I'll see you and the others soon."

Kaya bounced and initiated our handshake, humming "Always Like a Bridge" as she did so. I hummed with her as I executed my part of the handshake.

"I can't wait."

"Sames."

With that, Kaya hung up. But I still couldn't breathe.

"When I went to join the empire, I snuck into Molina's bedroom in the middle of the night just to remind her how easy such a feat was for me," P'Ken said, turning to me. "Do you think you'd need Aarif and Jellz's help? If just sneaking and infiltrating the palace really was your only goal, I mean?"

I clenched my fists, looking into her smug eyes. "What game are you playing?"

"It's your game, Layla. I'm just trying to figure out the rules." She stuck my cuffs back on me. Without the Glass Striker, it wasn't worth even trying to fight her. "I may be the only one who still cares about our family, but I won't allow any of you to harm each other or get yourselves killed fighting for a lost cause. We are not the good guys. Stop pretending otherwise." P'Ken turned me around and had me march out of her office, into the arms of two guards. "Return her to her quarters. She must be well rested before her audience with the princess and empress."

I sighed as the guards took hold of me and escorted me down the hall. My plan was a mess at this point, but I could still hold it together. I just needed to get a little creative. Not a problem for me.

Kaya had been working under the assumption that I hated her, and yet she'd called.

Despite how she was acting, this was a cry for help. But much as I did want to see Kaya and help her, that wouldn't be happening just yet if I did things right. I could only hope I didn't hurt her too much in the process.

No, there were only three people I really wanted to hurt right now. And one of them I very much could.

"Thanks for staying quiet, Juri," I whispered. "But we need to go kick Foodgiver's ass."

# CHAPTER 10: KAYA

I should have been skipping for joy. I should have been rushing to my mothers to tell them about the conversation I'd just had. I should have been making Molina equally excited about the reunion that would take place in just a few days. I should have been heading straight to the royal spa to make sure I looked my best before Layla arrived.

But I wasn't doing any of that. I was sitting frozen, alone in my room, staring at my reflection in my blank and empty tablet. I hadn't been honest. I hated liars, but I'd just done almost nothing but lie to my EZ Sister's face. She was going to be mad when she got here and found out what a mess I was. She hadn't promised to always forgive me. She wasn't Yael.

Yael. Layla hadn't even brought her up. That was weird.

I scratched my nails against the tablet's screen, the keratin in them strong enough to claw through the inferior material. My performance was perfect. Layla believed that I was the perfect princess happily waging war and thrilled to rule the universe with my mommies. She believed the lie I'd been telling myself for a year.

I tucked my knees against my chest and wrapped my arms around them. I didn't understand what had happened at my birthday party, but I'd made sense of some of it. Namely, Kaybell had never changed. She'd always been soft. She'd always cared a disproportionate amount about her letter. The remarkable Cykebian princess she'd been in her 20s was well and truly gone forever.

She'd never changed. All the time since I'd returned to Cykeb, she'd never loved me. She'd only ever hated and feared and been disappointed by me. Her slap had made that all too clear.

My Mommy, the woman who'd created me and loved me and wanted to give the universe to me on a silver platter, would never be a part of my life again. I loved her so much, but she just couldn't be. I couldn't help who I was, dammit! She, more than anyone, should have been able to accept me no matter what.

Molina… something was wrong with her. Something about Yael. Of course. But I didn't get what. Right now? I didn't want to. Right now, I knew that she loved me and supported me. I couldn't handle anything else right now.

Empress Molina Langstone Bythora now ruled over the empire unilaterally. And with me as her sword, we would end this war.

Closing my eyes, I hummed "Always Like a Bridge." Maybe Layla wouldn't actually care. It wasn't as if she'd ever even met Kaybell, and before meeting me, and even before hearing Yael's horror stories about her, she hadn't been a fan. If I could just put on a smile, and if Molina allowed Layla and the engineer back into her circle like she had Griffin and Captain Amatyn, then she'd never find out. And then once she was here, maybe I wouldn't be so lonely.

I tossed my tablet aside and laid my head on my pillow. I'd wanted to call her for so long.

I'd wanted my best friend at my own side. Now, I needed her more than ever. I didn't know if P'Ken had lied when she said she gave Layla my message. I didn't want to know. I hated lies, but I couldn't deal with a single one more right now.

Would Molina accept her? She wasn't actively against us, but she didn't support our glorious conquest either. Usually for either of us, that would be unacceptable. But this was Layla. Molina had been her professor for three whole years. Longer than I'd been alive when we met.

She had to be willing to embrace her, faults and all. Just like me.

Pursing my lips, I hopped out of bed. I'd had an idea. It wasn't an appealing or appetizing one, but it seemed practical. Yael was gone forever and Chancellor Shun was a traitorous bitch whose head would one day hang on my wall. But there was still one other member of Yael's family who wasn't set to appear at the upcoming reunion. Marcos. I'd never so much as bothered speaking to them. I'd only even tortured them once or twice. But if they were to be turned on our side as well, not only would we have a hacker of said-to-be unrivaled ability to aid us in finishing off the Authority, but the prospect of everyone possible coming back together could sway Mother toward trusting Layla.

Yes. I liked it! I had to take action like a proper princess, not just sit around and mope, and this was the action I could take. I wouldn't be speaking on my own to Marcos, though. I'd be bringing their old crush.

---

"Are you certain this is a good idea, Princess?" Griffin asked, the soft-faced, but handsome young man accompanying me in the elevator down toward the dungeon Marcos was being kept in.

"Do not question me on this," I told him, dressed in my military uniform. "I know what I'm doing."

"I'm sure you do. Just as I'm sure that I'm only still alive because

I'm one of the only people you and your mother *permit* to question you. And for a reason."

I seethed. His lack of ego, at least in comparison to us, and his training under Yael did allow Griffin to provide a unique, occasionally useful perspective from time to time. And, with my plan partially hinging on him anyway…

"Fine. Spit it out." I stared down at my flexed-out nails. "You have until we arrive."

"Thank you, Princess," he said with a nod. "I just don't understand how you plan on selling them on your idea. Marcos isn't me. Or Captain Amatyn. They have no respect for the crown. And they have even less respect for the empress."

I wrinkled my nose in thought. "Why?"

"Didn't you ask them that when you were torturing them? Because I can't imagine that helped."

I shot him an annoyed glare.

"That aside, Marcos spent their childhood being worked to the bone and exploited by their parents. Like my other old classmates, they were a prodigy among prodigies. And one of the rich and powerful forces that had a use for Marcos' natural ability was…"

"…the empire. I see."

Used in childhood to serve an elder relative's purposes? I could relate, gross as that thought was. I didn't regret what my aunts had made me… most of the time… but perhaps I could help them see the brighter side of their past.

"Anything else?" I asked.

Griffin side eyed me. I wanted to gouge out his stupid eyes, but not because of how he was looking at me; it was because I knew why he was looking at me that way.

"Right."

Griffin tensely nodded. "I respected the professor for her skill. Layla respected her for her ideals. The woman underneath it all was Captain Amatyn's best friend. Marcos? They longed for what she *had*. A successful career as a criminal totally under their own control. To never be held back or used again. Freedom."

The words did indeed carry weight and worth. It was genius of me to hear him out.

Yes... this would be tricky. But not impossible. I'd just need to make a few promises and deals on Mother's behalf. Hopefully after my disaster of a party, she'd be willing to give me some leeway.

The elevator arrived at its destination. The doors slid open, and Griffin gestured politely with his arms and a bowed head for me to step out first. There were no swears or screams thrown our way by animals as we made our way down the dark, decrepit hall. Each cell on this level was a solitary, sound-proof block made of four solid, metal walls. Molina hadn't shown her old student any mercy. She understood how dangerous they could be and took the necessary precautions to see they would never escape. I had to imagine seeing the conditions they'd be living in had they stuck by their friend played a part in Griffin's wise decision to switch allegiances.

Arriving at cell 111-278, I input the code on my tablet needed to open up a hole in the wall facing me. Inside, Marcos was asleep on their cot. I could see the bags under their eyes from across the cramped room, and smell the sweat in the beard they'd grown since last I'd seen them. Apart from the cot, the only other objects in the all-black cell were a dim, silver, light fixture; a ball; some ancient, dusty books Griffin had brought them for entertainment; and a toilet. They obviously couldn't be trusted with any form of technology. A little evil, even for us, but that included their chair.

They were short. They were all skin and bones. There were weird, icky marks all over their light skin. They hardly seemed formidable at all. But I needed them.

"Wake them up."

Griffin did as ordered, approaching Marcos and shaking their body until they jolted awake.

"What?! Who?!" Marcos glared at Griffin with hate and disgust, before turning those same disrespectful eyes toward me. "You."

"Marcos, please stay calm," Griffin requested. "This isn't what you're thinking."

"You mean her royal pain in the ass isn't gonna strap another battery to my tongue? Lucky me." Marcos spat on the floor as they brushed their hair out of their face. "And just go back to calling me Platyperson, Posh Boy. Hoodie's gone, but you don't deserve to say my name."

Solitary confinement and sensory deprivation for a straight year would drive most people to unrecoverable madness. From what Griffin and Mother had told me, Marcos had barely changed at all. According to an analysis one of our therapists had run, their experience spending days at a time on a computer without any human interaction, combined with them passing the time by replicating that experience and writing code in their head, had allowed them to maintain the perception that they were fine, even if they definitely weren't underneath.

"No, I am not here to torture you," I said, standing tall. "Fun as that was, we have a proposition for you."

Marcos laughed. "How many times do I have to tell you arrogant, badly dressed, potpourri-scented, genocidal nutjobs that I'm never working for you?"

I snickered back at him. "That your resolve still stands is

impressive. Foolish, but impressive. I have a different but similar proposition for you."

"Oh, this should be rich."

Hands behind my back, I stepped closer to the enby genius. "Layla and Aarif will be arriving on Cykeb in two days."

*That got them,* I thought, as their eyes bulged.

"Captain Amatyn picked them up. And I'm going to ensure that they stay here. I do not wish for you to serve the empire. I only want to make your family whole again."

They masked their true feelings on the matter, whatever they were, by shutting their eyes and laughing. The fact they felt the need to mask like that at all was a good sign.

"Yeah, hate to tell you this, Prin-Prin, but I never bought into the whole 'family' crap. Your stooge can tell you that. And even if I did, I think your mommy and Shun turning out to be cunts of the highest magnitude would have put the kibosh on that. Oh, and, of course, you murdering my teacher."

My first instinct as those words reached my ears was to raise my arm and fry this pig like the livestock they were. But I didn't. Lashing out didn't help me. It never helped me.

"Marcos!" Griffin cried, outraged for me.

"What I say about my name?!" they screamed back at him. "Not like I'm wrong."

Griffin grunted. "I understand your rage. I do. But I know you care about Layla. At least, as much as you care about anyone."

Marcos sneered at Griffin. "You really want to go there?"

"Go where? Empress Molina telling me you were in love with me and the two of us finally getting on the same page, only for you to backstab me?"

"You backstabbed me!"

Gods bless Griffin. Jumping in to defend me and taking over the conversation when he noticed I was struggling? That's what I needed to see in a man. That and being hot. If Griffin were 10% hotter and Marcos were 25% hotter, they'd be putting on a good show.

"I made the decision that was in my own best interest and was practical!" Griffin spat. "Yes! Like you said, Yael was gone. We didn't turn against the empress initially because of her politics. We did it out of loyalty. The moment she died, we stopped having a reason to resist."

"Except, you know, not resisting meant swearing loyalty to the woman who cheated on her and the girl who killed her."

"Stop saying that!" I cried by accident.

"Oh, touch a nerve?" Marcos snickered.

Griffin shoved Marcos against the wall by their shoulders. "We didn't need to 'swear loyalty'! Layla didn't! Aarif didn't! We just needed to not make waves."

"As if the empress would have given me the same freedom as the rest of you. I wouldn't be here if that were the case. And by your own logic, what's your excuse for licking the boot?"

"I have no excuses, because I stand by my decision. I was prepared to try and make a life with you, you uncouth imbecile, but when that wasn't an option, I made the best life I could for myself."

"At the expense of literally everyone else."

"I am a cog in a machine. One that has not directly hurt another soul. That's all almost anyone is. No matter how independent or free you think you are, you still live your life by the grace of the masters of the stars. You serve a function you're allowed to serve. I play my part. And I live well. Better than rotting or being crushed, no?"

"You wouldn't even be a cog," I jumped back in. "I want Layla. That's it. I just want to be able to offer her her old friends and professors, all back in her life. If you agree to putting on a smile and living in the palace, then not only will I set you free, and not only will you live in the same level of luxury as Griffin, but I swear on my honor as a princess that Mother will not force you to work for her, nor will any harm ever come to you again."

Still held against the wall, Marcos' arrogance failed them and fell apart. And to shatter whatever will to resist they still held... "Additionally, I offer you the opportunity to study our technology for your own personal interest. In this day and age, a year is an eternity in technological development. You've fallen behind. I will allow you to fix that."

Marcos shook as I gestured for Griffin to release them. I wasn't done.

"Griffin is correct that very few possess true control over their own destinies. I know that freedom is what you seek. I... understand what it's like to be used. And yes, I do regret what happened to Yael. More than I will ever allow anyone outside your little group to ever know. But true freedom was not something you were ever going to achieve. Say yes, and you'll have as much as anyone outside my family will."

Marcos continued to look away, distantly. Griffin rested his gloved hand on the side of their face and nodded at them affirmingly. Surely, a mind as brilliant as theirs couldn't be foolish enough to pass this up. They had to see there were no alternatives.

Marcos turned to me and smiled in a way that didn't ooze contempt. "You've got yourself a deal, Princess."

I clapped my hands together. "Splendid! We shall get you out of here immediately and—"

"HA HA HA HA HA HA!" they cut me off with mocking laughter. "Yeah right. Get fucked, you little psychopath."

Griffin struck them before I even had the chance, a right-hook to the face, knocking out several of the peasant's poorly maintained teeth. As Marcos grunted in pain, Griffin rubbed his blood-stained, white-gloved hand.

"What a waste of time," I said, refusing to let this insect's words get to me. "Let's go, Griffin. We have preparations to make. And Marcos has a long life of rotting in solitude to get back to."

Marcos shot one last look at Griffin, tears in their eyes. Griffin's own eyes showed hurt, but he nonetheless followed behind me without another word. Once outside the cell, I shut it behind us.

"Do not worry, Princess," he said through heavy breath. "This was a good idea, but Layla is coming to see you. That will be enough."

I walked with my head cast down, my eyes on my reflection in my scratched-up tablet.

"Of course you did."

"She will always blame you." "Murdering my teacher." "The girl who killed her."

"Get fucked, you little psychopath."

"I'm not going to support the murders of countless innocent people."

"but that… has never stricken me as a realization, so much as a trauma response."

"Yes," I whispered. "You're right."

# CHAPTER 11: LAYLA

Please go easy on him.

"Nope."

Now that I was less a prisoner and more a... coerced guest? with an invitation to the palace from the princess, it wasn't difficult to convince the security personnel to allow me to see Aarif. For all he hated Kaya, he could have helped prevent the deaths of all the people she'd killed this last year if he'd just given me her message.

P'Ken was to blame, too, but I couldn't take my anger out on her just yet. For now, I'd have to settle for the professor I'd been stupid enough to put my trust in.

As I was escorted down a corridor, I took careful note of every surface, every control panel, and every member of the personnel around me. Much as I wanted to see Kaya, now, and as likely as she was to be enraged by my not coming as I said I would, I couldn't set foot on Cykeb. The instant I did that, the game was lost. I wouldn't be able to escape, and it was far too late to just talk Kaya down.

I had a plan to get off the *Mangalarga*. It involved doing something I really didn't want to, but Captain Amatyn would never see it coming. I would get the Glass Striker back, I would rescue

Jellz, get to *Cascade*, and escape the *Mangalarga*. All without getting my ass kicked again. I could do it all. But not before I got all this unhealthy rage out.

The doors to Aarif's quarters, which were nearly identical to the ones I'd been given, slid open. I stepped inside to find my old professor fast asleep as the security personnel shut the doors behind me.

I was half-tempted to let Juri take control and lick the bastard awake, but that would probably be worse for me than him. He still hadn't showered in the time we'd been together, and I was pretty sure he'd never been touched by a woman in the entire time I'd known him. Marcos used to joke he fucked Juri, but I hadn't even humored that idea by asking her.

Still, I needed to get him up somehow. Given the circumstances, the direct approach seemed appropriate.

Standing right over where he lay on the soft mattress, I popped out my claws and slashed him across the face.

"Wake up, you son of a bitch!"

Aarif jolted awake, heaving and grunting as he sat up, pressing his hand against his face.

He was lucky I'd gone shallow.

"Layla? What's going on?" He pulled his hand away from his face and looked down at the blood on it. "Did you just scratch me?"

"Why didn't you give me Kaya's message?!"

"Kaya's what?" Aarif questioned, reaching for a tissue to wipe off the blood. "I don't know what you're talking about."

I picked Aarif up off the bed by his shirt collar. "Kaya told you to tell me that I was welcome to go to Cykeb and be at her side. Juri's listening right now. And she knows what I know. Are you about to lie to her, too?"

Aarif nervously swallowed. "Come on, kid. This isn't your style. I promise I'm not—"

I threw Aarif across the room, slamming him against the wall. Instances where I'd used my cyborg strength before were few and far between. It felt good.

"Don't lie to me!"

I didn't say that. For a second, Juri had taken control. That didn't feel so good.

Sorry.

"We'll talk about that later," I whispered.

"Out with it, Professor!"

Aarif cracked his arms, grunting more and he stood up, hunched over. "Fine! You got me! P'Ken and I were given that message and decided not to tell you. Happy?"

I shook my head at him. "Why wouldn't you tell me?"

"Is that a joke?" His voice cracked like a prepubescent teen's. "She'd just murdered Yael! She was holding the body! And she'd made very clear the kind of person she planned on being. We couldn't endanger you by letting you follow her, and we knew if you got that invitation, you'd head straight there."

"Because it would have been the right thing to do!"

"No, because you can't accept that the world we live in isn't one for dreamers. You'd have gotten yourself killed in a week, after disagreeing with her highness one too many times."

'You don't know that."

"And you don't know that you could have changed anything."

This jerk. Out of all my professors, he'd been the one I was least close to. Shun and Marcos had spent way more time with him than me. He'd just been the only option I'd had, and now I wanted to wring my hands around his neck.

But I still needed him. I couldn't do this alone.

I sighed, tugging on my hair. "Okay. Okay. I hate you right now, but I can figure out what I want to do about that later. Right now, we need to get out of here."

Aarif squinted his eyes. "How are you even here right now?"

"P'Ken didn't spill the beans about the message. Kaya did. She called me and, long story short, now we're being taken to Cykeb."

Aarif snorted. "Isn't that what you want?"

I shook my head. "It's too risky. I believe in my plan, and I can't jeopardize it on this kind of gamble."

Aarif chuckled.

"It's not the same! Molina has hurt her in ways I can't even imagine. Talking won't help her now. The only way to save her, and everyone else, is still to bring down the empire."

"Okay," Aarif said, bobbing his head and plopping back down on the bed. "So how do we escape? Last time I was trapped on this ship, Juri cut a path for us. But now, all of their security personnel are even more advanced cyborgs than her. More advanced than you."

I smirked. "Yeah. They are more advanced. But they're just soldiers." I sighed. "I really didn't want to have to do this."

"What? You've got another trick up your sleeve I don't know about?"

*We've got another trick up our sleeve I didn't know about?!* Juri followed. *How's that work? We're always together!*

"Yes, we are," I whispered. "But not in my dreams."

Aarif flung his arms out and popped his lips. "Fucking Banshee magic."

I begrudgingly nodded to confirm. "Remember how I said the Glass Striker was kinda a Banshee thing? I'm not sure who was teaching me, it's all pretty hazy, but someone in my dreams taught me about The True Adventurer. She said she was a Banshee who didn't approve of how my g-gma had treated me. She couldn't give me the full power. I can't do any of the really crazy, reality-warping stuff, but whatever higher power is out there that lets it work, I tapped into it for the Glass Striker's power source. It was the only way to forge a weapon that could handle Kaya. That's also why it's, admittedly, not the most practical weapon. The True Adventurer is about stories and experiences. About doing and living as much as one can. To make that work with an object, I had to tell a story with it; my story.

"Mmhm, mmhm," Arrif nodded, half-way mockingly. "Insane. Kinda cool, but insane. But how does this help us now?"

I widened my grin. "I said I couldn't do any reality warping. Didn't say the Glass Striker was *all* I had. Enjoy the body, Juri."

Aarif expressed confusion at that, but I didn't stick around long enough to hear him. If I was alone in my head, I wouldn't be able to do anything with The True Adventurer without the Glass Striker. But thanks to Juri, there was a mind, a soul, to keep my body occupied while I went elsewhere. I couldn't alter people's perceptions or survive being killed over and over again through non-existent versions of myself, or conjure things that weren't real, but I could utilize The True Adventurer's most basic principle: I could do two things at once.

And so while my main body was grounded by Juri in Aarif's quarters, I was going to see Captain Amatyn in her office, with my claws at her neck.

"Hey, Professor."

P'Ken jumped in her seat. Finally. I had the upper hand. She was afraid.

"Layla," she said, trying to sound composed, but with a slight tremble still present. "How are you here?"

"Just got done explaining that. Don't really want to again!" I dug my claws just barely into her neck." You're going to let Aarif and Jellz out, you're going to give me the Glass Striker back, and you're going to let us all leave on *Cascade*, or I swear, P'Ken, I'll cut your throat."

P'Ken breathed heavily through her nose. "You don't have that in you."

"Bet your life on that?"

Yes, it was a bluff. I hated her just as much as I did Aarif for betraying my trust, and I hated way, way more for everything else she'd done, but unless it was in self-defense, I still couldn't imagine myself taking her life.

She'd gone through all the same training I had under Yael and more. I just had to hope that I could still outbluff her.

P'Ken chuckled. "The True Adventurer, hmm? Madame N'gwa must be proud."

"She doesn't even know about this."

"Sure she doesn't." Acting unconcerned about my claws, P'Ken leaned forward. "I won't pretend I understand anything about how you're doing this, but regardless of why you didn't use it against me, it's impressive."

She picked up her mug and sipped her coffee. In retrospect, I should have used The True Adventurer sooner. I had even less practice with it than I did my weapon, but it was still more practical. But that was g-gma's power, not mine, and I hadn't wanted to use it. My mistake.

"You know this only gives you more to offer," she said. "Not only could you be the princess's closest friend and lady-in-waiting, but a valued warrior capable of fighting alongside her. You're throwing away everyth—"

I cut her off by digging my claws a little deeper into her neck. "No more talking. Move. Slowly."

She breathed through the pain and set her mug down. P'Ken did as I ordered, rising from her seat without any sudden movements, and led us out toward the doors to her office.

"Give the order to your men," I said. "No one tries anything. Or I'll show you what else I can do."

If something in my voice had given away that this was all I could do, I was done. But sure enough, P'Ken didn't hear anything wrong. She turned on her com, and informed her crew that she'd been taken hostage, but none of them were to act; she would handle it. Perfect.

"You still haven't told me."

"Huh?" I questioned, marching P'Ken down a corridor as her frustrated, trigger-happy men shot me the stink-eye.

"What you're actually doing. You're threatening to kill me and rejecting living in luxury with people who love you, and I don't even know why."

I took a heavy breath. "Take a guess."

P'Ken hummed. "Do you wish to end the war? Assassinate Molina and, hopefully, Shun? Return Kaya to the girl you befriended?"

My silence was her answer.

She giggled. "Of course. The drawback to letting you attend art school. You realize all of that would be much easier to accomplish once on Cykeb, don't you?"

"Sure would," I said with a hint of enthusiasm.

"Then you must be after something else as well. Layla, I'm sorry you've gotten it in your head that I am your enemy, but, before we part ways, I have to see if you'd be willing to compromise."

The two of us stepped into an elevator.

"Glass Striker, first," I said. "What kind of compromise are you talking about?"

P'Ken exhaled. Her posture eased. She still wasn't actually *at* ease, but it was more like when I'd see her in the teacher's lounge, or drinking the night away with Yael and Aarif.

"I am not a warmonger. I am not a cruel woman. You know this about me."

"I did."

"I have only been doing what I felt was right. But perhaps there is a better way. I would love for the war to be over, and for the bloodshed to end. And I have my own idea for how this could be achieved."

"I'm listening."

"Kaya was hiding her true emotions on the call. I'm sure you saw that, too. What you don't know is that at her birthday party, Emperor Kaybell suffered a complete mental breakdown, and was confined to her quarters. Molina was finally able to seize the last bit of power from her and assume total control of the empire. Which also means that if anything happens to her, Kaya becomes the new emperor. Here's my offer. We return to Cykeb. Integrate you into Kaya and Molina's lives. Wait a couple weeks to throw off suspicion. Then, I kidnap Molina. You know I could. Kaya takes the throne, with you as her most trusted advisor, we pin the kidnapping on Shun, and, with my help, the two of you lead a full-scale invasion of Utozex Prime. Between Jellz, your Banshee abilities, and possibly even Marcos, Kaya could have the support she needs to break through the Authority's home world defenses, wipe out the Authority's leaders, including Shun, and force their new leaders to submit to a peace deal. No more fighting, no more conquering independent worlds, and Shun pays for what she did. When it's all said and done, you just have to be willing to let Molina live. I know we can make this happen. And I know you can't accomplish any of your goals without me."

That... wasn't the worst offer. It was nice at all hearing some real humanity out of P'Ken. And she was right that her plan probably had better odds of success than my own. But her plan hinged on me being able to sway Kaya toward peace. With Molina out of the picture, but... she didn't get it. So long as the empire stood, Kaya would never be free. So long as Molina was alive, Kaya would never be free.

We were two floors away from our destination. I had time for one question. "Molina's life really that much of a dealbreaker?"

P'Ken took a disappointed breath. "No one else in our family dies."

I nodded regretfully. "Thought so."

The elevator doors opened. I walked us out into a heavily guarded storage facility. A good place to keep both important cargo as well as contraband, like my Striker.

"I suppose there's nothing I can do, then," P'Ken sighed as she led us to where my weapon was being held. "And there's nothing left to say."

P'Ken led us into the back of the vault, performed a retinal scan, performed a voice command, and opened up the door hiding the Glass Striker behind it.

"There she is," I said, kissing my blowpipe and strapping it on my back.

"Aarif, next, I presume?"

"No. Jellz first."

P'Ken shrugged, hopefully just thinking I was going for the tactical choice. I couldn't be sure what she'd do if she walked into Aarif's quarters and saw Juri occupying my other body.

The elevator ride to the containment cell where Jellz was being kept was silent. P'Ken had said there was nothing left to say, and she'd apparently meant it. If only I could have made her see somehow that just keeping everyone Yael cared about alive isn't what she would have wanted. But I had no idea how to do that, nor the time to figure it out. I'd thought about it during my time as a prisoner, even tried standing on my hands, but nothing I thought of seemed right.

"BWAHAHAHA!"

Jellz cackled as he exited his cell.

"There is nothing funny about this situation," P'Ken said.

"Really? Cause I think this is hilarious. Only thing funnier would have been if she'd scratched an eye out."

He turned to me. "Good work, kid. You'll have to tell me how you pulled it off later."

P'Ken knew how to maintain a stone cold look no matter what, but Jellz's words seemed to crack it just a little. It definitely wasn't just from the sting of defeat. If I had to guess, despite how she was treating him, she wanted to be the one getting praise from Yael's old boss. It couldn't be easy, selling out your beliefs for the people you love and almost none of them being grateful.

Was that a way in? Making her feel like everything she was doing was for nothing? No, it was too late for that kind of thinking. We just needed to get Aarif and get out of here.

"Layla."

I pressured my fingertips against her neck, surprised to hear her address me again. "Yeah?"

"Whatever happens next, I'm sorry. And I hope you will forgive us."

I turned my head anxiously to Jellz. "Us?"

Jellz raised his hands up. "Don't look at me."

What was she talking about? Had she alerted Kaya somehow and gotten here already? Molina? No, that was impossible. Did she have a Banshee on board? She knew I already hated most of them. Had she somehow gotten Pena and Rachel to enlist?

"Guh!"

Looking down, my stomach was bleeding. Scratch marks. "What the Hell?" Jellz muttered.

Panicking, I slammed P'Ken into a wall. "What did you do?!"

She shook her head. "Nothing. You brought this on yourself."

Another scratch appeared. Much deeper. I wasn't a fighter. I wasn't used to pain like this. I screamed and doubled over. And that was all P'Ken needed to break hold of my grip, strike my gut and throat, and backhand me out cold.

My eyes flickered as my soul returned to my original body. One that was in just as much pain. What was even happening?! What was I missing?!

"Juri… girl… please tell me she didn't hack you or something."

Sorry, human. No.

My eyes finally opened and my vision cleared up. I was seated on the bed, with Aarif standing over me, flanked by soldiers with guns pointed down at me.

"Aarif," I practically whimpered.

He clenched his eyes and mouth shut. "Surprise."

## CHAPTER 12: KAYA

An interesting, fairly new business had caught my attention on Popcorn. Known as Cadere, they claimed to offer clothes that shifted with one's mood. The ones shown off their webpage were gorgeous, and suitably expensive for my tastes, but I was self-aware enough about my own… instability… to know that, if the clothes actually worked, the colors could be switching up constantly. Although, they could be even cooler if so.

I hummed to myself as I thought about this, the light of my tablet shining in the darkness of my unlit room. Cozily wrapped in my blankets and sitting in bed underneath the canopy, I should have been getting to sleep, but I couldn't just yet. If nothing else, I needed the perfect new outfit to wear when Layla arrived, and it needed to be something that was my style, but still artsy.

"Mmmm. Why not?"

I purchased a few of their dresses and sets, but continued shopping for backups. It wasn't as if gidgits were in short supply, not when I was willing to beggar a planet or two, so if I didn't like the pieces, I could just wear something else, and burn Cadere to the ground later.

Stretching my arms out, I let out an extended yawn. It had been a long day. A long few days. A long year. But Layla would be here soon. And then none of this would matter. Not the war, not what I did before, not my moms, not Marcos. Even if she didn't stay, even if she hurt me again, the time she spent here would be magical.

"Hmm. I wonder how I'd look in leather pants."

"And you will keep wondering about that." I nearly leaped out of my bed in shock as Mother entered my bedroom. She'd never come to visit me in the middle of the night. Ever.

"At least until you're older."

"H… how much older?" I asked, a smile creeping up my face. I wanted to ask what she was doing here, but she was *here* and just talking to me like a person; I wasn't about to shut that down.

"Let's say several decades. And beyond."

I giggled as Mother crossed the substantial distance from the entrance to my room to my bed. Dressed in a long, burning-orange nightgown, she climbed the steps up to my bed and sat down next to me.

"Didn't you used to wear a lot of leather before you became empress?" I asked.

"I did. Almost exclusively in fact, regrettably so. Did Yael show you pictures?"

My face fell, but Molina laughed and rested a hand on my shoulder before I could say anything. She smiled warmly. "It's okay. We can talk about her."

I tried to speak, but all that came out of my mouth were weak tats. Molina was never like this with me. She hadn't even spoken directly to me since the party. What was going on?

"I… I don't want to," I eventually spat out, putting as much confidence as I could behind the words. "Is there something you wanted to talk about?"

Molina laughed, no, cackled, as she fell onto her back, sprawling across my mattress. She waved me over to her, but I stayed frozen. This was too weird.

"What?" she questioned. "Too old to cuddle your mother? You know you're only really three."

I continued to stare at her with my eyes wide and my mouth agape. Meanwhile she continued smiling without a care in the world, her amber eyes big and full.

"Are you sick?" I asked. "Are you dying?"

Molina laughed even harder. "This must seem strange, hmm?" I nodded furiously. She tilted her head and looked up at the canopy. "I haven't been a very good mother to you. Frankly, I've been a horrible one."

"That's not true!"

"Don't," she said, waving her hand to silence me. "I know that you've been hurting. And I haven't done anything to help you, or even understand you better. And now with Kaybell so sick... it's not an excuse, but there is a reason for why I've acted how I have."

"What do you mean?"

Molina cracked her neck. She gestured once again for me to cuddle her. I didn't know what was going on, but I'd wanted her to hold me like this for such a long time. No matter how confused I was, I couldn't pass this up. I set my tablet down, crawled into her powerful arms, and let her continue.

"I... have made many poor choices. From when I was younger than you to today, I've never been the picture of Cykebian perfection. Just an "average commoner" who was fortunate enough to have a father who'd worked his way up from nothing to greatness. Just an Autistic little girl who somehow won the love of the greatest woman to ever live. And I'm not talking about your other mother." Molina rested her chin on my head. "You took them both from me, Kaya."

I shook and tried to jump away, but Molina held me tight. I wasn't sure if my strength had just abandoned me, or if Mother had gotten a *lot* of work done.

"Hey, hey," she pet my hair. "I'm not mad. Honest."

I welled up, my nose getting stuffy and my stomach churning. "How?"

"Well, I was. Deeply so. You heard about my reaction to learning you'd murdered Father. And, after you returned to Cykeb and informed us of what had happened to Yael... I shut down. I shut down, I became completely unavailable emotionally, and I preemptively started the inevitable war with the Authority because I needed to stick myself back into the only thing I'd ever been remotely good at: being a soldier. And Kaybell was right. I did want to hurt her. I wanted to hurt her so, so badly. Because what I said at the party was true. Regardless of my initial reactions, none of this was your fault. You didn't ask to be born, and Kaybell failed you once you were. And so I decided to hurt her where it would hurt most. She'd grown a conscience. She was a monster for the decade we were inseparable, but while I was away, she'd turned over a new leaf. And that new leaf, along with the opportunity she offered, caused me to make the biggest mistake of all."

She sniffled. My unstoppable empress of a mother actually sniffled.

"I never should have left Yael. I should have left Cykeb and rendezvoused with you all before you ever arrived, and I should have stopped all of this. It should have been us raising you. I'm sorry you'll never have that."

While Molina was just starting to cry, tears were streaming

down my face and my heart was pounding. Was I dreaming? This felt like a dream. Mother had stayed so strong, so invincible while Kaybell and I were breaking down at the party, but was she just as fucked up on the inside?

There were so many thoughts racing through my head, so many questions, but before I could get answers to any of them, there was an answer she'd already offered I needed to hear.

"You didn't say how you decided to hurt her."

"Right, right," she moaned, petting me still. "War doesn't need to be waged the way we've done it. It's not a way I ever thought I would fight a war. I left the Sunrisers originally just because Kaybell enjoyed torture. So quaint and insignificant in hindsight. But Kaybell, not you, had taken everything from me. And so, with her new, kind-hearted, egalitarian way of viewing things, I decided to become everything I hated to punish her. I decided to seize power from her, take control of the war effort, and commit unspeakable horrors across the universe in her name. The war was an inevitable and necessary evil, but I chose to weaponize it against her. I refused to let her wash her hands clean of what she'd done. She made me empress, she put me in this position, and she would always have to live with what she'd done."

This was crazy. But I knew it was no dream. Because even in my dreams, when Molina would hold me tight and tell me things, it was never anything like this.

Molina cupped a hand under my chin. "Are you ok?"

I rapidly nodded. "Would it be all right if I asked some questions? I'm so confused, Mother."

Molina smiled through her tears. "Ask whatever you wish."

I took the best breath I could. I hardly even knew where to start. "Do you love her at all? Do you love me?"

"Oh, baby." She pulled my face into her chest. "I loathe your other mother with every fiber of my being." My eyes jolted open as a wave of horror crashed against my mind's devastated shores. "I was so lost when we reunited. And she offered me everything. Only to hurt me worse than anyone ever had before. No, I do not love her. But, my beautiful daughter, I do love you. You are what will make life worth living when this war is over and done with."

After springing open, my eyes clenched shut. I was hysterical and I couldn't stop crying.

Thrusting my arms forward, I pushed Molina away. "So you've been lying to me?!"

Molina sat up straight. "I am sorry. I needed to keep you in the dark so I could prolong—"

"So why now?!" I screamed, sitting up and popping my katars out of my arms.

I didn't know what I was doing, arming myself against Mother. I was starting to think I didn't know anything.

"Because this horrible era of our lives is almost over," she said. "Our new weapons are going to make all of our problems go away. Kaybell has been driven mad. And the Authority is no longer any kind of match for us. In one week, we will launch our final invasion of Utozex Prime. We will raze their cities, annihilate their infrastructure, complete our conquest, and capture and execute the evil woman who deigned to try and kill you. Then, quickly and quietly, I will kill Kaybell. You will become the emperor of the entire universe, and I will finally be the mother you deserve."

My whole body shook as I forced my eyes open. Mother's smile was gentle. I didn't know if what she was saying was true. I wasn't sure if I'd ever be able to tell the difference between the truth and a lie again.

*"I just wanted to make sure you were doing this because you wanted to, and not because she was making you."*

"Your sword."

"What?"

"That's what I'm known as. The empire's ultimate sword. But I'm really just your sword. One to plunge into Mother." I clenched my fists. "You used me! You used me to steal power away from her, you used me to spearhead your unnecessarily ruthless campaign, and you used me because you knew me being the one to commit all of these massacres would hurt Mother even more!"

My arm moved on its own and tried to skewer Mother. Thank the gods, she was quick enough to dodge, leaping off the bed and onto her feet.

"Yes, I used you and I'm sorry. But Kaybell does not deserve your sympathy or your love! If she'd called me after you were born, if she'd been even a half-decent mother to you, no one would be dead. And the two most powerful women in the universe wouldn't be so utterly miserable."

Molina hung her head. "No one knew Yael liked I did. No one loved her like I did. But I know she was important to you, and I know you loved her, too. And Kaybell is just as responsible for what happened to her as Chancellor Segisteel." She picked her head up and glared at me. "I have hurt you and used you and lied to you because it's been the only way to liberate us both from the past. To liberate the universe through the glory of the Holy Cykebian Empire. But what has she done for you? She's just continued to ignore you, but not because she's busy. She ignores you because she's disgusted by you. Because she regrets making you."

She put her smile back on. "But I couldn't love you more. I am so happy every day knowing that I have you as my daughter. I will always accept you for who you are, Kaya. And no matter how mad I ever get, I will always forgive you."

The words. They were so much like Yael's. And yet they sounded so different. A free spirit vs. an empress. The woman who needed me to change vs. the one who accepted who I was. There was a warmth behind Yael's words that I missed. But there was no warmth inside me. So maybe it was better this way.

I retracted my katars.

"Layla is coming here," I said as I tried my hardest to compose myself. "It's a long story, but Captain Amatyn picked her up. Aarif too. They're all on their way here. They want to see us."

"I see," Mother said with a pop of joy as she wiped off her face, struggling to get a hold of herself as well. "Is that what your visit to Marcos was about earlier? I hope you weren't too rough with them this time."

I let out a small giggle. Mother giggled with me. Wow.

"No, it wasn't too bad. But yes. I thought them being free, working for us like Griffin and Captain Amatyn, would help convince Layla and Aarif to stay. For me. And for you."

Continuing to smile and laugh, Mother rested her head in her hand. "Who says you aren't a sweet girl?"

Mother gingerly stepped back toward me and, without any resistance on my part, she wrapped her arms around me. She was a monster. She'd tortured Kaybell this past year because of what I'd done. She'd slaughtered millions just to make her suffer more. And yet, she really did seem to love me. For real.

She wasn't like me. She was so much worse.

I hugged her as tightly as I could without breaking her. "I love you, Mother."

She was everything I'd ever wanted.

"I love you too, my princess," Mother said, kissing the crown of my head. "I will begin making preparations of my own for our family's arrival in the morning. I am so relieved you understand me. If you couldn't..."

"...no one else could."

Mother and I stood in silence for the next several minutes, just holding onto each other.

Two monsters alone at the top of the universe, hoping to not be quite so alone soon. I wished this was the Mother I'd had for the past year, and I wished either Yael could be alive to join us or Kaybell could have been a better mother. But one of them was dead and gone, and the other would be soon. Our pain, our troubles would be gone. We would revolutionize our lives and the universe. Utopia would be achieved. And as we continued to hold each other, it was as if Molina was plunging a sword through my heart.

# CHAPTER 13: LAYLA

No talking.

I didn't know if it was the animal inside me, though probably not considering Juri had just stabbed me in the back, but I didn't stay put on Aarif's bed to ask him what was going on or why he had betrayed me. I just lunged at the bastard and hoped I was faster than the Sunriser's trigger fingers.

No, there was no "hope" involved. I just wasn't even thinking about it.

The sounds of blaster fire and an exploding mattress rang as I gripped Aarif's throat and slammed him against the wall. Fangs out. Claws out. Vision better than ever.

"Layla, wait," Aarif begged as I scratched and squeezed his throat. The soldiers had spun around and gotten their guns back on me. One of them was shouting at me to stand down immediately. Or maybe he was telling his men to get him coffee and a Danish. I wasn't paying attention. "I'm sorry."

A thought was all it would take to kill him. My heated blood wanted to. I wanted to. I had the Glass Striker back. It was my move to make. I could kill them all so easily.

I threw Aarif around me, flinging him at the soldiers. They caught and steadied him. In the moment they'd been unable to act, I'd drawn the Glass Striker. Not to kill them, though. This was new. This was something I had to be wary of. If this was a part of me now, it was one I had to stay in control of. No matter how much I wanted to kill this piece of shit, I had to remember who I was. What this war was making me do wasn't me.

Oh god, oh no, oh god, oh no, oh god oh no.

"Shut up, Juri. You're a bad girl." I panted as Juri whimpered.

"One of you tell me what's going on."

Aarif, breaking out of the soldiers' arms, panted. His fat stomach pumped up and down. Juri went back and forth between grating on my ears with her moans and repeating those four words on loop.

"I did what I had to do to protect you," he said. "Both of you."

"What are you talking about?" I asked.

He nervously swallowed. "If Yael had walked into that bar and told me she was going to burn down the empire, I would have welcomed her back to life, bought her a drink, and followed her right into the flames, because she could make any magic happen, no matter how insane. You aren't her. You can have some of her magic, you can have some of her brains, you can carry on that spirit, but you'll never be her." He shook his head, as I realized just how fucking tired I was getting of hearing about my old professor. "You're not winning. You asked me to come with you, and I wasn't gonna do anything, because it was your life to throw away; I'd already protected you once, not that you're grateful, and I was in no position to tell someone else life was worth living."

He pointed a shaking finger at me. "But then you showed me that that wasn't the only life you had control over. I don't know how Juri is still alive, maybe that's a Banshee thing too, or maybe it's the love I put into sticking you two together, but I knew that I couldn't let you render that miracle meaningless."

I glared at Aarif as I processed, truly processed what he was saying. And how it all amounted to him having thrown me to the mutated wolves for his damn dog.

"P'Ken didn't have any spies on Jellz, did she?" His silence was deafening. "While we were on our way to Migdhilt, you contacted her. Told her what we were doing. Got her to come pick us up. All that rage and hate toward her was all just an act."

"No! I am not on her side. I'm sorry, I really a—"

"Save it!" I cut him off, the image of biting out his jugular with my fans crystal-clear in my head. "You're just like everyone else in my life. Wanting to control me and turning on me when I don't do what you want."

"This wasn't about you," he pleaded. "I just couldn't let you get Juri killed."

"And you knew about this, girl?!"

No! No, human. I just learned. We just talked while you were gone. Foodgiver said he was keeping us safe. Like always.

I cringed. Was I really about to get mad at the dog in my head? It's not like it would do any good. There was no getting rid of her. Especially not when giving her temporary control of the body was seemingly making me more like her. She was a dog, and she'd just trusted and obeyed her master. My ire needed to stay where it belonged.

"Sorry, Juri," I sighed. "You're not a bad girl."

I glared back at Aarif. He really did look guilty, but I didn't care. He was the one person from our old family I thought I could trust to help me, but he'd betrayed me like all the rest. At this point, even if I did get out of here, I probably wouldn't be able to save Jellz.

The doggo and I were on our own.

"Please, Layla," he said. "Just give this up and we can all just go back where we were."

I shook my head. "What was it you said to me? Oh, right. You can go give facism a blowjob like everyone else."

"Not a bad idea at all."

My face wrinkled as Captain Amatyn arrived on the scene, cane-whip in hand and bandages around her neck. With that smug look I was getting sick of her on her face, she stood next to Aarif.

"From the sound of things," P'Ken continued, tapping her com, "you've already worked out most of what's happened. Juri, I am so happy to see you alive and well. But, Aarif, while I'm grateful for your cooperation on this matter on a professional level, you must understand why I wouldn't want to drop you off on that backwater planet so you may return to drinking yourself to death."

This fucking…

"Allow me to once again make the same offer I have before. Be my chief engineer."

She smiled at me. "Perhaps, with your mind and our resources, we can find a way to put Juri in her own body that doesn't strain our dear student."

"Don't call me that," I breathed. "Neither of you gets to call me that."

What were my options right now? I had the Glass Striker, I was prepared to use The True Adventurer a little more, I was more than ready to let my wild side out, and I'd already accepted that I wouldn't be getting Jellz out of this; I'd apologize to him if I ever got the chance. There was no question I could overpower P'Ken and everyone else here and escape. The question was just how bloody I was willing to make my getaway.

Aarif breathed heavily as he stared at me. Was he really about to turn? I couldn't hate him more, but if he really did go and join the empire, I'd lose the last speck of respect I had for him.

Sweat dripped down his cheeks, his nose already damp. His intense eyes were focused entirely on me. With each breath he took, his substantial gut shook.

Aarif bowed his head. "I'm in if they're in."

"Fuck off," I immediately spat out without even thinking.

"I was listening to your conversation on the coms," Aarif said as P'Ken's smirk widened an inch. "She isn't going to give up. She isn't going to lick the boot. But if Layla and Juri agree to go along with your compromise, and consent to risk-averse experimentation to separate them, yeah, sure, I'll serve your command."

P'Ken and I both opened our mouths to speak, but Aarif continued first, picking up his volume. "But it has to be both of you! I'm not torturing the two of you by turning you against each other. I already hate that I had to do that once."

There it was. Aarif had sold out. He'd sold out and was giving my opinion on what happened with my body the same value as his dog's. I was more disappointed than I was insulted. He'd have valued Juri over any living person.

"Thank you for being reasonable," P'Ken said, hand on his shoulder. "I'm looking forward to us working together again. Truly."

Aarif cringed, at least clearly aware of how wrong he was for doing this. "Yeah. Yeah, I know you are."

P'Ken grinned at me. "We'll give you two some privacy to talk things out. You have five minutes. If you both agree, then that's wonderful. If you don't, then when we arrive on Cykeb, you will be left to make your own mess." She reached out her hand. "The Glass Striker?"

Soldiers surrounded me to take my weapon. My breakout was now or never. And while I'd had a knife plunged into my back, and P'Ken had been one step ahead of me this whole time, there were still two things neither of them was aware of.

*Juri, we don't have much time, and if we don't do this extra fast, they may catch on to the fact I don't need to speak out loud to communicate with you*, I thought extra hard. *Are you with me?*

*I don't want to fight Foodgiver.*

*I don't want to fight Foodgiver, either. But you're a good girl. The best in the history of existence. And you know that Aarif is hurting himself by doing this. You're man's best friend, you're that man's best friend, and it's your job to do what's best for him. If he was in a burning building, and he didn't want to leave, you'd still drag him out with your teeth, right? Same thing. The only way we help him is to stop this.*

My mind was racing a mile a minute because it had to. P'Ken was already getting antsy about me handing over the Glass Striker. Hopefully the example I'd given that would have been debated and discussed to death in Mr. Fra-0's philosophy class was enough to win over and convince a dog's more simple mind.

*Please, Juri*, I anxiously added for emphasis.

The wait for Juri's response was long. At least it was in my head. Thought traveled faster than almost anything, and the world around me was moving even slower than usual.

*Yes*, Juri said, making me hold in a sigh of relief. "*We must help. I am... the best dog.*"

I hung my head and smiled. She'd scratched me up good, but we were still gonna be grabbing her favorite foods when we were out of here.

"Professors," I started. "It was your job to teach me. To prepare me for the future. And you did. Even if I didn't always appreciate it in the moment. But that's when you'd always say…" I grinned as manically as I could at them both. "You'll thank me when you're older."

I reached for the Striker on my back and removed it from its strap. The soldiers moved to take it from me, but P'Ken could already see in my eyes that I wasn't handing it over. She was ready to strike me down once again with her whip, but, in what must have been a reflex, Aarif grabbed her arm as she pulled it back. He may not have been as strong as her, but he delayed her for just an instant. And in that instant, I played my last card.

Using The True Adventurer, I split myself off into a second body, positioned several feet behind P'Ken. I could only imagine the look on her eyes as she saw the Glass Striker disappear from my original body. It was made from and powered by The True Adventurer, and that meant it was subject to its control, and transferable between all four of my hands.

As I brought the mouthpiece to my lips, P'Ken ordered her men to shoot, but she was too late; she shouldn't have underestimated me.

The simplest of commands. Blowing as hard as I could. A flurry of rainbow-colored shards flew out at the same rate and with the same velocity as the most powerful of machine guns. The shards filled the security personnel's arms and legs, even those in armor completely defenseless against them, as they fell to the ground, disabled and writhing in agony. The shards would dissolve once I was far enough away from them. The damage they did? That would stick.

I made sure none of the shards hit P'Ken. I still didn't have it in me to hurt her like that, even if she'd probably assume this was me underestimating her now. It was a moot point. I'd given one last order to Juri before I'd split off from her, and before P'Ken could make her own move against me, Juri grabbed her, picked her up, and threw her into Aarif, leaving both of the traitors on the floor.

"Don't go back to Cykeb!" I called out, merging my original body into my new one and racing out of the bedroom. "Just a piece of friendly advice!"

*Woah!* Juri cheered. *I feel bad… but that was awesome!*

"Yeah, I'm awesome, I know." I paused. "Shit, I really am talking like her."

Aarif and P'Ken would get up. P'Ken would call for medical attention for her troops.

Even with how far she'd fallen, there was no way she'd become the type of heartless captain to disregard the well-being of her men. They weren't catching me. And if P'Ken was as smart as I knew she was, she wouldn't bother calling for more troops to apprehend me. She'd seen what the Glass Striker and my version of True Adventurer could do now, and she was probably thinking about what Yael had been able to do with it. The only move she could make was to fortify her men around Jellz, but that was just because I'd already given up on him.

Wiping a stray tear from my eye, I raced toward the elevator, letting Juri take the driver's seat when needed to knock out everyone in our way. It was possible P'Ken would also position troops in the transport room, believing that I had a way of breaking *Cascade* away from the *Mangalarga* without Aarif or Jellz, but I wasn't so greedy. We were on our own now. All I needed was a basic cruiser, and one of those could be stolen easily.

*That's good… but how do we win without Foodgiver or Jellz? You said we needed them.*

"I did. And I meant it. They were the good options." Sitting down at the controls of a cruiser and strapping myself in, I bit my tongue before giving an order I knew would come back to haunt me. "Juri… respond to Shun's most recent message. Tell her we're interested."

# CHAPTER 14: KAYA

Entering the throne room this morning had been as thrilling as my stomach was empty. I wanted to look my best not just for Layla's arrival, but for the dawn of the new era that was fast approaching, so breakfast had only consisted of half an orange and an egg. As for the throne room, Mother had told me she was having it slightly redecorated overnight to suit how things would be working from now on.

The empress' and princess' thrones had been removed. There was no need for them.

Mother would sit in the lone emperor's throne until dominion was achieved, with me standing at her side, and once Kaybell was dead, I would inherit the throne for her, and she would stand by me. I wouldn't have an empress for years to come; I'd need to actually learn to talk to boys before I could achieve that.

For the last three hours, I'd stood proudly at Mother's side as she went through the day's court matters. It was largely all insignificant. The true planning for the final push was occurring in backroom talks, away from the ears of common nobility. Backroom talks I was finally being permitted to take part in. Still, my interest had been kept as, between dealing with each advisor and general, Mother and I cracked jokes to each other. I'd never realized she could be so sassy!

Plus, Griffin now stood prominently among the court. While he'd previously been relegated to the back while in attendance, Mother was finally in a position to properly reward him for his loyalty. We had coms in our ears, and, whenever he'd notice I was drifting off, he'd make a funny sound. Apparently one of his older siblings had taught him how to make a lot of them. "They weren't all bad," he'd said.

My interest was further raised as an uncommon face among the court stepped forward and kneeled. It was my Aunt Morphea, Supreme General of the Sunrisers. She was dressed in her military uniform, one nearly identical to my own. She had long black hair with pink highlights, and awful bags under her eyes she really needed to do something about. Like Captain Amatyn, she was usually away, so I hadn't gotten to spend any real time with her, but hopefully that would change. She couldn't replace Aunts Wink and Jolla, but she was still family.

"General," Mother said. "Your report?"

"The final round of testing for the new Cykerdroids has been completed," Aunt Morphea said. "Barring any unreported developments on the Authority's end, their upgraded blasters should be capable of penetrating the strongest ground-level defenses on Utozex Prime four times over. Likewise, their most powerful weaponry is three times weaker than it needs to be to even damage the new Cykerdroid chassis, let alone the interior circuitry. Mass production on the scale of the previous model will take another few months, but we've completed the number requested for the final push. They will cut through Utozex Prime one stomp at a time."

Snore. All of this had already been disclosed to Mother last night via tablet, and she'd informed me and her closest advisors about it. Still, it was good for show, as the court applauded. Many of the nobles present had been serving as major financiers for the Cykebian military, and if the results of the military's recent R&D paid off, they'd be rewarded handsomely and inclined to reinvest. Even once the universe was in the palm of our hand, further progress would always be necessary to keep a firm grip.

"Excellent news, General," Molina said, playing along with the idea that this was news. "I knew I could trust you to oversee this project."

"The Sunrisers serve the Holy Cykebian Empire," Morphea said. "As Supreme General, it is my duty to not allow any of your enemies to stand in your way."

Her speech was almost as robotic as a Cykerdroid with a voice box. Not that that was too different from most career officers. I liked blowing stuff up and I liked cute uniforms, but actually subscribing to a military lifestyle? Yuck. Everything I'd heard from my mothers had made it sound so boring, lame, and soul-crushing.

"Thank you, sister," Molina said as she rose from her throne. "Our victory is at hand! Soon, in a matter of days, all worlds *will* be under Cykeb!"

Mother and all of the court saluted, as the court applauded once more, and Morphea returned to her place among them. Molina looked down at me. "I believe that's a high note to end on. How would you like to spend the rest of the day?"

Yes! This! This was all I wanted! But what did I say? A meal? Too boring. Sparring?

Maybe. Perhaps we could just sit down and talk more so I could ask her more stories about funny stuff she did before becoming empress; she might enjoy that. Or maybe–

"Oh Moliniiiiina!"

That voice. That obnoxious, disrespectfully bold, common voice. And if he was here, that meant...

There was a twinkle of disbelief in Molina's eyes as the court gasped and whispered over someone addressing the empress in such a fashion, while not even in the same room. What they didn't realize was their empress put more stock in this loser's life than a thousand of theirs.

I bounced on my feet as I listened to the pitter patter of footsteps from outside the throne room. As excited as I was for the day with Mother, this would be so much better.

Aarif entered the throne room, escorted by a cringing Captain Amatyn, with all eyes turning to them. There was no sign of Layla.

"Where is she?" I whispered.

"Do not do anything rash, your highness," Griffin whispered, cupping a hand around his mouth. "Let's hear the situation."

I grit my teeth and seethed, but I did as he said. Not like there was anyone I could get away with blowing up right now.

"Been a long time," Aarif said, kneeling before us. He'd become a fatty in his time away, and he clearly hadn't been taking care of himself otherwise, but P'Ken had evidently done her best to clean up him before their arrival. He'd showered, his dark, curly beard was freshly trimmed and his hair recently cut, and he'd been dressed in a form-fitting black suit. "I can't say this was where I expected us to chat next while you were bitching to me about your disrespectful students in the teacher's lounge."

The court's volume picked up. The outrage over this type of speech and behavior wasn't surprising. I was only unsure of what he thought he was accomplishing by doing this. P'Ken's brow was furrowed in frustration, so this wasn't her idea.

Mother evidently had some idea, however, as, without a word, she stepped down toward them, raising a closed fist to silence the nobility. She stared down at the two and jutted her head up.

"What?" Aarif asked as the two stood. "Nothing to say to me, your—"

Mother cut him off as she wrapped her arms around them both. I couldn't see her face, but her body shook. She softly laughed. The laughter picked up. Within seconds, she was belting, momentarily tilting her head back and allowing me to see the tears in her eyes.

"Your highness!" some elderly duke shouted, "I am sorry, but I cannot stay silent on this matter! This behavior is more irregular and—"

"Oh, do shut up," Molina cut him off. She backed up from her friends, a pleased smile on P'Ken's face and a guilty one on Aarif. "Take him away."

The rando duke was seized by guards and dragged out of the throne room kicking and screaming like a child about how this was just the type of thing he feared from allowing a commoner so much power. Moments after the doors shut behind them, the sound of blaster fire echoed through the hall. No one dared to speak again.

Molina turned to me, grinning like I did at EZ Street concerts. "Kaya, come here. You as well, Griffin."

My burning desire to ask about Layla was somewhat quelled by just how happy Mother was. She'd spent the previous year doing everything to make Kaybell suffer, but with who she'd been before all of this, that couldn't have been easy on her. To a point, she'd been torturing herself. It was no wonder she'd always been so sour and uptight.

From our respective places, Griffin and I approached Mother and the others. Molina laughed once more.

"Lords and ladies," she spoke. "Your emperor may never be fit to rule again. Prince Megz and Princess Morphea are fine generals, but that is all." Out of the corner of my eye, I noticed Morphea shrink. "As our dominion nears completion, a new age approaches! A new age with new bloodlines! New gods! Gaze upon your idols!"

P'Ken, Aarif, and Griffin were all overwhelmed with confusion, and even I was uncertain as to what exactly she was doing, much as I like the sound of her declarations. But the court took the message as to what they were meant to do and kneeled before us all, saluting and chanting "All Worlds Under Cykeb." Mother continued to grin with triumph.

If Mother was doing what it seemed like she was doing, then it seemed too early. I had to ask.

"Where is she?"

Aarif and P'Ken's confused faces fell as Molina's lip curled. I wasn't going to like the answer.

---

P'Ken scrolled through her tablet, face in her screen, while Aarif poked around at the ancient Cykebian relics that lined the walls of Mother's office, only to have his hand slapped away by Griffin; Aarif laughed at him, while Griffin shook his head in disapproval.

I sat quietly at Mother's desk, observing the reunited strangers as I circled my thumbs around each other and kicked my feet. Mother had some things to tend to before she joined the rest of us, but it was hard to focus on anything with the non-answer my earlier question had received. The fact that Layla was something we needed to "discuss" worried me.

Still, it was fascinating watching how those waiting with me interacted, or, rather, didn't interact. The memories of my time on *Ricochet* were burned into my mind more than any concert or massacre. As different as Aarif and P'Ken were, they were still Yael's right and left hands, best friends in their own right. Yet now, they hadn't even looked at each other once since we'd come in here. And while I'd never seen Griffin with the two before, he'd still been their student, and now his eyes were filled with nothing but contempt for Aarif.

Mother wasn't lying to me anymore. She'd finally given me the full, horrible truth about her motivations and plans and feelings. But there were still things I didn't understand about what had gone on between all of them, and what was now going on including all of us. Once she came in, she wasn't going back out without telling me everything.

"Hey, Kaya."

My head spun toward Aarif, staring daggers at his eyes for addressing me by my first name. P'Ken looked to him as well, while Griffin's eyes landed on me, no doubt fearing an outburst.

"Before Molina—do not ask me to call her anything else, I'm not an officer just yet—comes in, there's something you need to know."

I pursed my lips, pouting and crossing my arms. "And what is that?"

Aarif cast his head down and scratched his tattooed hand. "Layla misses you so much." My heart nearly escaped my chest. "There's no one in these stars she cares about more. And whatever crazy crap she's getting up to, in her mind, she's doing it for you."

A heavy breath escaped my mouth as my heart continued to pound. What did that mean?

"You should have brought her here," Griffin said.

"I tried," P'Ken said. "But there aren't exactly any known tactics for countering a girl/dog hybrid with The True Adventurer."

W-what? What did she mean by hybrid? And Layla had The

True Adventurer now? But we'd broken her away from her great-grandmother! Still, if she was that strong now, then that was too perfect! We so belonged together.

She better not have been putting herself in danger.

After about another two minutes of kicking my feet in silence, now with my hands firmly clenched around each other, Mother entered.

P'Ken and Griffin saluted, but she waved at them to ease, kissing my head before taking her seat across from me. Her stern stoicism was present, but there was no malice or pain behind it; this was just a serious situation that required her full attention.

Mother sighed. "First things first, Aarif, I really am happy to see you. I know from the previous times P'Ken has reached out to you, you haven't had the kindest thoughts about me."

"Still don't," he said, leaning against the wall. "You know why I'm here."

Molina bobbed her head. "P'Ken, thank you for finally getting him here. And… I apologize for being so distant these past months."

"No apologies necessary, your highness," P'Ken said, even as a small smile crept up her face.

Mother briefly smiled back at her. "Aarif, you did the right thing contacting her. I promise we'll find a way to separate Layla and Juri."

"What do you mean separate them?!" I asked.

"I'm still not sure you should be giving him so much leniency, your highness," Griffin said. "He'd kill you if he got the chance."

Molina snorted. "Griffin, show some respect to your old professor." P'Ken and Aarif both laughed.

"He's not wrong, though," Aarif followed with a smug look on his face.

"Good to know." At long last Mother's gentle eyes landed on me.

"Yes, Layla and Juri are currently sharing a body. The only way Aarif was able to save Layla from the injuries you inflicted on her was by surgically implanting pieces of Juri. Somehow, it seems The True Adventurer resulted in Juri continuing to live on in Layla's mind."

"That's crazy."

"Very. I've never gotten to see this power in action like you three have, but I aim to fix that; the empire requires it."

"I'm sure Layla would be happy to use it for us. We could even hunt down and kill the Banshees so she'd be the only one left with it. So where is she?!"

Mother bit her lip. "She… ran away from the *Mangalarga*. From what Aarif and P'Ken have shared with me, she sees me as nothing more than an evil tyrant, and you as my poor, innocent victim."

"What?!"

The reaction was without thinking. I did get why she would think that. We *were* evil. But despite my own fears, we were evil *together*.

"It's unfortunate. And, even more unfortunate, she claims to have a plan to bring down the entire empire. Do not worry about that, no one could accomplish such a thing, and, even if Layla could, she needed Aarif and Jellz, two men she's no longer with."

I hung my head. "She lied to me. Layla lied to me."

"Do not allow yourself to spiral, Princess," P'Ken said. "She's just confused. Like Aarif said, she thinks she's helping you. It's up to us to help her."

"She's right, your highness," Griffin followed. "She's your best friend, right? Friends help friends."

I nodded along. Yes. This made sense. She'd always been confused. I should have reached out myself, sooner, to clear everything up.

"Where is she?" I asked. "Is she still on the move? Do we know where she's heading?"

"We do," Mother said. "And it's nowhere good. It appears that since her plans to bring us down have fallen apart… she's now turning her attention toward the Authority." As I grimaced, Mother grinned. "There's no question she loathes them as much as we do, and Aarif has already confirmed that her intentions are to bring both empires down. The good news is, we can use this. Layla stands just as good a chance against them as she did against us. But I have no doubt she can cause trouble. We will take advantage of that. Our fleets, led by you four, will take advantage of that, and we will destroy Utozex Prime, and bring Layla home in one move."

P'Ken nodded calmly, while Griffin seemed shocked, and Aarif sneered. This sounded as good as any option to me.

"I'm sorry, the four of us?" Aarif questioned.

"Yes, that did catch my attention as well," Griffin followed.

Molina smiled. "My performance in the throne room had meaning. The universe will belong to Kaya and I, but you are still my family; my true family. Prove to the nobility and common folk alike why you deserve to be, and help me put an end to all this violence." She brushed her hair back with a glide of her hand. "It's what she would have wanted."

There was a brief pause.

"As you command, your highness," P'Ken spoke first.

"I'm honored by this chance," Griffin said.

"Not like I can say no," Aarif said next.

It was almost over. It would soon be over and perfect. The only thing standing between me and my perfect, dark future was my own ability to succeed.

I smirked. "I won't fail you, Mother." I turned my head one more time to look at Yael's family. My family. "We won't fail you."

# CHAPTER 15: LAYLA

I didn't drink.

Despite all my time being taught by functioning alcoholics, that habit had never rubbed off on me. No matter how stressful an assignment or deadline had gotten at school, no matter how much certain friends wanted me to go out with them, I'd say, "No thanks! Hyper-nutrient blueberry and brussels sprout smoothies for me!"

I didn't want to drink. But being taught my functioning alcoholics didn't let me learn many other coping skills for when faced with absolute crushing despair and loneliness.

Alone in a cramped cruiser in the dark, endlessness of space, without a friend I could call upon or an ally I could trust, I downed the second beer of a six-pack I'd just purchased at a small outpost and sat back down in the pilot's chair. I had a date with the woman who'd made this whole mess.

Preparing for takeoff, I thought back to the first time I'd met Shun Segisteel. Griffin and I had been studying for an engineering test while Marcos watched a movie ten feet away from us, loudly munching on chips and laughing at us for not already understanding everything. The next thing we knew, our headmistress was being kicked through a wall behind us.

"Wooh!" Yael cheered from the ground, snapping her shoulder back into place. "You do pack a pretty punch. I could go for some punch right now if you're interested!"

The girl I'd soon know as Shun stepped through the hole in the wall, cracking her knuckles. "Honestly? I was expecting more."

"You know what, fair? I don't usually lose scrapes. But hey, I never claimed to be the best fighter ever." Yael grinned. "I am a dirty cheater, though."

Sure enough, Yael had stuck one of her favorite tools, a Hercutious lima bean, down Shun's shirt while the two had been trading blows. Shun may have been stronger, but that didn't do her any good while she was trapped in a sticky, green, gelatinous substance that tasted like rotten shark. I hadn't been surprised that Yael had tasted the stuff, she was the curious-type and got easily hungry, so much as I was that she knew what rotten shark tastes like.

"Good fight," Yael said as she stood up and dusted herself off. "Kids, say hello to your new classmate!"

Shun, eyes cold and lips pressed, nodded at us. Marcos didn't pay attention, while Griffin and I waved back; I didn't want to be rude, and he was a little scared. That wouldn't be a concern of mine for our reunion.

*Those were fun times,* Juri moaned. *Why did they have to end?*

"They didn't," I said, blasting off. "Bad people made choices. It's what happens everywhere in a universe consumed by greed and a hunger for power."

You really think they were always bad?

"At this point?"

I didn't need to say the rest for Juri to understand where I stood. In fairness, there was still little I actually understood about

Shun, and who she was. All I knew was what she'd told me in her transmissions and by her actions as Chancellor. There was no question Molina was the bigger threat, but that didn't mean Shun wasn't running an equally brutal campaign, one just as harmful toward independent worlds, or that the so-called "meritocracy" that had allowed Shun to achieve the highest level of power in the Authority while still under 21 wasn't rotten to its core.

*What will you do when you see her?* Juri asked. *If she's bad, why are we working with her?*

"Two reasons," I said. "First, we have nowhere else to run."

*And second?*

I snorted, taking in my own hypocrisy. "Because we were never the good guys."

---

Roshjita was the capital city of Utozex-Prime and the birthplace of the philosophies that now governed the Authority. Unlike the chrome skyscrapers of its Cykebain counterpart, Roshjita's skyline was almost entirely empty. Credit where it was due: that left their stunning pink and yellow sky clean and clear. To the city's founder, the Cykebian desire for grandiosity was overcompensation for their lack of true greatness. Utozin structures weren't actually too different in size, but they kept their architecture close to the ground and used hypersonic particles to make them bigger on the inside.

Accessing the planet, let alone Roshjita, without clearance was a guaranteed death sentence for most right now, with security raised a thousand-fold in light of the war. I, on the other hand, was being directly escorted to a secret military base far, far away from the capital. I'd refused to talk to Shun ahead of time, but I'd made myself clear. Let me in, let me talk, let's see if we can help each other, do not call me again, and respond by authorizing clearance.

It had only taken her three hours to do as I requested. She was desperate.

*I still wanna eat her face,* Juri growled.

"If I wasn't vegan, I might just let you when we're done."

Then stop being vegan!

I laughed.

"I know none of this is easy. But I'm glad you're doing a little better."

We will help Foodgiver. Like you said. We will.

"Yeah," I nodded. "Yeah, we will."

The remaining flight took another couple hours, and I could tell we were circling back around at points for security reasons, but I was eventually given permission to land outside a positively stunning, moss-covered mountain. Hypersonic particles didn't just work on metal and wood.

Stepping off my stolen cruiser, dressed in a floral button-down with a cream blazer, pants, and tennis shoes, and the Glass Striker strapped to my back, I was met by three Utozin soldiers. All three were over six feet tall and at least 225 lbs, and were dressed in head-to-toe brown tactical gear, their helmets completely obscuring their faces.

"Follow us, Ms. N'gwa," one of them spoke in a deep, modulated voice. I couldn't have told you which. "Please, for your own security, refrain from any sudden movements."

I nodded, and followed behind the men as one of them slid their finger across the moss in a pattern I was barely able to follow. As he finished, a door on the side of the mountain opened.

*Cool,* Juri thought.

*A necessity,* I thought back.

Once we were all inside the mountain, the door automatically slammed shut and locked behind us. The soldiers walked me down a long hallway where identically dressed, and identically built, guards lined the walls. Also in the rocky walls was a series of doors. Utozex military bases weren't just hidden, they were mazes. Half of the doors on either side of me would lead to an office or a facility, while the other half would invariably lead to a death trap.

We stopped at the sixteenth door on the left. One of the guards opened it, leading us down another halfway. This time, a different guard gave the vocal command, "Strength in Equality", to open the fourth door on the right. Another hallway. Finally, the third guard drew a knife from one of his pouches, removed one of his gloves and cut his palm so that he could place his blood on a scanner to unlock the sixth door on the right.

As I stepped through that last door, I finally took in a sight other than the brown mountain's mossy walls, and entered Shun's office, where the Chancellor was seated at her desk.

Juri barked up a storm and my heart raced as I set our eyes on her. Trying not to breathe through my nose too loudly, I stared at the woman I used to play paper football with during class. Her dark skin had been cleared of all blemishes, her twin braids were now long enough to nearly touch the floor, her muscles had grown even larger, with signs of additional augmentation, and she wore a brown cloak with a gold chain over a simple, pale-green uniform.

Looking up from her monitor, Shun smiled at me in a way she never had before. "Layla. Thank you so much for finally agreeing to meet. I know you think you understand me, but I'm looking forward to showing you the true—"

"RUFF! RUFF!"

I instinctively covered my mouth with both hands. That wasn't Juri. I'd just barked. Shun blinked in confusion. "Okay. You can explain that later. Please, have a seat."

I took a deep breath, shoving whatever was going on in my head to the back, as I sat across from her, and the soldiers exited without a word.

Shun's wooden desk was bare save for her monitor. Behind her was an Utozex flag, with a green triangle on a brown background, and five screens. There was carpeting underneath my feet with a texture I couldn't quite describe, making me wonder if they'd made it out of the moss. Shun hadn't had the nerve to purchase any of my sculptures, but she'd gone one step further by making the only piece of decoration in the office a framed photo of all of us from the school days. In it, she was crouched down next to Marcos, with Griffin and I posed on either side of them, and our four professors behind us—Yael and Molina making out. The smile Shun wore was the brightest I'd ever seen on her. We'd taken it just after she'd received her bounty.

"Put that up just for me?" I asked. "I don't have time for mind games."

Shun looked over at the photo, then back to me. "No games. I just enjoy remembering the happiest year of my life."

"Yeah, sure."

"You doubt me? You know that I've spent my entire life in the military. That I've spent it either undergoing excruciating training or fighting a losing war. I did my duty when I had to, but it shouldn't be difficult to believe that I loved playing school with you all."

I stared into her cold, brown, emotionless eyes, trying my best to read her. No luck.

Everyone I was playing this game against was better than me. She was right, though. Her time with us was probably like a damn vacation for her.

"What do you want to talk about?" I asked, getting to the point.

Shun folded her hands in front of her. "In the next two hours, this planet is going to be invaded."

"What?!"

"Obviously these aren't the circumstances I hoped to meet under, but I count myself lucky to have you here at all. The empire's weaponry has advanced by leaps and bounds... again. The 'progress' of absorbing everyone else's. There hasn't been a day where this war wasn't in their favor, and if our intel about their new weaponry is true, our defenses will prove completely ineffective. Especially with the princess leading the charge."

I slammed my fist down on the desk.

"It gets worse. All our old friends are with her. Well, not all of them; I pray that Marcos is still alive. Still, it seems they're prepared to finally overwhelm us, and end this war."

Fuck, fuck, shit, gods fucking...

Kaya was coming. Did I have something to do with that? Did they know where I'd gone? Would they have really based their military strategy around me? Or was it just a coincidence? I'd hoped to come here to get the Authority behind me on my plans, but now I was getting drafted as their last hope.

"Mmm," I hummed, eyes and mouth clenched. "This wouldn't be happening if it wasn't for you."

"We don't have time for this."

"We have time for what I say we have time for." I opened my eyes and sneered. "You tried to kill Kaya. You set her off. You got Yael killed. Yael would have stopped Molina a year ago!"

"I did what I had to do."

"You didn't have to do shit. You didn't have to try and murder a little girl!"

"The Authority would have already been exterminated if not

for me! You've seen how Kaya has ravaged planet after planet. Imagine what she'd have 'achieved' by now, if instead of a third-rate Sunriser my tactical enemy had been Yael. I infiltrated the school to scout Yael as a potential ally for the Authority, and with how fond she became of me, I believed in my chances, but once it became clear she was going to side with the empire… one of them had to die, and I cared for Yael, I did, so, yes, I targeted the child; I underestimated her."

I shook my head. "The Cykebian Empire had no intention of starting the war at that point; that's on your council."

"And the council knows best. They are those who, by their own merit, have achieved more in life than anyone else. My duty then, as it is now, is to carry out their will. And I stand by their decisions. The Empire wasn't just going to stop because the royal family suddenly wasn't a bunch of barbarians. Peaceful co-existence was not an option. Not if we didn't want the Authority 'nicely' absorbed and erased in the next thirty years."

"I hear you, and I get that, but—"

"But what?! Obviously I took no pleasure in trying to kill her, not like I would now, but that girl was always an existential threat to our existence from the day she was born. And I understand you bonded with her for, what, a few days, but child or not, you cannot say that her life is worth more than a civilization. A civilization with an actual culture. With scientists, artists, and philosophers. Not the homogenized, empty vanity fueled by the suffering of others that is the Empire."

"Shitty as their nobility may be, people tend to be happier living on Cykebian worlds."

"And those with merit on Utozex worlds live far beyond the means of the peasants of Cykebian worlds."

"And that being 'fair' doesn't sound at all to you like the attitude of the nobles you despise?"

"Enough!" Shun panted.

I panted with her. Neither of us had breathed once during that volley.

"We are not going to see eye to eye on this. You are not military. You are not Utozin. You do not understand sacrifice."

I bit my tongue.

"Be that as it may, you are the granddaughter of Madame N'gwa, potentially the most intelligent woman currently on this planet, and a wielder of The True Adventurer. You are the only one who can save my home."

She paused. "I am sorry for whatever pain I've caused you. And for whatever part in this you believe to be my fault. I will get the council behind whatever plan you have to take out the empire. But first, I need your help getting us to that point. Please."

I tapped my foot. Eating her face sure seemed like a good strategy right now, but I held back. I was going to help her. Not like I couldn't. I still needed her and the Authority, and after ditching her, Kaya was either in the mood to kill me or forcibly drag me back to Cykeb for 're-education'. But there was one thing I needed to ask before I agreed.

"You're not stupid."

"Obviously not."

"Uh huh. And enough people have been telling me this lately, but I'm no Yael. Am I smarter than you? Maybe, I dunno, intelligence is actually pretty difficult to measure objectively."

She opened her mouth.

"Do not bring up your dumb metrics. Point is, you were a child prodigy. You're in this position now because your oligarchs thought you were the best fit to lead. Even if I am a little smarter than you, I don't know anything about military tactics. And The True Adventurer can't stop a fleet. At least, not my version. So what are you really banking on me doing here?"

Shun leaned back in her seat and sighed. Just as I'd thought.

"You want me to work the emotional angle," I said. "Everyone hates you, but the entire leadership of the incoming fleet fucking loves me. And you think I can, what, turn them to our side? Turn them against each other? Mess with their heads enough for you and your forces to gain the upper hand?"

"Whichever option you prefer."

Grabbing the Glass Striker off my back, I brought the mouthpiece to my lips, blew and twisted to make the pipe into a hammer, and as Shun leaped across the desk at me, I slammed her in the face with pink and yellow glass as hard as I could. She crashed through the side of her office, flying through layer after layer of rock and dirt.

Walking through the tunnel I'd just made, I stared down at Shun, bleeding all over with what looked like a broken shoulder, but still conscious. We shouldn't have been in this position. We were just two eighteen-year-old trans girls who should have been enjoying the kinds of lives people like us weren't always able to. But she'd been brainwashed from childhood, and I was the only one stupid enough to attempt what I was. So here we were, trying to figure out what to do about the menace of the fourteen-year-old being used as a bludgeon against the universe.

None of this was right. And I hated it. And I hated everyone and everything. And I wished I could have just been sipping smoothies and smoking weed and making art that makes the universe a more beautiful place, and I wished there could be peace, but none of that was an option. Not unless I did some bad, bad things first. Like everyone else.

I reached out my hand to Shun. "Let's get started."

## CHAPTER 16: KAYA

It was like something out of a dream.

Seated in the captain's chair on the *Winjolla*, twirling my hair, P'Ken and Griffin sat in front of me at the helm, flying me toward my destiny. They were communicating with Aarif who, with heavy supervision, was performing final checks on all our systems. Mother's blessing was with us, and 300,000 soldiers and Cykerdroids heading toward Utozex Prime were with me.

After a year alone, I had all of this. I had all of them. I could only imagine how happy it would have made Yael if she could have seen me leading her family into battle like she used to, all on the same side, to save our missing friend.

"I'm proud of you," I could hear her say, imagining her standing behind me, wearing her standard jacket-button-down-jeans-combat-boots combo, and her brown, curly hair longer than ever, with a hand on my shoulder and the dorkiest smiles on her face.

"I know," I whispered, nearly inaudibly.

"ETA is 22 minutes, Princess," Captain Amatyn said, spinning around, the final leg of our voyage set. "Will any of us be joining you on the surface?"

"Negative," I answered. "I will not risk allowing anything to happen to any of you—even Aarif. The invasion will require my full attention. I cannot be distracted protecting you."

A small smile cracked through P'Ken's stoic face.

"What is it?"

"Oh. Nothing, Princess."

I frowned at her, but only for a moment, before I felt an impossibly light hand slide across my shoulder.

"You're reminding her of me," Yael whispered. "You're doing great."

I looked at my imaginary mother and giggled. "You look different than how I remember you."

Yael shrugged, blood dribbling down her chin. "Can't drink when you're dead."

"Uh... I..."

"Apologies, did you say something, your highness?" Griffin asked, having also spun around.

I shook my head. "Yes. Have there been any updates from Utozex Prime?"

"Still nothing out of the ordinary," he reported. "If Layla is causing problems for them, she's doing it slowly and quietly."

"I'm sure she's all right," P'Ken said, as if she knew the concern I was about to voice. It was one that had been stuck in my head over the days we'd flown. "I was hoping to hear about her causing a little chaos and destruction in Roshjita before we arrived, but it won't matter soon."

"You're a psychopath, P'Ken," Aarif said, coming up the elevator on the bridge, now dressed in uniform as a proper chief engineer. "You're all psychopaths. And if you're at table with all psychopaths, then..."

I rolled my eyes as he came to stand at my side. "There is no shame in joining the winning team. Not when there's a seat already prepared with your name on it. And not when Juri's life is worth more than every last Utozin's." I looked up at him, softening my gaze. "I apologize for putting you all in this position. There is obviously a lot I wish I could take back about what happened on *Ricochet* that night, but there was no reason for me to hurt Juri and Layla like I did."

There was a time when the thought of apologizing to someone like Aarif would have made my stomach turn. Both because he was a commoner and because a Cykebian princess was never supposed to apologize. But I wasn't the naive little girl parroting her despicable aunts anymore. I was on my way toward being a woman. And Aarif, annoying and gross as he was, wasn't a commoner; he was family.

Aarif snorted. "Whatever, kid."

Really?! I was giving him the honor of being respectful toward him and that was how he responded? Oh, he was so—"

"Ha ha ha."

Yael cut off her laughter, catching her not-breath. "Give him time. It's just how he is."

"Be nice to your princess, Aarif," P'Ken said, smirking. "You're going to have to get used to being around us psychopaths eventually." She looked around the bridge, smiling at each of us. "This is life now."

"Precisely," Griffin said. "We're all young, even you, Aarif. We have long, wonderful lives ahead of us. There is no need to be weighed down by bitterness."

"Ahh, I see," Aarif said with irritating sarcasm. "And does Marcos also have a wonderful life ahead of them?"

Griffin's face fell. "They're young, too."

This was going to keep being an annoyance until the problem was resolved. Either Marcos was going to need to make a change fast, or I was going to have to kill them so everyone could stop talking about them.

"Aarif, this is a historic, celebratory moment we're lucky enough to be a part of," P'Ken said. "Either get into the spirit or get off the bridge."

Aarif slammed his hands together as he jumped up with both feet. "Yeah! Murdering thousands of innocent people! Awesome!" He bristled and sneered at us all.

"You are a ridiculous man," I told him.

"When the whole universe has gone crazy, I'll take that as a compliment."

"BWAHAHAHAHA!" Yael was bent over, laughing, keeping herself balanced with a hand on my shoulder. "Oh, man. You guys are all a mess. I really wish I could pull your asses out of this fire, but you're gonna have to do that on your own. Please try not to kill too many people? For me?"

I blinked, as Yael disappeared, my head aching as she did so. "Wh... what?"

---

The first shots were fired fifteen minutes before we arrived on Utozex Prime. Their pitiful defenses would be easy to smash through with our new weapons and shields, but the distance and accuracy of them was still more than adequate. But against the most advanced society ever known, adequacy wouldn't save them.

We couldn't fire on Utozex Prime indiscriminately. Even if Layla wasn't there, I wanted to look Shun in the eyes when I killed her. So we settled for counter-attacking, targeting and destroying their ground- and satellite-based defense systems.

Multiple squads, consisting of hundreds of single-person manned fighter ships, attempted to intercept us before we reached the planet. They hoped to use their speed and agile nature to fight back against our absolute power. They were more annoyingly successful than I would have liked, managing to take out three and a half of our warships, the crew of the fourth managing to largely evacuate and survive before it went up in flames.

It was so annoying to take any losses at all. But an annoyance was all it was. Every fighter was destroyed, every pilot killed.

"HA HA HA HA!" I laughed. "They really don't stand any chance. Just as it should be."

"This is…"

"War, Griffin," P'Ken cut off his timid words. "Did you not realize what you were stepping into?"

"I did," he said, his voice still quivering. "It just isn't how I imagined it." He turned to P'Ken. "How did you get used to this?"

"This is no time for chatter," I spat.

"It is fine, Princess." P'Ken remained entirely focused on the helm as she answered. "We have a brief moment before we arrive. To answer the question, destruction was nothing new to me. Only the death. Funny thing is? It was a lot easier to get used to."

Griffin hung his head, not pleased with that answer. Was he really going to go all lame on me now? Weak.

"Not as romantic as being a gentleman thief?" Aarif mocked, still on the bridge, but now standing in the corner, intentionally not paying attention to any of the screens and likely grateful that the vacuum of space kept him from hearing the screams. "Why didn't you just do that after Molina let you out of prison? I'm sure P'Ken would have been happy to teach you, and it would have kept you both out of this."

Griffin sighed, rolling his shoulders and refocusing himself. "I'm loyal to my empress."

I kicked my feet, smirking at his correct, not-lame answer, as Utozex Prime came into view.

"Okay, people. Time for the fun part." I rose from my seat. "Captain Amatyn, you're to command the *Winjolla* and coordinate the global assault with generals Megs and Morphea. My mothers and I have complete faith in your ability to keep up. Griffin, you know where to send me."

Griffin nodded, his fingers clicking away on one of the control monitors. Our intelligence efforts had gained us Chancellor Segisteel's current location. These Utozins… what kind of general needed to hide? While I was constantly out on the front lines, acting as my mother's ultimate sword? Such cowardice. With leadership like that, they never stood a chance.

"Got it."

I smirked, cracking my fingers and ejecting my katars as I snickered. "Beam me down. Once Shun is dead and we have control of the planet, finding Layla will be a breeze."

"Could always send out a scouting party in the meantime."

Our eyes all turned to Aarif in surprise.

"What? I want to find *them* as much as you. And if I'm stuck playing the bad guy, I can at least not be a useless one."

P'Ken smiled triumphantly. "Don't get ahead of yourself."

My smile widened alongside P'Ken's. "Do as he said. And wish me luck."

"We all know you don't need it, Princess," Griffin offered.

"Shun will regret the day she was born," P'Ken followed. I bit my lip, hard enough to draw blood.

"All worlds under Cykeb!" I shouted with a salute.

"All worlds under Cykeb!" the other three, even Aarif, shouted back. A moment later, I was gone.

When my molecules came back together, I stood in a long hallway, surrounded by rocky walls and endless doors. Our technology wasn't the most advanced possible just yet, so beaming me down directly to the location of someone in a secured location who we didn't even have the DNA of wasn't possible. Not a problem, though. It just meant I got to hunt.

I closed my eyes and allowed my advanced hearing to do the work for me. I tuned out the sounds of the explosions going on outside and focused only on my surroundings. Soldiers were scurrying all about in response to their end of days, screaming, crying, or barking orders. Most of the noise was coming from a single location, though. Their command center.

The only question now was which of these doors would lead me to it. Mazes were so annoying when you were the one trapped in one. I understood the appeal, though. I'd run a few unfortunate souls through my own mazes; obvi none of them had survived, but unlike them, I wasn't a loser.

Whatever traps they'd set up behind these doors, there was nothing that could hurt me.

Never again.

"You're so far, so afraid," I started singing as I blasted down the first door on my left, leading into another, identical hallway. There was a single Utozin soldier present, who sounded like they were saying goodbye to their family. I shot them dead without stopping. "Fearing that you have strayed, but I know you!"

As I stepped over the threshold, I tripped over into a pit of spikes. I didn't even bother flying to avoid falling onto them, instead just letting myself collide with them. I'd been morbidly curious if I would even feel it. Of course I couldn't.

"You're taking steps, day by day, I'm coming to meet you, no matter which way," I continued to sing as I flew up out of the trap and back into the hallway, mulling over which door to enter next. "Just take my hand, and we'll find what's next, I can feel your breath, all over my neck."

Opening the next door revealed a dead end, with a single blaster shot painlessly shooting me in the forehead. It would have been almost funny if the great Cykebian princess had gone out that way.

"I'm running towards you! I can see you! Don't run away! Don't look over that riiiidge…. Always Like A—"

My awesome belting was cut off as my instincts took over, someone attacking from behind. Without even processing who it was, I grabbed their weapon, threw them over my shoulder, and slammed them into the floor.

I stumbled back against a wall. Oh gods. What had I just done?

"Not again, not again, not again," I whispered, near silently. "Layla?"

Layla, from the floor, groaned.

Alive. Good.

"Damn, Kaya," she laughed, picking herself up and dusting herself off. "I just wanted to play with my EZ Sister."

I was confused, and frightened, by what Layla was doing here, and about if she was being honest just then, but I wasn't going to jump to conclusions; not this time.

I giggled as I ran up to her and initiated our secret handshake, flipping our hair, bumping our fists together, wrapping our pinkies around one another's, clapping our hands three times each, and flipping our hair again. Layla giggled with me.

She was so beautiful. Maybe I hadn't appreciated how pretty she was the last time we met in person, or maybe she'd just blossomed. Either way, her light skin was glowing, her curly brown hair was shimmering, her hourglass figure was, near, flawless, her tie-dyed tactical gear was adorable, and in her hands was the Glass Striker.

"I've missed you," I said, hugging her so tightly and never wanting to let go.

"I've missed you, too," she said, hugging me back and resting her head on my own.

I didn't want to bring up what was going on, where we were, and what she was doing. I just wanted this moment to last forever. But if I wanted my happy ending, I needed to work for it.

"What are you doing here?" I asked, pulling away. "Why didn't you come to Cykeb?!" I already knew the answer. But I wanted to hear her version.

"Before I answer, let's just make clear that I would have if I'd known you were about to bomb this place to Hell."

"We're bombing it *now* because of you," I said. "Everyone is worried about you."

She hung her head. "Everyone?"

"Yes! Everyone! Mother has been wonderful ever since she took out Kaybell, Griffin's always been great to me, and now I have Aarif and P'Ken too. We all want you to be happy with us. And you will be! I know you'll love it, it'll be just like your school days, only way better."

Layla laughed that pretty laugh. "I'm happy for you. You're doing better than when we talked before."

She was so smart, so intuitive, so in touch with emotions... "I am."

She picked her head up. "I don't support the empire's actions. That isn't new information."

"And you won't have to, soon," I pointed out. "This war ends now. Well, logistically, probably more like in a few months for it to be totally done, but still!"

"And that's great. But where does that leave us? The universe is the empire, and the empire is the universe. That's good for you. It could be good for me. But countless people would suffer."

"Countless people are already suffering," I snarled. "I know you know the Authority isn't any better."

"I don't know if the Empire or the Authority are worse. From the eyes of an outsider, it's impossible to support either."

I curled my lips. "And that's why you want to destroy both."

"No," Layla shook her head, not at all surprised that I knew what she was doing. "It's because I *do* support you. Because I know no matter what you say, you're not happy. And you won't be until you're freed from the system that made you."

"Aarif said you'd say that. I believe that you believe that. But you need to believe me. You're wrong. Do you think I'm lying?"

"I don't. I think that you're confused and scared, and being us—"

"Why are you here?" I cut her off. "We knew you were on the planet, but we were surprised when we weren't hearing reports of what chaos you were bringing to it. We thought you might have lost, again, but none of us expected to find you here."

Layla cringed, like she was about to cry. Veins were visible in her neck.

"Kaya, please come with me," she said, reaching out a hand. "Leave with me. You're down here for a reason. Your fleet doesn't need you to finish this war. And once we're out of here, we can figure out what to do next. Find a solution that works for both of us. Please. I didn't take your hand when I should have. But you're smarter than me. You can take mine."

The last time we were here, I shot Layla. I shot my best friend. I wasn't going to make that mistake again. But I wasn't going to enable her delusions either.

"I can do something even better," taking her hand. "I can save you from that big, common brain of yours."

Layla's hand tensed up inside mine. "Please let go."

"No way," I said. "I'm not letting you run away again."

"I'm not trying to run away."

"No, you're trying to ruin my life." I paused, gripping her hand tighter. "You didn't say why you're here."

Layla breathed on my face. "I will never lie to you. P'Ken ruined my original plan by stealing Aarif and arresting Jellz. This was plan B. Using the Authority's resources against the empire before taking them out, too. Yes, that means I've been talking to Shun, but I've also been plotting to kill her, I swear."

I still had no idea what her actual plan was, but getting access to the Authority's resources was the best bet anyone could have against us. In her hands, she could have even had a small shot at success. It was kinda funny too. Shun had infiltrated the school as a spy, and now Layla had infiltrated her base of operations, waiting to betray her. Shun going out that way would be hilarious… but I needed to kill her myself. And more importantly…

"I believe you." Flexing out my arm, I flung Layla away, diagonally, so that she collided with the wall, not too far away.

"There is no need for any deceptions," I said, as Layla ached on the floor. "We are going to kill Shun right now, along with every single other wretched Utozin who stands in our way. You can follow me and watch… or you can fight me."

Saying those words was like hammering nails into my tongue. But I didn't have time for Layla's nonsense right now. Even if it was under threat of ultimatum, I needed her to stand with me. Now.

Layla stood up, twirling her pipe. "Please don't make me do this."

"What? You wanted to play before. Let's play."

Much as it killed me to do so, I rushed toward Layla with my katars. Once she was knocked out, I would have her beamed up and secured. This would all be settled once we were safe on Cykeb.

Plus, I really was dying to see how strong she'd gotten.

As I swung my katars, Laya blew on her pipe and surrounded herself with a blue glass shield. My strike cracked it but didn't shatter it completely. I'd been briefed about the Glass Striker, but it was so cool to actually see it in action.

"How did you make this?!" I asked.

"I wish I had time to tell you."

Layla breathed in, the glass making up the shield forming around the other side of the pipe and forming a spear. She wasted no time in striking back at me. I easily blocked.

"That's the first time you've ever tried hurting me."

"I did gas you once."

"Totally different."

I kicked her back, but she kept herself from flying away by stabbing her spear into the floor almost immediately after impact. I fired lasers out of my palms at her, but she hopped away, yanking her spear out of the ground, and deflecting every one of my shots.

"Woah!"

Both of us fell over against the walls as the ground shook. The bombing was increasing in intensity. This planet's destruction was a certainty, but if I didn't finish this fast, Shun could get away. I couldn't let that happen!

"Stop this, Layla!" I cried. "Even if you beat me and took me away, all the Authority's resources you hoped to use will be gone or ours soon. You can't win! So just let yourself be happy! Please."

"I really wish I could." she said from behind me, tripping me over, before sealing me in a red glass sphere. The Layla I'd been looking at faded away as I glared up at the one who'd caught me. Damn True Adventurer. "But nothing will make me give up on you."

Sneering and growling, I punched at the sphere she'd locked me in, but all I could do was slightly crack it. The Glass Striker was no longer cool.

"Let me out, Layla!" I screamed. "Now! That's an order!"

"I don't take orders from my friends," she said. "Princess, general, or otherwise."

I seethed. I didn't like enclosed spaces. I didn't like not being able to move. It reminded me too much of… of…

"Friends don't do this to each other!" I continued punching at the sphere, enlarging the cracks. "I hate you!"

I didn't mean that. But I did hate her right now. "I know. And I'm sorry."

"No. You aren't. But you will be."

Screaming at the top of my lungs, I charged up my energy, and released a ginormous electrical blast, completely destroying the sphere I'd been trapped in and totally screwing up this base's electrical systems, the lights flickering. Layla protected herself with another shield, but I wouldn't give her the chance to trap me again. Without wasting another moment, I fired another high-intensity blast at her.

She was a cyborg. She had The True Adventurer. She would survive. She wouldn't learn.

I knew that now. But I would still be ready to teach her.

BOOM!

Bright, shimmering, pure glass that was every color all at once filled my sight. And that was all I could see before I fell over, writhing in agony, only able to see darkness.

# CHAPTER 17: LAYLA

"Layla to bridge. How's everyone doing?"

"What the Hell have you done?!"

I nervously laughed, huddled over Kaya's unconscious body, secured and alone in Shun's office. "I grabbed the one bargaining chip I could."

The "Rainbow Art Show" was one of the two main attacks I'd developed for fighting Kaya directly. It channeled all of my experiences as an artist into a single, stunning wave of concussive, refracted light. I knew it would be enough to counter Kaya's relatively weak, by her standards, attack, but I hadn't counted on it knocking her out.

Of course, one of Kaya's abilities was to adapt to any major harm she faced. That meant the attack wouldn't work on her a second time. If we fought again, I'd have to go with the move that would have brought the whole mountain down around us.

*That. Was. Wicked!* Juri cheered.

*It was like seeing my entire life as a single portrait,* I thought back.

"Dammit, Layla!" P'Ken screeched over the com, Kaya's com now in my ear. "Where is Kaya?!"

"Taking a nap," I said, brushing a stray, blonde hair out of her eyes with my fingertip. "You've got Aarif and Griffin with you, right? Put them on speaker. I want to say hi to the traitor and my old buddy."

P'Ken was seething, no doubt. But right now, she was stuck doing whatever I wanted.

She knew I wouldn't hurt Kaya, but there was a lot more than that I could do right now. "Layla. I wish we were—"

"Reuniting under better circumstances, yeah, yeah, Griff," I cut him off. "You suck, by the way."

Griffin grumbled.

"Kid, you need to let us get you, Juri, and the princess out of there right now," Aarif said. "It's a damn war zone down there."

"And whose fault is that?" I asked. "You can stop dropping bombs and start calling back troops whenever you want."

"That's what this is?" P'Ken snarled. "You wish to trade Kaya in exchange for a withdrawal? How do you think that would go? We'd pull back, you'd hand her over, and the second she woke up, we'd be back. Neither she nor the empress possess the honor to stay true to an agreed-upon ceasefire."

"Considering I just took out your ultimate sword with one hit and you can't touch me from orbit right now without hitting her too, it's on you to propose some other options here."

"And if we don't?"

"You don't think I prepared an escape route? I'll take Kaya with me. You can have your fancy computers run simulations for all the ways that could go, but by the time you've read them all, your boss, who's totally still your friend, will have already cut your heads off for letting this happen."

My heart was pounding. Again. I was really gonna have some

heart problems by the time this was done, if I survived. It was exciting though. To execute a plan and turn the tables on a far more powerful force than yourself. If this was the thrill that had made Yael love being a thief, then I finally got it.

Over the speaker, I could hear P'Ken tapping her cane-whip against her hand, trying to figure out the next move. Of course, I already knew what she'd say.

"Okay, Layla. You win." Aarif and Griffin both screeched, the former surprised and the latter appalled. "Don't make fools of yourselves. She has us. We cannot allow her to kidnap the princess, and the degree of force it would take, either from orbit or deployed into the base, to apprehend her would only further endanger Kaya's life. What are your exact demands?"

"Glad you asked," I said, sitting back in Shun's uncomfy chair. "Like you said, full withdrawal comes first. Then, I hand over Kaya at an agreed-upon third-party location. And lastly and most importantly, I don't want any of you there. Or any soldiers or Sunrisers or Cykerdroids. Just me, Kaya, and Molina."

"You know that isn't possible," Griffin said. "The empress will not travel to some backwater planet alone with you."

"Sounds like a her problem."

"Please see reason! Do you really think we're all evil? Every single one of us? Do you think I truly believe everything the empire has done to be moral and just? Nothing about the current state of the empire's leadership resembles the noble honor I believe in. The amount of hurt and death I've indirectly participated in… it keeps my eyes open at night."

By the time I'd arrived on Utozex Prime, Shun had viewed pathos as my only meaningful weapon against the empire. But I'd known that Kaya would want to come right for her. Which was why I'd leaked her current whereabouts to Cykebian intelligence, and then immediately evacuated her. Kaya came right to me, with no potential trigger from Shun in sight, and I'd taken her down, a prospect Shun had found difficult to believe but put her faith in.

And now, it was the invasion's leaders who could only play on pathos.

"Sounds like a you problem," I said.

"Stop making light of this, stop talking like her. None of us like this. None of us want this. But the universe is a dark place, has always been a dark place, and we're just doing what we have to."

"Like good little soldiers."

"Would you shut it?!" Aarif and P'Ken weren't speaking up. They were seemingly content to let Griffin take his shot here. I wondered what they were thinking about the fact Griffin was clearly welling up. "Aarif only betrayed you because he's smart enough to understand that you're going to get yourself and Juri killed. I'm pretty sure he hates the empire, and us, more than you. He cannot shut up about it."

"It's true," Aarif commented, shortly.

"And that's why I have a sliver less hatred for you than them. At least you were just a coward and not—"

"Molina would have killed Marcos!" The com went silent. On both ends.

"What?" I asked a moment later, energy gone from my voice.

"Griffin, don't," P'Ken breathed heavily.

"No, I'm doing what I need to. Just as I've been doing. On the way here, Aarif asked me why I didn't seek P'Ken out after I was freed from prison. The two of us could have had a nice, comfy little, thieving life away from all the death. But if I'd left Cykeb, Marcos would have been stuck by themselves." He wasn't just welling up anymore. "I couldn't leave that self-righteous idiot alone. We all know what Molina's become. Without her minimal investment in keeping me happy and loyal, the third or fourth time Marcos refused to serve her, she would have executed them so they could never be used as a potential weapon against her."

Griffin continued to weep, banging his hands on a surface. "Marcos needed me. And soon after I began serving the crown, it became clear that Kaya needed me as well. I'd never met her. But the way she'd speak of Yael and of you, and the way every second I spent with her I could feel her pain…" he cut himself off, gulping. "I'm sorry. But we all just want the same things."

He was playing me. This was his move. His strategy. Sure, it was Griffin, but he'd still studied under Yael with me, and had spent the last year with Molina. He was good. Better than we ever gave him credit for. That's all this was.

It did make sense. It did. But then…

"You already told me your story, P'Ken," I weakly said, holding my shaking fist. "Are you about to tell me you left out a detail that makes you just another victim?"

P'Ken… sniffled. She was crying now, too. What the fuck was going on? Did they really think I was buying this? Was I buying this?!

"I didn't—"

The transmission was cut off, static as max volume blasting out my ears. I tried turning my watch off, but it didn't work. What was going on now? Was this part of P'Ken's plan? Were the Utozins backstabbing me?

"Hello, Layla. I think it's about time we had a chat."

My heart sank so low, it dropped right out of me. A hologram had projected out of my watch. A hologram of the face of the big bad bitch herself.

"Molina," I said, sitting up straight and trying my best to compose myself. "I couldn't agree more."

RUFF! RUFF! RUFF!

As Juri barked internally, I dragged my claws through Shun's desk, peeling off the glossy surface. For the past year, Molina had haunted my nightmares. Over the past year, Molina had become responsible for the deaths of millions. She'd betrayed us. She'd manipulated Kaya. And now, I was finally face to face with her. Would I even recognize her?

Molina, seemingly seated on her throne, sipped wine from her goblet. "Up until now, I have permitted you to operate. I removed your bounty so that you could attend art school in peace, and had you ever come to see me, you would have been welcomed with open arms. I allowed P'Ken to handle you as she saw fit after Aarif alerted her to your horribly illegal activities, and I gave Kaya the chance to pursue you after you escaped her; she loves you so much, dear. But…"

Molina sinisterly giggled as she set her goblet down. "Now you've actually managed to gain the upper hand. I don't blame my subordinates for falling prey to you; you're very good. And ultimately, it is a matriarch's job to protect her family. Just as it has always been."

I took a deep breath as I grabbed a drink of my own, a taro, coconut, and carrot smoothie I'd been able to have prepared. I took a sip before setting it back down.

"You've been watching somehow? Listening in? You know where things stand?"

"I do. And, for old time's sake, and for Kaya, I'm giving you one last chance to surrender. Should you fail to stand down and bend the knee, I will have no choice but to stop treating you as a misguided child and to begin treating you as an enemy of the empire."

"Well, you can go ahead and treat me like that if you want, because that's exactly what I am," I said. "Before we get down to business, I have to ask: was this always you?"

Molina elevated her head. "What do you think?"

"You want to know what I think? I think you're pathetic. A loser who was so insecure over not having achieved enough that you gave up everything good in your life so you could feel powerful. So you could hurt people who love you. So you could be special. Well, congratulations, Molina! You're special, all right. A thousand years from now, every last history book will document you as one of history's greatest monsters. And biggest losers."

It was hard to feel good about anything right now. The smoothie was for nerve control, not taste. But it felt damn amazing getting to say all that to her.

Molina sighed. "History is written by the winners. I'm sure you know this. And while I can admit I was a pathetic 'loser' for most of my life, the thought I could ever lose this war hasn't occurred to me once."

"Not when you can send your pre-teen daughter to kill anyone who threatens you, right?"

Molina's lips curled in disgust. "I have already broken Kaybell for creating her. She will suffer for decades to come. And I have brought Kaya to the brink of complete collapse. Once the war is over, and the universe is under my dominion, I will shatter her once and for all. And I will make her subsequent death quick."

I bit my lip and nodded furiously. This goddamn… "There really is no good in you at all, is there?"

"Good is just another term defined by winners. Try again."

I shook my head. "Other people always questioned how you managed to land Yael. Why was she so in love with you? I don't wonder that. Even now. Love's a fucky thing. The only thing I don't get is how she never saw what a monster you were."

"I've thought about that one myself," Molina said almost immediately. "One of the universe's supposed greatest geniuses not being able to consider that someone who'd torture the woman she loves and be the closest friend and companion to a demonically evil princess for a decade may not be a very compassionate person is just sad."

No. No, I didn't recognize her at all.

"Okay," I nodded. "Okay. So… how about that withdrawal?"

Molina cackled.

"Even if you hate your daughter, you still need her! And now if you leave her with me, I can tell her everything."

"You think she'd believe you? Not only have I groomed that girl to perfection, but you have The True Adventurer. Even if you've been recording this, she would believe it to be fake. More nasty, nasty lies."

"Doesn't change the part where your military strategies are built around her."

Molina shrugged. "Not anymore they aren't. The latest models of our warships and Cykerdroids haven't made her redundant, there's still no more powerful warrior in the stars… but to say I need her? No. No, I don't."

I would have reached for my smoothie but I didn't want her to see my shaking arm.

What the Hell was this?!

"So that's it? You want me to take her so you can continue your assault?"

"Don't look so mad at me. This is your fault."

"Don't even. You're here now because of me, but this was inevitable."

Molina snickered. What now? "No, no it really wasn't. My dear, the Cykebian Empire doesn't develop its own weapons. It's above that. It feeds on all others in its presence." Molina leaned forward, and halfway across the universe, a darkness fell over me. "Do you really think I haven't been watching you?"

Uhhh. I feel weird, Human.

"Yeah. You and me both, girl," I said, my clouded mind not in a position to speak to her silently.

"Little Layla wanted to be an artist," Molina said, her voice... different. "A painter, a sculptor, oh no, my mistake, a glassblower. Whatever that means. You thought you could get away. You thought you could beat me. You thought I wouldn't have people watching you, you thought you could take that brilliant mind of yours and waste it. You thought you could keep your potentially universe-shaking invention for yourself and squander it as a weapon of war!"

I fell over in my chair. Frozen. I knew who was talking and it wasn't Molina. But how?

What was going on?!

"Molina" cackled, now in her true voice. Her true, but still familiar voice. "Figured it out? Then you know why the thought of losing this war has never once occurred to me."

The face in the hologram took on its true form as panic seeped into my soul. "For I am Madame N'gwa! And I always win!"

My g-gma laughed her haunting laugh at the top of her lungs as I curled up into a ball, unable to close my eyes even a little. I had no idea what was going on anymore. I had no idea what I was supposed to do. I couldn't think. Each of my senses dulled, one by one. Smell, then touch, then sight, then speech. But not my hearing. Not when I needed to hear the laughter.

# CHAPTER 18: KAYA

Had I lost?

That wasn't supposed to be possible. I was invincible. The ultimate sword. The peak of Cykebian ingenuity. Yet here I was, lying in my bed, back in the palace, my last memory being of bright light, then nothing.

Layla. Layla had beaten me. That was wicked. It only made things even more clear why I'd become so attached to her so quickly; despite the nature of her bloodline, she was my equal. Oh, if she were only a boy…

Growling, I fired a laser out of my hand and blasted a hole in the wall.

No matter how cool or smart or sexy she was, she'd defied me again. She'd gotten in my way. She'd hurt me. That bitch.

I flew off my bed, my nightgown I'd been changed into bristling, and pressed my fingers against my ear, only to find my com was gone. Dammit! I needed to find out the status of the invasion immediately! I needed to talk to someone. But not Mother. I'd failed her. Regardless of if we'd been victorious anyway, I couldn't bear to face her with this shame.

Fortunately, I didn't even need to hunt down any of my other family or any nobility. If we'd won, if Utozex Prime had finally fallen, then the wondrous news would have been announced to everyone on Cykeb.

"You!" I shouted at a maid who seemed to be around my age. Her knees buckled at the sound of my voice, before she dropped to the floor and bowed. "Has Utozex Prime been conquered?!"

She trembled, naturally terrified of me, but she was able to spit out an answer without further prompting.

"I don't know, Princess. I haven't heard anything since the assault was announced. I swear."

No report. Enough time had passed for me to be brought home. Not that this simpleton would understand, but if victory hadn't been announced yet, then that meant Mother was keeping the truth close to her chest to prevent bringing shame upon the empire and the crown. We'd lost.

"But how?" I questioned myself. "The rest of our forces should have still been able to crush them. Captain Amatyn had everything she needed."

I looked back over at the servant girl and scowled. "Leave!"

She grabbed her dress, stood, and scurried off as quickly as her weak little legs would carry her.

It was going to hurt, I knew that, but Mother's words would only drive the sword of shame inside further in. I needed to know. I needed to know what happened. I needed to know that they were okay.

I flew down the spacious halls of the palace, avoiding people when I could and knocking them over when I couldn't. I needed to make it to the throne room ASAP.

The doors were shut when I arrived, but the guards saw me coming from down the hall and opened them, so I didn't have to stop for a second. As I flew in and touched my feet back down on the floor, my stress gave way to confusion. One of my mothers was here. But not Molina.

"Kaya!" Kaybell cheered, stretched across Molina's throne with a leg up on one of the arm rests and, shockingly, she didn't have any wine on her. "Thank the gods you're okay."

"Mother?" I questioned, approaching her. "What are you doing here? Where is Molina? What happened on Utozex Prime?!"

Mother smiled, lips shut, and waved toward me with both hands. I stopped walking.

"Please don't be mad at me," she said. "I'm sorry for how I acted at your party, but I've had time to think and re-evaluate my actions. Just as I have before. I've even stopped drinking. Not that any of that has been easy. Or entirely by choice."

Kaybell sat up straight. "Whatever I did, whatever I said, I can't even really remember. But I love you. And, more than anything, I'm sorry if you've doubted that."

I bit my lip and tapped my foot. Kaybell was the enemy. She hated me. She hated me for the evil monster I was. She hated everything I believed in.

But she didn't look like she did. She looked at me no differently than when she believed me to be her little angel. And I still needed answers.

"I am not sitting on your lap," I said, closing the gap between us.

"Because you're a big girl or because you're mad at me?"

"Both."

"Heh. That is fair."

She... actually seemed like my Mommy again. Like the amazing woman who'd raised me and not the bitter, hateful, weak-hearted loser she'd become. Had it just been that nasty alcohol poisoning her? Had Molina done something to her? Was this a gift? I certainly didn't deserve one of those right now.

"What happened?" I asked.

Kaybell cracked her knuckles. "We won."

All those nerves abandoned my body. Well, most of them. A smile crept up my face. "I don't understand."

"Utozex Prime fell," Mother began to explain. "Even without you leading the charge, the Authority was outgunned. And with Chancellor Shun absent, Megs and Morphea were easily able to outmaneuver her lessers. The planet was conquered, and the follow-up attacks we had in place gave the Utozex Council no choice but to surrender."

Of course her explanation would only give me more questions. Of course it would!

"What do you mean Shun was absent? And why were Uncle Megz and Aunt Morphea leading the fleet? What happened to P'Ken and the others? Why hasn't everyone been made aware of our triumph?"

Kaybell rose from the throne, not looking very happy about what she had to tell me. "From what our intelligence was able to gather, Shun was never on Utozex Prime. At least not by the time we got there. We have no idea if she's dead or alive."

Layla must have sent her somewhere as part of whatever she was planning. Another reason to be pissed, but it was also a relief; I'd still get to kill her.

Wait. Layla! If we won… "What about Layla?!"

"The same status as Shun. The same status as Captain Amatyn, Griffin, and… I'm sorry, I'm forgetting his name."

"Aarif."

"Right. We have no idea what's become of any of them. Molina was speaking to Layla, attempting to negotiate your release after she bested you, but part-way through, the call cut out. In the following two-minutes, Captain Amatyn and the others disappeared from the bridge of the *Winjolla*."

I clenched my fists, but not in additional, frustrated confusion. On the contrary, I knew exactly what had happened. The only people who could have just stolen my friends off the *Winjolla*'s bridge and taken down someone who'd beaten me and possessed The True Adventurer... was with The True Adventurer.

"The Order of the Banshee."

"What?"

"Do not be daft, Mother! I told you about them shortly after I returned home last year. They aren't ordinary women. I still don't really get how, but they have powers. They can warp reality around them. I've only gotten to see up close what novices can do with it, and both times I have, I've lost to it. I can't even imagine how powerful Madame N'gwa is."

Kaybell chuckled. "Apologies. This isn't the time for that. But this does explain why Molina reacted the way she did."

"What do you mean?"

"I mean that as soon as you were safe in bed and confirmed by the doctors to be stable, she left Cykeb on *Ricochet Supreme*. I'd thought she was only going to meet with the surrendered Utozex Council, but if she knew about this as well..."

"...then she wishes to fight them herself."

Mother tilted her head back. "Six years ago, The Order of the Banshee crushed my life when engaging them led to Molina leaving me. Now, they seek to crush those around me. But why?"

Another obvious answer.

"Layla turned her back on them," I explained, my heart racing.

I may have been confident in my hypothetical understanding of what was going on, but being right also meant we were all in far more danger than the Authority had ever put us in. "She turned on her great-grandmother and all her plans for her. And Yael helped her do so."

I'd been so stupid. Madame N'gwa had sworn revenge, but after everything else that happened, and all the time that passed, I'd forgotten. And even if she hadn't, it clearly hadn't been at the front of Layla's mind; I had been.

"And with Yael dead, she seeks revenge on those she loved," Mother voiced. "Your theory tracks, darling."

"I know."

Was I in top shape? No. Did I probably look a mess? Absolutely. But I couldn't let my Mommy fight these criminals, these terrorists without me. If anything happened to her, or the others, I wasn't sure what I'd do. I had to believe Layla and everyone else was still alive; they had to be.

"I'm following after her," I said. "But first: what are you doing here? And why wasn't there an announcement?"

Kaybell hummed as she twirled a finger in her hair. "Molina is seeing to this new threat herself. Had the announcements been made, she would have been kept occupied by countless obligations. To say nothing of how doing this at all is beneath her station. As for me, Megz and Morphea are still away. You were unconscious. She couldn't trust any of the nobles to oversee things in her absence, which left her poor, half-divorced wife as her only option. I'd sobered up, and she trusted me to not push things further into chaos during such a sensitive transition period."

She laughed. "I cannot lie. Doing so anyway and dragging this whole, miserable universe down to Hell with me does sound fun."

I shook my head at her as she continued to laugh in disgrace. With all the answers I needed, I turned around to leave so I could get changed and have my ship prepared.

"Wait, wait, wait."

I stopped at the entrance, rolling my eyes. "What?"

Kaybell took a breath. She strutted across the throne room so that she was once again close enough to hold me. Not that I would let her.

Kaybell beamed. "You seem different."

I scoffed. "You mean less miserable than you've made me this last year?"

"I was the one making you miserable?"

"Of course you were. With all of your silent hatred of me, isn't that what you wanted? At least Molina had a good reason to hurt me."

"There is never a good reason for a mother to hurt her child."

"Coming from the mouth of a deposed emperor who cares about innocent lives?"

"Coming from the mouth of a woman who's been forced to watch her family's legacy and her people's culture corrupt the people she cares for most to their very core."

"I wasn't corrupted!" I screamed. "I'm evil. I always have been. You made me. And you made me bad."

Mother shook her head. "No one is born evil. Especially not you. You were my angel."

I shook my head back at her.

"I failed you completely by allowing them to, but it was my sisters who made you what you are."

"Wrong. Do you know what's different about me? Acceptance. I know what I am, and I'm done caring. I'm the villain, and that's everyone else's problem, not mine."

"I know I never read you many stories, but surely you know what tends to happen to villains."

"In fantasy. In real life, look around. We always win." I giggled. "Just look at you. How life was when you were awesome vs life after being enslaved to common morality."

I shouldn't have even been wasting my time here. I needed to go, now! But something compelled me to stay and remain engaged.

Mother rubbed her refreshed but still-tired eyes. "Do you know why I spent the past year drinking as much as possible?"

"Because you were depressed and pathetic."

"Because I didn't wish to feel." She licked her lips. "Those warm elixirs, be they of grain or of fruit, may only crush you on the inside more, but on the outside, they are an escape."

"Like I said. Depressed and pathetic. What's your point?"

The bitch smirked at me.

"Why do you think Yael drank?"

"Don't you—"

"Compare myself to her? Never." She tilted her head up. "There's no lifetime where she and I would have been friends. Still, I would have loved the opportunity to meet her for real. The thief who shook the stars."

I shook my head, sneering. What was she even talking about?!

"I can only make my own assumptions," Mother continued. "I drank to dull the pain and the guilt I felt over what I'd allowed to happen. It's possible Yael merely needed her senses dulled so she could have the courage to live as freely as she did. But I have had a lot of time to think. And I believe that there was something else."

She held out her arms. "93 billion light years. Within that space, over 5,000 substantially populated planets, and over twice that many where human life can be found at all. Over 4,500 planets a part of the Empire or the Authority, home to over twenty-five trillion people. And of those people, how many were truly happy?"

"I don't care."

"Of course you don't. But Yael did. Those who rule, those who make the rules, are the only ones with true freedom. That is what we tell ourselves. But is it true? Are we not confined by rules of our own? By expectations and the society around us? By even, at times, our own people? No, just because our chains are gilded does not make them any less tight than on those shackled in mines. I believe Yael understood this. That's why she broke her chains. And why a selfish thief could never say no to taking in anyone who wished to break theirs. She did not drink for courage; she already possessed more than anyone did. She did it because there is nothing scarier in this world than being the only one responsible for your own choices."

I clenched my fists. What she was saying made a lot of sense. But why was she saying it?

Mother looked down at my hands before looking back up at me.

"The closed fist. The symbol of the chains we all wear, and your first instinct to wrap yours around—"

I shut her up with a smack upside the chin, launching her back, across the throne room, and through the throne.

"Oh gods." I'd just destroyed the ultimate symbol of Cykebian power. The one I'd long dreamed of sitting in. But whatever. It was time for a new dawn anyway.

Mother lay in a pile of rubble, injured but alive. Her power was nothing compared to my own, but even in her disgusting state, she still stood among the strongest. She could take it.

I leaped across the room and landed where Mother had, picking her up by the collar. "Get to the point! Tell me what you're trying to say already, or I'll cut out your tongue, you damn bi—!"

Mother caught me off as she wrapped her arms around me.

"My point is that I love you. My point is that there is nothing more I want than for you to grow up and live a long, happy, and fulfilled life, free of the chains I put on you in your crib. For you to find the bravery to realize you aren't evil, and to figure out what it is you truly want. To find what makes you happy, surrounded by those that you love… even if that doesn't include me. I know those chains may feel loose, and the darkness may be comforting, but they will always find a way to hurt you."

In her arms, I was warm. But I didn't want her warmth. Or her love. Or anything she described. I'd found my place, and my comfort, in the darkness. Maybe I wore chains, but I was too powerful to care. Being enslaved to the destiny of ruling over all other life didn't sound so bad at all. I was going to live a long, happy life, delighting every second in tormenting those beneath me.

It's not like I had any reason not to. It was what brought me joy. And everyone who mattered supported me. Mother supported me. P'Ken and Griffin had my back no matter what… but Aarif might not have. And if he left or turned on me after getting Juri back, then what? Would P'Ken still stand with me? Would Griffin still be my friend if I killed them both?

Layla. Layla had fought me. She'd refused the gilded chains. Of course she had. She'd broken her chains, and now she wanted to break every last human being of theirs. She was never going to put new ones on, no matter what I did.

If the Banshees hadn't killed her, then I'd have to. Just like Yael. I couldn't live my happy life knowing she was always out there, hating me.

Why? Why did I feel like this about her? We'd barely gotten the chance to know each other before everything went wrong. Was it just because she'd been my first real friend? Still the only *real* friend I'd had? My EZ Sister?

Or did I...? Yes. Yes, I did. "Baaaaaa!"

Tears and snot raced out of my face in an instant. It burned, it hurt. They gushed and they wouldn't stop as I heaved. I loved Layla. She was a girl, but I loved her. I loved her more than any boy band member, or any of my "friends," or any of my siblings, or even any of my mothers! I'd made the biggest mistake of my life when I killed Yael. I couldn't make that mistake again. If freeing myself of my chains, of escaping the darkness, was what I needed to do to live my life with her, then I would. I was Kaya Langstone Bythora, daughter of Kaybell, Molina, and Yael, princess of the Holy Cykebian Empire and heir to the throne, and the most powerful cyborg in existence.

Nothing would ever hold me back!

"Thank you, Mother!" I cried through my tears, hugging her back. "I... I don't know what I feel. Or what I want. I don't know what I want to do once this is all over. But I'll figure it out! I'll break my chains! I'll be free! I promise."

She didn't respond. Her powerful arms had gone limp.

I pulled back, holding my Mommy. The light had left her eyes.

Screaming, I tripped my feet and fell over to the floor, dropping my mother's still-warm body.

"No, no, no, no, no." I crawled inches forward and shook Kaybell. "Please! Please come back! I'm sorry! I'm sorry!"

She didn't listen to me. Bad things always happened when people didn't listen to me. Heaving and shaking, I grabbed the biggest piece of rubble I could find.

# CHAPTER 19: LAYLA

Had I lost?

It wasn't too surprising. I'd been completely outgunned from the jump. All I'd had going for me was a pretty good head on my shoulders. Well, that, a cyborg body and The True Adventurer. But I'd been feeling pretty confident, gripping the Cykebian fleet by the balls. Yet here I was, lying in my bed, my last memory being of bright light, then nothing.

I gasped. As my eyes fully opened, I realized where I was where I was.

The mattress was the softest I'd ever slept on, and the silk blankets the most fine. The poles holding up the canopy above me were gilded, the room itself was huge, and along with art that looked to be hundreds or thousands of years old, it was decorated with both my own sculptures and boy-band collages.

I was in Kaya's bedroom.

This didn't make sense. How was I here? What happened on Utozex Prime? Where was everyone else?

"Juri, what's going on?" No answer.

"Juri, talk to me!" Nothing.

Something came up my throat, but nothing came out. She wasn't here. It didn't even feel like I was still a cyborg. Not even connected to her in a separate body, for the first time in so long, I wasn't just alone; I was alone, all by myself.

If I was in the Cykebian palace, then maybe Aarif had already taken her out of me. But he couldn't have figured out how to do so in what I had to hope had been a short timeframe. And even if he had, even if he was a coward, he wouldn't have done something like that without me being aware of what was going on.

I squeezed my face, noticing as I pulled my arms into view that I'd been dressed in a silver nightgown. This was exactly where I didn't want to be. If I was going to end up here either way, skipping the whole trip to Utozex Prime and coming straight here would have been far more advantageous. Now, I'd pissed everyone off, and likely sped up the destruction of the Authority, and the completion of the Empire's dominion.

But…then why was I in Kaya's room? How had I lost? I could have sworn I'd been speaking to Molina when something happened, but I had no idea what. If I'd really gone down somehow against her and the fleet, there's no way I'd be getting even better treatment now than I had when I'd been captured by P'Ken. Something was up.

I leaped out of bed. The first thing to do was get changed. Whatever was going on, I'd probably be ending up in a fight soon and—

"Good morning, Layla!"

I lost my balance as my heart pounded. I turned around and looked up to see Kaya, in a matching nightgown to mine, brushing her hair and sitting above where I'd just been lying. I hadn't been sleeping under a canopy; I'd been sleeping in a bunk bed.

"Kaya," I said, smiling back at her. "Good morning."

Kaya pouted. "What's got you so jumpy?"

Was... was she serious?

"Do you not know?"

Kaya, continuing to look at me like abstract art, hopped off her bunk. "Is this about last night? I told you Mother didn't mean anything bad about your hair; she was just making a suggestion!"

What the actual fuck? Molina hadn't said anything about my hair, that obviously wouldn't be what I was focused on if she had, and just because I hadn't been able to wash my hair in coconut water lately didn't mean...

"I know that. Hey, what would you say if I told you the last thing I remember, you were invading Utozex Prime, and I was trying to stop you?"

Kaya's eyes widened, her lips curled, and, soon enough, she was cackling.

Kaya held my hands. "I'd say you had a bad nightmare, and maybe too much to drink." She giggled as she turned away, looking at herself in a mirror as she resumed brushing her hair. "Yael needs to stop encouraging you."

I tensed up. My heart stopped. "Yael?"

"Yes, Yael, my favorite magical, functioning alcoholic mother." She giggled again. She turned around, tossing aside her brush, and floated over to me, feeling my forehead. "Are you all right? Do you need to see a doctor?"

There were a few possibilities as to what was going on. Option one was that me and Kaya had died and gone to Heaven with Yael, but there was no chance of any of us going there, even if it existed. A more likely possibility was that this was a dream. The less likely, but ideal option was that everything else had been a dream, and this was real.

But I knew what the most likely option was. Because I knew

what forms of magic existed in the stars. I even had access to them myself. And I knew who the greatest master of them was. I didn't know what the limits of The True Adventurer were, but I was beginning to suspect it was whatever this was.

I'd neglected Madame N'gwa as a threat. My g-gma hadn't bothered me once while at college, so I'd figured she wasn't interested in taking me on directly. I may have been an idiot.

I laughed. "No, no, sorry. Definitely just a bad dream I had to shake off."

"Well, good," Kaya said. "My lady-in-waiting isn't allowed to get sick."

We laughed together and performed our handshake, before Kaya called in servants to dress us and prepare our hair for breakfast. Despite my being a couple inches taller than Kaya, we shared a closet. High-class Cykebian dresses worth more than some planets weren't my style, but wearing one did remind me of the Benkinian dresses Yael would sometimes stick Shun and I in. The designs were completely different, Cykebian dresses being much more loose and less modest, but the quality of the material was the same, and both definitely weren't good for a planet's environment.

"So what's on the agenda for today?" I asked.

"Boring stuff. I was thinking we ditch and go check out that Ivanna Fruxy exhibition you haven't been able to shut up about. Maybe seeing it will do the trick!"

My heart ached at how wonderful going to one of Ifruxy's shows sounded right now. That Kaya was so relaxed and at ease, and just happy only made it sound better.

I braced myself as we entered the dining hall. I knew who I was about to see. Whatever was happening, I wasn't ready.

The guards opened the doors for us. We strolled into the

magnificent, if ostentatious, dining hall together, arm in arm, and were greeted with a chorus of "Good Mornings" from Molina, Kaybell, and, of course…

"What's up with you, Layla? You look like you've seen a ghost."

I nervously laughed, uncontrollably, as my eyes wettened. It was Yael. Just as I remembered her. Well, not exactly. Her hair was up in an elaborate knot, with her head adorned with a silver crown and jewels. Her makeup was heavier than she'd liked to wear it, and she too was in a regal Cykebian dress. But the smile? The smile was all her.

"Excuse her," Kaya said as we took our seats across from each other. "She had the silliest nightmare."

"Is that so?" Molina asked, her face as soft as I remembered it, without a hint of the cold dictator found in her propaganda. "What was so silly about it?"

I forced a giggle, needing to keep playing along for now. Even though all I wanted to do was race to the head of the table, where the three crowned, seemingly married rulers sat together, and hug Yael.

"Kaya was leading a fleet to invade Utozex Prime, on your order, and I was fighting her." The emperor and, I supposed, her two empresses laughed.

"I cannot even fathom how your dream-self got into that predicament," Emperor Kaybell said. "The only part I'm unsure of is what's more unrealistic: the Authority going back on the peace agreement we formed only six months ago, or you and Kaya fighting."

"She did try to kill us three times, so I'm gonna say the former." Everyone jovially booed Yael's attempt at humor.

"What is the matter with you?" Kaybell teased.

"Eh, sometimes you just gotta say something to say something."

"Which is why it's a good thing one of my many talents is shutting you up." Kaybell and Yael kissed. I held back my barf.

"Have I mentioned you two are disgusting?" Molina vocally agreed with my sentiment, but clearly teasing.

Both Yael and Kaybell kissed her cheeks. While I was holding back disgust and omnipresent confusion, Kaya looked at her mothers with a twinkle in her eyes.

This was what Kaya had wanted. All of her mothers happy and together, with me as her lady-in-waiting. There was no telling where the others were in this make-believe world, but Prince Megz and Princess Morphea were absent as well, so there was no reason to worry. Not that there was a need to worry about anyone but myself right now. This was all fake. G-gma's game. Right?

"Everything is all right now, though?" the emperor asked.

Kaybell was the one person at this table I'd never met. I'd heard stories of a monster, imagined my own of a fascist conqueror, and learned that she'd been rendered a hapless victim of those that she had corrupted. Looking at her here, I didn't see any of those women. I saw an impeccably presented emperor and mother who'd sought out peace, who loved her family, and whose family loved her.

"Of course," I said. "I'm no child. That's Kaya's job."

"Oh my goooood," Kaya groaned. "Why is everyone bullying me today? Is it because I blasted the newest Duroc Boys album over the loudspeaker? I already said that was an accident."

Everyone laughed again. This time, myself included. I wasn't even faking it. Seeing my friend so happy like this in a universe at peace? It was everything I'd been fighting for.

The palace's servants brought us our food, the first of multiple courses. As I enjoyed my delectable vegan quiche, with at least two vegetables inside I'd never tried before, I mainly sat back and listened as everyone else talked. Molina rambled about an exhibition she'd organized to uncover "the lost blades of Venus," Kaybell explained to Kaya the matters they'd be going over in court later, clearly boring her and guaranteeing she'd turned on her internal music player, and Yael...

"...and after that, I'm gonna meet up with P'Ken and her crew. Apparently my 'all grown up' apprentice still needs my help from time to time."

"As if you didn't jump out of bed when you received the request," Molina said.

"I never said I didn't appreciate the occasional chance to still do my thing." She looked directly at me. "You're not really needed in court today, Layla. Why don't you come with us? Been forever since you've gotten any action."

I wanted to say Yes so badly. Even if I'd never wanted to be a thief, it would have been a lie to say I hadn't enjoyed working with Yael. I'd missed her so much.

But she wasn't real. For all I knew, going would lead me to the part of this where G-gma tortured me. If it really was her behind this, then there was no way she'd have stuck me in...

Paradise.

"Fun as that sounds, my responsibility is to be here for whatever Kaya needs." Kaya snickered, knowing we'd be sneaking out. "Remind me, who's in the crew these days?"

Yael belched into her elbow. "I think just P'Ken, Aarif, Griffin, and Marcos. Pretty sure P'Ken dumped the new guy she brought in off on a poisonous swamp world after he tried getting in between Marcos and Griffin."

"A love triangle," Kaybell hummed.

"Not something any of us have the least bit of experience with," Molina joked.

"Right. She mentioned she got rid of that jerk. I doubt anyone will ever top Shun in that department though, right?"

I had to know. Their responses to what I'd just said would tell me everything. And they did.

"Why would you say that name?" Yael asked, grimacing.

Smiles had been exterminated from the hall, and across from me, Kaya was hugging herself, with her head lowered. Molina and Kaybell scowled at me.

"I'm sorry," I said. "I forgot that it was taboo."

"Taboo?" Kaybell questioned rhetorically. "That monster tried to kill your princess. If you hadn't been there to gas everyone on *Ricochet* so that she could be detained and executed, there's no telling what harm she could have done."

The knife pierced my heart, shaking me on the inside and the outside. That was the game.

The True Adventurer had the power to let you warp reality to your whim, under the condition that it be used to live multiple lives, experience multiple stories, at once.

I had no idea of knowing if G-gma was alone, or if her gaggle of gray-haired hags was working with her, but I'd only ever seen a taste of their power in action. This had to be the next step beyond. Forcing someone else to experience an alternate timeline, still based on just a single decision.

Everything had gone wrong on *Ricochet* in the middle of the night. I'd been exhausted. And when I'd been woken up by the fighting, I was terrified. I panicked. I'd made the wrong call and attempted to talk Kaya down. But if I'd just used a gas grenade on her, as I had before, if I'd knocked the whole crew out with her, I could have secured Shun and Kaya in separate cells and taken us all to our expected destination of Cykeb so that everything could be reasonably worked out.

I'd hated myself for the past year for not saying the right pretty words. I'd hated Aarif and P'Ken for keeping Kaya's message from me. But my biggest mistake was the one I'd chosen to ignore. I could give myself some leeway for not being able to save Yael and the universe by saying the exact right words to an unwell girl I'd just met, but there was no excuse for cracking under pressure.

Kaybell had created Kaya and corrupted Molina. Molina had embraced corruption. Kaya had been an unwitting pawn and killed millions. Shun had been doing her job, which she thought was the only way to protect her society.

But more than any of them, everything was my fault. My fault for not being good enough. My fault for not working and training harder as a thief and instead practicing my art. That was what this was. That was what Madame N'gwa was showing me. This was her revenge.

And I couldn't imagine anything more painful.

"I'm sorry," I repeated, standing up. My lip was quivering, and my knees were barely doing as I wished. I needed to get out of here before I caused a scene. "Please excuse me. I think I need to get some better sleep after all."

No one said anything as I walked out. I wasn't even sure where I was going. My chambers? If I wanted to break down and cry, that was the place to do it. And oh, I wanted to. It wasn't as if there was anything else I could do. I'd already been trying to use The True Adventurer this whole time. In this timeline, I'd never gotten a mysterious helping hand.

My watch beeped. Holding back tears, I checked the message I'd just received.

I can tell something is wrong. And it isn't just a bad dream. You know you can tell me anything. When you're ready. I guess. Waiting is lame though.

I had to smile a little. Oh Kaya…

The smile didn't last long, disintegrating before I even stepped out into the hallway. I could have tried leaving the palace and looking for a ship or asking a guard to point me to my workshop that Kaya had mentioned I had, but there wouldn't have been any point. I was powerless here. If all I could do was cry in my chambers, then that was what I'd do.

I laughed as I walked up the stairs. I'd spent a year working as hard as I could preparing to bring down the empire, I'd fought as hard as I could, and now it was all for nothing.

Preparations I'd made would never be put into action, pieces I'd aligned would never be moved, and the universe and the people in it I loved descended further into darkness, I would be here, enjoying a utopia; at least until G-gma got bored and decided to finish me.

"Wonder what would happen if I tried hunting her down in this world," I said, opening the door to me and Kaya's chambers. "Would killing her here do any—"

I cut myself off, shrieking, as the door slammed shut behind me.

Wrapped in a wine-red cloak, with fingerless white gloves stretching down her arms, bells decorating her from head to toe, and her eyes unnaturally bulging out, Madame N'gwa stood by the windowsill, grinning at me.

"Layla," she said. "How nice to see my favorite great-granddaughter again. Tell me: are you enjoying your present?"

I stumbled back against the wall, knocking over one of my own sculptures from a shelf, sending it crashing into pieces on the floor.

"Madame," I breathed.

"Oh, don't sound so scared or surprised. Please. It's beneath you. You're many things: impudent, disobedient, naive, misguided, self-destructive, absolutely, but you were put in this position in the first place because, unlike those useless parents of yours, you're no fool; you know exactly what's happening here."

Clinging to the wall, I sneered. "Yeah. I do. Doesn't make it any less of a normal reaction to be terrified of you."

"HA!" G-gma laughed. "That's fair. Despite my acknowledgment, I can only imagine you'd be tempted to do something foolish, like attempt to fight me, if you could. But, take away your weapon, your power, even your body, and so without the ability to fight, you take flight."

I grit my teeth, trying to keep my breaths quiet, peeling myself off the wall. "Are you really here?"

"Are any of us really anywhere? In the scope of the vast, endless stars, do any of us really exist? Or are we blips defying the rules of nature, waiting our turn to be purged?"

"I really do not have it in me to listen to your nonsense right now."

"This isn't nonsense! This is what I was always trying to teach you. None of us matter. Nothing we do matters. Life is a gift and a miracle, and spending it for anyone but yourself is a waste. Whether you're the power hungry dictator or the artist trying to fill the world with beauty, your time will come soon, and the relevance of even the most important historic actions will, in the grand scheme of everything, eventually be irrelevant. Except for stories. Stories can live on forever if they're exciting enough. All that matters is experiencing as much of the universe as you can, living life to its fullest, and sharing those experiences with the people you love. Living for yourself, telling the best story possible, is all you can do."

I'd been hearing speeches like that for half my life. I'd never bought it at all. I could enjoy a good story, but there was more than one way to tell one; my sculptures were my stories.

And I refused the notion that in a universe of twenty-five trillion people, the best way to live was for all of us to only think about ourselves.

"I can tell that you're listening, but I doubt that you're hearing me," Madame N'gwa continued, jingling her bells. "Which is exactly why this world will be your tomb. This world, where everything is the same, but where you thought quick enough to keep your fake family's crisis from getting out of hand and spilling out to the rest of the stars. It's almost impressive how badly you blundered. To the point my reputation would be sullied if it were public knowledge that you, Layla N'gwa, incited the bloodiest war in over 4,000 years."

I clenched my fists, nodding my bowed head. "Yes. You're right. And that's it? No twist?"

"No twist at all. The world will never be corrupted unless circumstances naturally go that way, but I doubt it. I will never directly harm you or attempt to end your life. No, no, there is no need for bluntness like that. You will live your life, enjoying all the splendors of being a lady-in-waiting for the princess of the Cykebian Empire. And not a day will go by where you are actually happy with all your luxury and your loving family, because no matter how hard you try to forget, you will always remember that the real world is suffering, burning to the ground, because of you."

Her words were sharper than any glass. They were all true. The dread of it seeping in that my only options were to live my long, Cykebian-tech extended life exactly as she'd described, or to kill myself, brought me to my knees, and forced tears down my eyes. I wouldn't have been surprised if she was hoping I'd eventually go for the latter, decades from now, just for the thrill.

Madame N'gwa snickered. "I'm truly sorry it had to be this way. I had such big plans for you. You were to be my successor. To continue the Madame N'gwa legacy. To experience the greatest adventures and live life to its fullest. Wouldn't that have been nice? Nicer than this, certainly."

I kept crying on the floor.

G-gma sighed. "Well, I don't do well with crying babies, so I suppose this is goodbye. But I can leave you with some final comforts: the real you and your old friends are all safe inside one of my homes. No physical harm will come to any of you, even as you each get to enjoy a tailor-made Hell. Former Chancellor Amatyn as well. For completion's sake. But I've also arranged for a date with the empress; seeing how Molina has ripened should be fun. And when I return her daughter to her, it will be with the blessing that she remains more obedient than you." Her smile finally faded, as she sneered back at me. "Make the most of this life, Layla. I mean that."

Madame N'gwa exploded into glass shards, many of them flying by and touching me, but without cutting me, as bells rang directly in my ears.

She was gone. And I'd barely been able to get a word in. Damn her. Damn the power she'd always had over me.

"You're bullshit!" I screeched. "You're full of it! We should all live for ourselves, but you're pissy because I wouldn't follow your path! You're just another jackboot! Fuck you, Madame N'gwa! Fuck you!"

I didn't care who heard. Even if everyone thought I was crazy, this would just be a single outburst. I'd be examined by a doctor, maybe put on some meds, and life here would become the new normal; life here would slowly begin chipping away at me.

She'd forced me into training to be a thief. Now, she was going to force Kaya to remain in the darkness, all alone with the monster who wielded her. There would be no one to stand against the empire as the universe devolved into an even hotter Hell.

"All my fault," I whimpered. "All my fault."

"Well."

My eyes jolted wide open.

"I wouldn't say that." Crawling around 180 degrees on all fours, there was Yael. Not dressed like an empress, but like Yael. Shitty button-down, jeans, combat boots, and barely any makeup. "Frankly I'd lay more blame at the feet of that mega bitch of a great grandmother. I really wasted my adult years fangirling over her, and I'm not sure I'll ever live that down."

Trembling, I pushed myself up to my feet. "What is this now? What are you?"

"Me? Gay, Autistic and ADHD, but I'm guessing that's not what you meant." She laughed as she hopped over to me, wiping away my tears with her hand. "There we go. No more crying." She turned her head around the room. "Wow? Did you make all of these sculptures yourself? Well, I guess you didn't, but a version of you did, which means you could! Awesome work!"

I didn't know if this was the same Yael I'd encountered downstairs, or if something weird was going on, but I knew she wasn't a toy of g-gma's. This light, this energy... this was her.

"Please tell me what's going on," I begged.

"Oh, sure, no biggie. Kinda thought you'd figure it out, but it's all chill."

Yael wrapped an arm around my shoulder. "So you know what's going on here, right? Crazy alternate reality stuff."

I nodded.

"Right, well, I'm not a part of that. There's another Yael down there who, dammit, I'll admit it, I'm fucking jealous of. I should steal her crown before we go. Did I ever tell you about the time I stole a crown right off the head of this narwhal-obsessed king while he—"

I cut her off, grabbing her wrists and clapping her hands against her face.

Yael giggled. "Sorry. Bad habit. Point is, I'm the one and only, real Yael Pavnick. And I can't pull some badass mojo and save the day, but I can get you out of this."

"How can you do that? How are you alive?!"

"Pfffft! You think I'm alive? I took one of the worst beatings of my life, pushed myself to my physical limits, and then I was skewered. I'm dead as Hell. It's just not as big a deal for me as it would be for most others."

I cringed. "Please tell me this isn't more True Adventurer nonsense."

"Afraid so! I was running that power overtime to keep up with Kaya in our last fight, which also didn't help with the whole "staying alive" thing, learning as much about it as I could as quickly as I could because what choice did I have? When Kaya took me out, the power was still active, even if I wasn't thinking about it. And I had some choice last words The True Adventurer seemed to like."

"Man... we could have had such an awesome story."

"The True Adventurer kinda took that literally and found a way for me to stay a part of everyone's story. I was speaking to her, so it gave me a chance to remain a part of Kaya's life."

I shook my head. "I don't understand. Are you a spirit? A ghost? Tell me you're not a god; I will kill myself right now."

Yael just smiled. "Ruff Ruff."

I instinctively took a swing at her face, because what the fuck! Yael took the hit and laughed before pulling me into her arms.

"Don't worry, I haven't been pretending to be a dog for a year. Although that does sound fun. It's just my "soul" or whatever was used to grant Juri sentience inside you. She's had your back from within, and I've been inside her." She let me go and I backed away. "Why did you hit me? I know you've been curious about this."

"Yes! I have been! And you could have told me at any point or, I dunno, helped me with anything else!"

"I wish I was a spirit or a god that could have done more, but I'm not that powerful. This? We're only talking right now because you're so heavily tapped into The True Adventurer. Fortunately, since I'm kind of a part of The True Adventurer now, I think, getting you out of this is the one thing I can do. On top of the few ways I have already helped you."

The realization dawned on me. "You gave me The True Adventurer."

"And helped speed things up on the Glass Striker. Not to brag. It was a gamble sharing the power with you, but I knew you could handle it. Not because you're the great-granddaughter of Madame N'gwa. Because you're Layla."

I resumed crying, heaving with a smile on my face. Finally, I had a damn break.

Courtesy of the woman who'd taught me everything. The one who should have been fighting this war.

"Hey, hey, why more tears?"

This time, I wrapped my arms around her. "Because I missed you! We all missed you, and we all needed you, and everyone did really stupid shit without you! Everything is so messed up and wrong!"

Yael hugged me back, resting her chin on my head. "I've seen through your eyes what's happened to everyone. Especially..." Yael trailed off, sniffling.

I nodded. "I'm sorry about Molina and Kaya. I'm sorry I messed up when you could have had all of this, and I'm sorry I wasn't able to save—"

Yael cut me off, kneeing me in the stomach, really driving it in. "No. None of that. No blaming yourself for any of this."

"But I—"

"You're one brilliant kid who's been trying her best as long as I've known her. And I am so proud of everything you've been able to do." Yael wiped her eyes. "You're no hero. But you could be. Problem is, like everyone else, you've been doing what you thought I would have wanted. Only, and I'm not sure how you all missed this, I sucked! I lied, I cheated, I stole, and I don't regret any of it, but we fucked up so many people's lives in the process, good and bad. You have a better heart than I did. You want to fill the world with beauty. Focus on that."

"I'm not sure anymore that the universe wants beauty."

"Of course it does. The universe is girls like you and me. Big evil empires? They're just a disease making people forget what's really important. Cure the disease, most optimally with some brutally wicked, overwhelming violence, and everyone will eventually get their heads back on straight." Yael shrugged. "I dunno. Just my opinion. A hope that, deep down, most of us just want to live free."

I nodded rapidly, her words doing just a little to soothe my soul. "Thank you. But, for the record, I'll never see you as a bad person."

"Didn't call myself one." Yael sighed. "You've all suffered so much. Most of you have helped cause so much pain. But I know you can all still get your happy endings. I know you can save them all."

I squinted, arms wrapped around my gut. "Even Molina?"

Yael cringed. "My Moli is gone. This empress or whoever? I don't recognize her. I just want to be with my wife again."

"I don't understand."

"You will."

"Right. And Kaya? You still–?"

"Love her? With all of what passes for my heart these days. I promised her I'd always forgive her, and I meant it. The things she's done are irredeemable, but some would say the same of me, and unlike her, I made all my own choices. She deserves a chance."

My grin widened. Yael got it. Of course she did.

Yael reached out her hand. "Let's finish this. So I can rest and so you can stop fighting. So you can all live." She raised an eyebrow. "I can bring everyone back to reality, but that's it. You got a plan?"

I shook her hand. "Who do you think trained me?"

# CHAPTER 20: KAYA

"I'm sorry, I'm sorry, I'm sorry." I gasped.

Opening my eyes, I wasn't in the throne room. I wasn't in the palace. I wasn't even on Cykeb. I didn't know where I was.

Sitting up on the miserable cot I'd been given to sleep on, my back ached. The room I'd been put in was oddly shaped, octagonal, and had more in common with a jail cell than any kind of living quarters. The floor and ceiling were stone, the only light came from a lit torch, and the walls were some kind of tinted glass.

I'd just been dreaming. Thank the gods. It hadn't felt like a dream, it had seemed so real, but I wasn't about to snap a gift horse's neck in front of its mother. Kaybell was still alive. And whatever condition she was in when I returned to the palace, I would set things right. I would be free of my chains.

But first, I needed to be free of wherever the Hell I was.

I fired out widespread electrical blasts at the walls, only to be met with forcefields. Yuck. I knew what the inside of Utozex prisons and ships looked like. I'd studied them. Unless this was something new, this wasn't them. If it wasn't the Utozins, was it the Banshees? Had they used their powers to mess with my dreams?!

I widened my stance as I spat on the floor. If the Banshees as a threat were real, then I wasn't their only prisoner. They had Layla and the others, too. These old bitches were gonna pay with their lives for messing with me.

Focusing on my chest, I charged up a special energy I hadn't needed to access since I'd been upgraded with it. Forcefields had proven to be a weakness for me in the past. Mother had seen to having that weakness removed.

A burning orange flash released from my body. The forcefield around the tinted walls fizzled out and disintegrated. I smirked. Maybe I didn't want to be the big bad princess after all, but being loaded up with all the best Cykebian tech was still awesome.

With a normal energy blast, I easily blew a gaping hole in the now unprotected walls. I raced out of the room and into a much finer hallway, still torch lit, designed with 1000-year-old Cykebian architecture. The walls were covered with framed photos, artifacts and trinkets in glass cases sitting beneath them.

A quick look at one of the photos confirmed my suspicions. It was a group picture of a somewhat younger Madame N'gwa and a bunch of other Banshees. I didn't know them all, but I recognized some of the big names like The Librarian. Looking further, all of these photos were of N'gwa with different groups of Banshee on different planets. The contents of the glass cases had to be trophies; the spoils of crime.

"Gotta be kidding me," I snarled. "Madame N'gwa's whole issue with Layla was that she found meaning in stuff, not experiences. Yet here she is, keeping mementos. I thought this hag couldn't get more hypocritical."

"Talk to yourself a lot, child?" I spun around, flipping my hair and ejecting my katars. "No one loves you, so I'm guessing you do."

Madame N'gwa walked toward me, aided by a cane, dressed in a blood-red cloak, with raggedy, fingerless white gloves stretching down her arms, partially rusted bells decorating her from head to toe, and her eyes bulging out like a total freak.

"Big words from the old bitch whose family doesn't want anything to do with her," I said, clanging my katars against each other.

"My family is the Order," she said. "My children, their children? They mean as little to me as a peasant does to you. My interest in Layla was based on her potential, not on blood."

I snorted, stepping toward her. "Explain it to me like I look my real age, then. How is this different?"

"How are you different from me?" She cackled. "Apart from all the obvious ways, I mean. Your love is just as conditional as mine."

"That isn't true."

"Isn't it? We both offer our affection toward those who share our views. Those who, in turn, offer us validation. We may still care about others, but if a little hippie girl cannot understand what's best for her, neither of us is going to accept that."

I took my stance, ready to fight, sneering into her smug eyes. "Fine. Maybe I was operating like you. But unlike you, I'm ready to change. That dream world you put me in taught me that I have to."

N'gwa laughed. "Oh, child. That was no dream."

Screaming, I launched my attack, swinging my blades at her. She was lying. Trying to get inside my head. That's what all her words were.

This wasn't my first time fighting a Banshee.

Madame N'gwa pulled the same trick Yael did in our second fight, making alt reality copies of herself to die in her place as I succinctly bisected her fat-ass waistline three times in a row. Each time I hit her, a new version of N'gwa appeared behind me, jingling her bells to signal her existence to me. And unlike Yael had back then, N'gwa didn't seem to be feeling any pain.

"You know this can't end well for you!" I cried as I continued to chop up dupes, waiting for her to make a move I could actually do something against. Gaaah! I hated The True Adventurer! "Whether I win or lose, you and your band of phonies cannot win against the Empire!"

"Who said anything about winning against the empire?" N'gwa said. "I have no interest in politics or revolution. All that is important to me is the Order. Yael Pavnick was my prized student, and a dear friend of mine, but she betrayed my trust and besmirched the Order by abandoning it and stealing away its legacy; you are here not for being a princess, but for standing with her, and encouraging Layla's bad behavior."

"I encouraged her to be herself! To break her chains. To do the thing Yael thought you believed in doing!"

"You should know better than anyone that that's a child's view of the world. No one can be truly free. Even the humble farmer living all alone on a small moon is restricted by the knowledge that stepping away even an inch from his home will change everything for him. You speak of chains, but not everyone is bound by them. What we are all bound by is our ties, our bonds, and the threat of violence from those more powerful than ourselves."

A chill filled the air as I cut apart the 14th or 15th Madame N'gwa. "But I am Madame N'gwa. I never lose. And I fear no one."

My eyes widened as I spat out blood and squeaked. Madame N'gwa had plunged her arm straight through my stomach.

She giggled as I gasped.

"Impalement is one of your favorite ways to kill, isn't it? It's how you killed Yael."

This isn't real, this isn't real, this isn't real…

"I do not enjoy killing. I am not a fighter. The Banshees do not wield weapons, and we are discouraged from ever wielding The True Adventurer like one. But that is simply because they are unsavory. We are not wielders of violence. But against a mechanized mistake plaguing the stars like you? I happily make an exception." She grinned. "The stars may even applaud me."

Madame N'gwa tore her arm out of me, and I fell over to the floor, limp. This wasn't real. I had to fight it. I had to make my brain realize I wasn't dying.

"Heh."

I had an idea. A stupid one. The best kind.

Gathering my electric energy, I targeted it internally, shocking my brain. In ancient times, a technique like this had been used to attempt to "cure" those deemed mentally ill. Of course, it never worked. But I wasn't trying to cure a disease. I just needed to tell The True Adventurer to fuck off!

"Ugggh."

I weakly groaned and laughed. The pain was gone. I didn't see any hole in my stomach. But I also couldn't move. I'd cooked my brain. And with the attack having come from within, my body wasn't adapting.

Crap.

Madame N'gwa clapped. "Well done. Your fate is still sealed, but to counter The True Adventurer is no small feat. Perhaps an iota of your boasting is justified."

I panted. "Mother's gonna kick your ass. And if she fails? The best girl in the universe has this stupid power, too, and if I was able to escape your dream world, so will she."

She stood over me. "Like I said. I fear no one."

Madame N'gwa raised her leg, seemingly ready to squash my

head like a grape underneath her heel. Shutting my eyes, I hummed "Always Like a Bridge" for the last time.

SHINK!

Opening my eyes, I was still alive. And another Madame N'gwa was disintegrating. Instead of that hag, Molina stood over me, armed with a bloodied, one-handed sword, and dressed in leathers.

"Mother?" I squeaked. "You came. What… are you wearing?"

Molina smiled sweetly. "Something more appropriate for this form of combat than a uniform. Are you okay?"

I nodded fiercely. "Of course!"

"That's my princess." Mother turned to face the newest Madame N'gwa, the smug look on her face wiped away. "Rest easy. I will finish this."

One by one, Madame N'gwa cracked each and every one of her bones in rapid succession. Loudly. She pulled up the sleeves of her cloak, revealing her wrinkly arms.

"If you have made it this far into my home, then that means you have murdered at least one of my sisters."

"Two, actually. I would have cut apart Lioness' mane, but I was in a hurry."

Madame N'gwa shook her head, as angered as I'd seen her back when we freed Layla. "That shouldn't be possible. Not from you."

Mother snickered. "Six years ago, you allowed me to catch you. You humiliated me and destroyed my career. I was your pawn. And rightfully so. I was pathetic. Average." She raised her blade. "I now stand on the verge of total conquest of the universe. Utozex Prime has fallen, and in mere months, all Utozin worlds and all remaining independent worlds will fall. The stars will belong to me." Mother cocked her head. "Why would I ever allow any of you Banshees to inhabit them?"

Madame N'gwa narrowed her eyes. "I was planning on offering your daughter back to you. That will no longer be possible."

"Nor is it necessary."

Mother dashed forward, Madame N'gwa taking a step back to ready herself. What was it that Mother had said about Utozex Prime?

Madame N'gwa continued to be cut apart by Mother. "You can attempt to defend yourself, but I ensured I would be protected from your tricks as soon as I learned of them." Both mother's eyes and her blade glowed green. "And I also ensured I would be able to fight against them."

Mother slashed Madame N'gwa across the chest, actually making the old thief scream.

She'd only even survived thanks to a shockingly nimble leap back. "H-how?"

"I won't even attempt to understand the science behind it," Mother said. "You and your 'sisters' have attempted to do so for generations, but to no avail. Is it really a surprise that the resources of the greatest empire the universe has ever known could do in months what a gaggle of nobodies couldn't do in centuries?"

Of course. I'd told Molina all about what I'd learned. And even if I'd been a total idiot and forgotten about the Banshees, my brilliant Mommy hadn't.

Finally, Madame N'gwa was pissed.

"You really think you're something else, don't you?" she snarled. "But I remember the real you! The you I used and tossed away! The you I chewed up and spat out! The only respect a failure like you deserves is for stumbling into the second-greatest heist ever performed. Stealing the hearts of the brilliant and the powerful, and being cruel enough to secure your throne."

"I've heard it before. I suppose next you'll say the greatest heist was the empire's stealing of resources from the rest of the universe? Spare me. If it was so easy, anyone could have done it. My empire deserves everything it has."

"Your empire is as meaningless as you. No story, no history, no culture, just brutality and a galaxy of lies." She huffed. "Your wife may have defied me, but she was special. It's why you and everyone you pretend to care for with your little black heart has shaken the universe over her death. She made an impact, just by being herself. Who the Hell are you?"

Molina waved a blade in front of her face. "You're so preoccupied with stories. Maybe that's the real reason you couldn't figure out The True Adventurer's secrets. More concerned with the legend and your own mythos and legacy than the power it offered in the here and now."

"Power is only the aim of the weak and short-sighted."

"Power is the only thing that matters. To decide what is right and what is wrong. To decide who lives and who dies. To decide which stories are told and which stories are burned away forever. The type of stories you relish are nothing but distractions, and instigations of rebellion. That is why they must burn."

Madame N'gwa shook her head. "Yes, stories distract. They inspire and educate and entertain. When those in power are never anything but the likes of you, how else are people supposed to pretend there is hope?" She snorted. "What good is power if it won't even save you from the inevitable?"

"Everybody dies. There is birth, then life, then death, then nothing. What happens after I am gone is irrelevant to me. Power is not just how you instill your will, but how you protect yourself from that of others. I have hurt so much. But I will never hurt again."

Mother dashed at Madame N'gwa with her glowing blade once more. Madame N'gwa influenced her own body with The True Adventurer to give her a physique on par with the female wrestlers Yael loved to watch. She clashed with Mother, dodging the swings of her sword and getting in punches that actually made Molina stumble.

But it was futile. Without the full aid of The True Adventurer, there was nothing she could do. In an instant, Mother drove her sword through Madame N'gwa's heart.

"It seems, Madame, that a little more power really could have protected you." She ripped the sword out of her and the corpse of the greatest thief in the universe fell over. "You lose."

Holy crap. Mother was the coolest.

Molina sheathed her sword as she breathed and walked back over to me, kneeling. She opened her mouth, but before she said anything, I found the strength to pick myself up and hug her.

"Thank you, thank you! I love you!"

"I love you too, my princess. One of our final worries has been obliterated. Soon, the last of them shall fall."

I pulled back, grinning. "I... I have so much to tell you. And so many questions. There's so much I do not understand. So many things I'm worried about. But also things I can see more clearly than ever. Things I'm so excited about."

Molina ran her blood-stained hand through my hair. "The Cykerdroids should be finished sanitizing the house by now. Let's get back to *Ricochet Supreme*. We can discuss all of that after we've left this dreadful place and reduced it to rubble."

"Nah."

My heart fluttered and Mother's face fell as we heard that beautiful voice. Layla stood across the hall, a cocky grin spread across her face and the Glass Striker in hand.

"I think we should talk now. After all, there are only ten minutes left till your empire is completely dismantled."

# CHAPTER 21: LAYLA

The look on Molina's face was priceless. A nice, healthy mix of absolute contempt and utter bewilderment. I would have laughed, but the unexpected corpse of Madame N'gwa laying ten feet away from me really killed the mood. I just wanted to howl and cheer over that bitch finally being dead, but I wasn't about to thank the empress for that.

"What are you talking about?" Molina questioned as she helped Kaya stand.

I smirked. "You okay, Kaya?"

Kaya nodded, glowing. "Better than okay. I knew you'd get out of that dream world too. Look! Madame N'gwa is dead!"

I cast my smile down at g-gma's dead body before looking back up. "I had a little help."

"No sidetracking," Molina said, taking a few, proud steps forward. "What do you mean my empire is going to be dismantled?"

I giggled. "Sorry, I probably should have kept that to myself and waited for the right moment to reveal it, but that's not my style. And this is my show! So, I'm gonna do what I want."

Molina continued to glare at me, and even Kaya now showed

concern and confusion.

"Quick question of my own, empress: How much of our conversation actually happened before Madame N'gwa meddled? Because that's gonna determine a lot of how this goes."

She hesitated to give an answer.

"We haven't spoken in over a year. From the recordings we have, you, Kaya, P'Ken, Aarif, and Griffin were all abducted by Electric Ellie and Moonriver, simultaneously, mid-conversation. Any interaction you had with me during that time was them playing with you."

I bit my lip as I nodded. "Okay. Didn't call that one. In that case, hi! It's been a while, Professor! This actually gives you a few different options for how this goes then. First off—"

"Wait!"

Kaya cut me off just as I was really getting into the rhythm of this performance, getting in between Molina and me.

"I can see where this is going, and I won't let it get there," she said. "No more fighting. Not between us. Please. Layla, I know what you think you're doing. Mother, you have every reason to fear what she just said. Let's just all try and get on the same page, okay? Please? For me?"

I stared Molina down, and she stared back at me. We both immediately understood the mini-game that had just been initiated. Something had obviously shifted in Kaya. And now, whoever came off unreasonable, whoever acted as the aggressor, would have Kaya turn against them. She had the advantage in that Kaya's default was fighting for her. I had the advantage that Molina was pressed for time, but if she pushed, she'd only make things worse for herself.

"I got the time," I shrugged. "For your sake, Molina, we should make this quick." Molina continued to sneer for a moment before shifting her face into a sharp smile.

"Fine. Let's."

Kaya breathed a sigh of relief. "Thank you. Both. The fourteen-year-old shouldn't have to be the adult in the room. Hello!"

Molina and I both feigned giggles.

"Okay... so what the Hell happened on Utozex Prime?"

"The invasion continued without any of you present," Molina answered. "We were unable to locate Chancellor Shun, but the council she answered to was forced to surrender, and every major city has been seized and occupied. We won."

Kaya's smile was replaced with dread. "Oh no. I thought you said something like that during the fight, but..." She looked at me. "Layla, you understand The True Adventurer better than either of us. We were put in dream worlds, right?"

"Not exactly," I said in a comforting tone, unsure of what she was so afraid of. "We were put in, 'What if?' scenarios. I was sent to a world where I'd gassed everyone on *Ricochet* our last night there." I looked at Molina. "Every single one of us was living happily together as a family."

Molina didn't look much like she cared.

"Where did you go?"

Kaya held herself. "I was back on Cykeb. In the palace. Kaybell was in the throne room, all better and she... she helped me realize some important things. Before I accidentally killed her." She forced a smile. "But that's okay, right? Maybe it wasn't a dream, but if it was a fake reality, then it doesn't matter. Mother's still alive, right?"

I shut my eyes. There wasn't going to be anything fun about this next part.

"Kaya," Molina said, stepping forward and putting a hand on her shoulder. "Of course she is still alive." My eyes jolted open.

"We agreed she wouldn't die until the Authority fell and Shun was dead; only half of that has been achieved."

Kaya breathed a sigh of relief. "Okay. Okay, good!"

"Of course. Now, what are these things this fake version of Kaybell made you realize?" Kaya looked at me, then back to Molina.

"I don't want to live in the darkness. I don't want to be the monster I was taught I had to be. If she's really done something to destroy the empire, I'm not even sure I care. I want to live. I want to find out who I am, really. And I want to do it with Layla."

I knew the basics of what she'd been told. I would have killed to be a fly on the wall during the conversation.

"You're smarter than this," Molina said. "I'm sure you and this fantasy Kaybell had a wonderful, eye-opening exchange. But it was a fantasy. You know that the real Kaybell does not love you. That she hates you."

"But Layla said it wasn't a dream!" Kaya cried. "It was real. Probably just like, 'What if I'd been taken back to Cykeb?' or something. That was her!" Her heart raced as she panted. "Please. What's so wrong with me being someone else?"

"Yeah, what's wrong with her being someone else?" I shot Molina a cheeky grin as she glared at me. "If you can't accept that, I'd be happy to let you return to Cykeb to see the disaster-in-progress and take Kaya from her myself."

Molina continued to glare. Then she laughed. The laughter started maniacal, but soon, it was almost innocent.

"I have not done all of this to be left with no daughter and no empire."

"And what exactly have you done all this for?"

"I've done it for us!" she cried back. "My body was violated by my closest friend. My wife and father were murdered by my daughter.

My daughter was nearly murdered by one of the first people she ever trusted. And what was the root of all of this? Not any one person, or any singular group. Just the nature of the universe, and of humanity. The building of societies, the nurturing of differing ideals, and the inevitable clashes between them. When all of the universe is the Holy Cykebian Empire, all under my control, divergences will be eliminated. Over the next several generations, humanity will finally come together as a homogenized people. There will be no such thing as ideals, only the laws dictated by me, and my descendants. If people wish to distract themselves from the harsh conditions my precautions will create with entertainment or other useless things, they will be more than welcome. Those that thrive above the rabble will be those who dedicate themselves fully to us, proving their loyalty and use. And then, our family, wielding absolute power and dictating the rules of reality, will never be harmed again. I will do what Yael attempted but ultimately could not; I will keep us safe." Molina, shaking, drew her sword and pointed it at me. "Now explain what you have done!"

It wasn't an explanation that made me happy. There wasn't one of those that could have existed. But it was good to at least get some clarity before this all ended.

I shrugged. "Well, for starters, I blew your palace up."

Molina's eyes popped as she raced toward me. Kaya cried out for her to stop, but she wasn't listening. Pulling the Glass Striker to my mouth, I forged a turquoise spear, and clashed against Molina's blade.

---

WHACK!

"Is that anyway for a proud young lady to walk?"

"No, Ms. Amatyn. I'm sorry, Ms. Amatyn."

"It's quite all right, Meredith. So long as it doesn't happen a second time. Now, try again."

With Yael using her special powers to keep us invisible, the two of us watched as Assistant Headmistress P'Ken Amatyn of the St. Shiala School for Girls instructed a class of spoiled little brats on how to properly walk through a ballroom in a ballgown.

"This is if she never went with you, isn't it?"

"Mmhm. I think I wanna barf. Don't suppose you've got a bag."

"Yael… where the Hell would I pull a barf bag from?"

Yael cackled. "Ready to say hello?" I nodded.

Yael snapped her fingers. The young noble girls screeched as we became visible. That was pretty funny. P'Ken screeched too. That was even funnier.

P'Ken didn't stay afraid though. After the initial shock wore off, she noticed who'd just appeared. Her face and posture instantly crumbled.

"Ms. Amatyn, who are these commoners?" one of the scared girls questioned.

P'Ken's eyes glued themselves to Yael, who clicked her tongue at her. "Girls, class is dismissed early. I will address these… commoners."

I waited until the trepidatious nobles had all gracefully exited the room to say anything. "Your status is as real as this world!"

Yael wasn't so patient.

"What is this?" P'Ken asked.

Yael stuck out her tongue as she used The True Adventurer. We didn't have time to explain the details to everyone, but she could warp reality so that P'Ken had already figured it all out herself.

"Sorry, I know that probably feels pretty weird, but hey, not like I never put you through weirder stuff."

P'Ken's eyes wettened as she tore her dress and raced to wrap her arms around Yael. In the high-heels she wore, she was even taller than Yael than usual. Yael hugged her back.

"Hey kid."

P'Ken sniffled. "You're alive. Yes, I understand that you are technically dead. But you're here." She pulled back. "I warned you something like this would happen. I told you the Banshees would come after us."

"And you also said you'd have my back no matter what."

P'Ken's face lit up. "Always."

I bristled, blowing hair out of my eye. "A shame you couldn't understand what she'd actually want you to do with her gone. But now you can hear that from the woman herself."

Yael giggled. P'Ken... smirked? Huh?

"Please do not be mad at me," P'Ken started. "But I've been doing as she asked this entire time."

I cringed, ready to explode. "What?"

P'Ken laughed into her hand. "When we were escorting Kaya back to Cykeb, the plan was for all of us to try and integrate into life there. However, Yael and I anticipated there was a chance that any number of us could become corrupted by Cykebian society. In particular, those who would be closest to the throne: herself and Molina."

"Sooo, I asked P'Ken for a solid. In the event we both went all evil empress, play along, do whatever we say, and take us down from within; use my own playbook against us, knock some sense into us, and above all else, keep all of you kids safe."

My eyes flickered. Were they serious right now?

"I sent you off to art school, and I initially returned here to the school after Yael got herself killed, like an idiot..."

Yael raised her hands defensively.

"Because I really did need time to heal. But in the meantime, I was able to get a message to Griffin. He'd already begun working for Molina to protect Marcos, so I asked him to keep an eye on Kaya and be there for her if she needed anything. I told him I'd be there soon both to look out for him, and to take his place with Kaya, but Molina put me out in the field, and I couldn't question her."

"Still, we brainstormed a ton of ideas for the 'Break Glass in Case of Fashy Lesbians' case, and I'm sure at least some of the preparations I expect her to have made will line up with your own quite nicely."

I was going to kill them. I was going to kill P'Ken and I was going to kill Yael a second time.

I pinched my forehead. "You really couldn't have let me in on this? This is what I'd hoped you were doing!"

"You weren't supposed to be involved," P'Ken said. "And once you were, I had to stay in character."

I breathed out a long, angry sigh. I hated thieves.

"So hey, out of curiosity, what do you think of this life?" Yael asked. "If you could go back six years, would you still run away with me?"

"If that shy little girl who wasn't good for anything hadn't fled with you, you wouldn't have even beaten the Sunrisers, none of this would have ever happened, and my hands wouldn't be caked in the blood of innocents." P'Ken held Yael's hand. "But you gave me the chance to decide for myself who I wanted to be. And I wouldn't trade our years together or who I am now for anything."

P'Ken hugged Yael one more time, before flipping herself over and standing on her hands.

"Layla! On your hands! Tell me what it is you've been planning this whole time."

---

"Just let me do it!"

"I do not need your help!"

"I know you don't, I'm just trying to be nice!"

"Can you do it somewhere else?"

"This is my room!"

Yael and I, once again invisible, watched as, even fully aware that something wasn't right about where he'd been dropped, Griffin was still bickering with Marcos.

"So, they were actually into each other, huh?" Yael asked. "Gay."

Yael snapped her fingers, making us both visible inside Griffin and Marcos' remote house, downloading all the need-to-know knowledge into Griffin's head, and knocking out the fake Marcos.

"Yael. Oh my gods, it's—"

This time, I'd made sure I was in punching distance.

"That was for not letting me know what you and P'Ken were doing, jerk!" I shouted after knocking him over. "We were supposed to be pals!"

Griffin groaned as he rubbed his chin, having narrowly avoided hitting his head on the kitchen counter. "*You* were supposed to be safe at school."

"You still could have asked me if I wanted to help!"

Griffin shook his head at me before looking up at the cackling Yael. "You're really here."

"I mean I hope I'm not fake. I'd be getting a lot of false hopes up."

Yael reached her arm out and helped Griffin stand up. "I'm sorry."

"For what?" Yael asked. "You're not the guy I plan on suplexing today."

"For not doing more. I've been the only one to have Molina and Kaya's ears, and I couldn't push them in the right direction at all. I couldn't even keep Marcos safe." Griffin, choking up, bounced his head. "I suppose I really wasn't ready for the field."

Yael nodded along with Griffin. She then proceeded to lift him up and perform a German suplex on him.

"WOOH!" Yael cheered. "Gods it feels good to do that again!"

"What… the Hell?" Griffin croaked.

"You've done awesome," Yael said, helping Griffin up again. "You've helped keep Kaya stable, and you're the only reason Molina hasn't killed Marcos. You've played your gentlemanly part perfectly."

"But Molina—"

"Is a grown woman responsible for her own actions. Don't worry. I'll have all eternity to wring her out for this."

I still had no idea what she was talking about there. Griffin smiled. "Thank you."

"Of course! Now listen up. Cause we're gonna need you and your future partner's help."

---

After seeing where we'd landed next, I'd asked Yael to handle this one alone. She had no complaints about not speaking to the one person wrapped up in this she didn't love.

Having changed to blend in, putting on the Juniper Remedial Academy school uniform, consisting of a dark green blazer and skirt with a black shirt and green tie, I approached Shun at her locker.

"Remedial school?" I questioned.

Shun, dressed in the same uniform as me, slammed her locker shut and started walking away, books held to her chest. Her muscles were non-existent, her posture was relaxed, and her hair, usually found in long braids, was instead worn up, tied in intricate knots.

"I was a prodigy from birth," she said as I followed after her. "Had I decided as a toddler that serving the Authority's interests wasn't what I wanted from life, just playing dumb wouldn't have been an option; they would have seen through that. I had to fully present my true self. I had to present myself as—"

"Mentally unfit."

"Cheeky, isn't it?" Shun looked all around at the other students and at the murals painted on the walls. "It's difficult to believe this isn't real. Yael is something else."

"Yeah. She sure was. Ripping this band-aid off, Utozex Prime fell. The land has been occupied. Your council is gone. The rest of the Authority is falling easily without leadership."

Shun took a moment to respond. I'd planned on taking out the Authority anyway, but for her, this had to be a lot to process.

"I see."

"I see? That's it?"

"I may understand that none of this is real, but that doesn't change what I see here, and how it makes me feel."

She raised her wrist to show me her watch. "I've been here long enough to evaluate the state of the universe. It isn't perfect. Criminal operations I had personally dismantled remain active, and the Cykebian Empire, led by its emperor and empresses, is more powerful than ever, but…"

"But there's peace."

"Please stop cutting me off."

Shun turned to face me. "But yes, there is peace. For now. It isn't something that can be trusted forever, but it is obviously better than a reality where my home has been stolen. One where, even if I were to help liberate it, you would just attempt to burn it down."

I narrowed my eyes. "Are you saying what I think you're saying?"

Shun smiled like an actual kid for once in her life. "You want my help, right? My remaining resources? I'll give you the names and contact information of everyone you need to talk to, and the right words to say to each of them."

"I... don't know what to say. Shun, this isn't real. This was meant to torture you."

"It seems real enough to me. It may have been designed as a prison, but I see an opportunity." She shut her eyes, pressing together and curving her lips. "I wonder how many other hidden geniuses are here. It's no wonder that, when the council typically had no place for people like me, they couldn't foresee what Yael as empress would mean."

She opened her eyes. "The year I spent playing school with you all was the best year of my life. So I'm going to keep playing school. And when I'm done? I can do anything I want to."

"But—"

"Why do you care?"

I looked at her with my mouth hanging open.

"Not so nice being interrupted, right?"

I shook my head. "I hate you. I do. But you're just as much a product of the Authority as Kaya is of the Empire. You can find freedom in the real world."

"You'll let me? Kaya will let me? No. This is my choice. This is where I will be free."

I wanted to argue with her. I really wanted to hit her with a giant hammer again. But then, that was part of the problem. Was she running away from her problems instead of fighting to fix them? Yes. But for the first time in her life, she wouldn't be hurting anyone.

That was her choice.

"Fine," I resigned. "But as soon as I get better with True Adventurer myself, I'm coming back here to check on you."

She smirked. "I'm starting to think you never had it in you to kill me."

"Heh. How could I ever be so heartless as to kill some random, high-school girl?"

---

This last one had to be all Yael.

Out of everyone in our family, Aarif was the oldest. He'd made more choices in his life than any of us. But the alternate decision he was living with was the most recent.

Griffin sat at the helm of *Cascade* with Marcos next to him. P'Ken sat in the captain's chair with a well-built Aarif leaned against the console. A happy band of thieves, in a universe not too different from the ones Shun and I had been stuck in. Yael was still dead, but I was off living in the palace on Cykeb with the royals, and the universe was not at war.

Aarif had given me Kaya's message.

Making herself visible, Yael sped across the bridge, knocking out each of the other crew members before reaching Aarif and delivering the brain download.

"Hey dude," she said. "Guess who's been an indescribable being living inside our dog living inside our student for the past year."

Aarif bear hugged her, instantly in tears. "Of course you are." Yael patted him on the back. She then German suplexed him.

"That was for siding with my evil wife over a dog! I love Juri too, but come on, man!"

Aarif peeled himself off the floor, unintentionally cracking bones in the process. "I did what I thought was right. I was trying to keep Layla safe, too." He held out his arms to his sides. "Really fucked that one up, huh?"

Yael smiled and held his shoulder. "Yes, you did. Ready to try and fix things?"

Aarif gripped her wrist as he took a breath. "Do you hate me?"

"No, I do not hate you. Not like I never made any big fuckups myself. You all really mythologized me way too much." She giggled. "It's you and me forever, Brother."

Aarif smiled back at her. "There has to be some way you can come back. Come back, use your magic to give Juri her own body…"

"It's not happening. Honestly, you're our penultimate stop, and I'm getting exhausted. This story isn't getting a nice, pretty bow wrapped around it. But we can still give everyone in the universe an apology present for starting all of this."

Aarif tried to speak, but the tears gushed as he fell back into Yael's arms.

"Hey, hey, no crying, please no crying. Didn't you hear I'm tired?"

"Sorry. I just… don't know what I'm gonna do after this."

"Do what I can't. Live."

Aarif laughed through his tears.

"Can I ask you for one last thing? Before we go? I know it's something you've got on-hand."

Yael narrowed her eyes, uncertain. "What's up?"

"Heh. Could you tell me your top ten favorite things about being magic?"

---

The last stop wasn't like the others. It was a quick one. Just to bring Kaya back to reality and go. That didn't make it hurt any less to see her sobbing over Kaybell's dead body.

"What happened here?" I asked.

"More than one thing," Yael answered. "It's tricky to decipher.

I think N'gwa must have gotten help from some other Banshees for her."

Since reuniting with her, Yael had been a presence, just like always. She'd shown plenty of different emotions, sure, but she'd stayed calm and in control all throughout. Seeing Kaya like this changed that.

"Thank you," Yael said, breathing heavily and choking up. "For caring so much about my daughter. I'm not sure if I already said that."

I put an arm around Yael. "She's my friend. And a victim. Nothing was gonna stop me from helping her."

"And you were prepared to burn down the entire universe to do so. Who taught you to do something as crazy as that?"

We laughed together.

"I guess this is where I get off, isn't it?" I asked. "The last goodbye?"

"For now. If you can ever figure out how to do all this, maybe we can meet again."

I looked up. "Sculpting an entire universe. The ultimate challenge for an artist."

Yael and I hugged.

"I want you to listen to me carefully. Okay? You listening?"

"Yes."

"Good. Two things. First, when you do figure out how to craft realities, I need there to be lots and lots and lots of noodles and beer and gummies and wrestling tapes and porn. I have been so hungry and so bored."

I almost fell over laughing, but I held it together. "And the second thing?"

Yael took one last breath, calming herself. "I love you. And once you're done cleaning up my story, you're gonna have a brilliant one of your own. And I'm so excited to see that through your eyes. Whatever you face, you're never alone."

I couldn't not cry again too. "I love you, too." I paused. "Nothing to say about Molina?"

"Nothing else to say. I'll take care of her. Like I've been saying. Just bring her back to me."

---

Molina was stronger than I'd expected. It wasn't too surprising that she'd obtained weapons and enhancements to counter The True Adventurer. That was how she'd killed Madame N'gwa. What was so surprising was then when she hit, she hit like Kaya.

In the initial clash, she'd cut the spear right off my pipe. I'd jumped back and started firing off shards and blocks to keep her at bay, but she'd run straight through them, tanking some and slicing apart others. A high kick to the face launched me up against the ceiling, cracking it, before she caught me as I fell in her free hand, holding me by my shirt collar.

"What. Have. You. Done?!"

"Both of you stop!" Kaya cried. "Stop fighting! I don't want to watch anyone else I love die. Please."

Molina glared into my flickering eyes. "Just talk."

"Okay," I laughed. "Sure. But you won't like it. See, Kaya didn't break out of the alternate reality Madame N'gwa put her in on her own. I pulled her out. And I also pulled out P'Ken, Aarif, and Griffin. Had some nice talks with them. Funny story, P'Ken and Griffin have been double agents this entire time."

Molina's eyes couldn't have been wider and filled with more rage. "Oh, they love you, Kaya, but just like me, they've been wanting to help you. And a good smacking was all that was needed to get Aarif's head on straight."

Molina tore the Glass Striker from my hands and put me through a wall. I landed in a cozy den that you'd expect to belong to a normal little old lady.

"Gets better," I said, forcing a smile while trying to evaluate how many bones she'd just broken. "Shun was in there too. Didn't actually want to come back, so I'm gonna have to take care of her body I guess, but hey, she gave the keys to the remaining Utozin forces!"

Molina tried to crush me underneath her boot, but I rolled out of the way, jumping up to my feet mid-roll.

"Now, as you might be able to imagine, those are all some very useful allies to have on my side, especially when no one knows your allies are traitors."

Molina came at me with her sword once more, but with each swing, I ducked and dived out of the way.

"Once I'd found everyone in the real world, we got to work. P'Ken was step one. Sending out a brief report from the respected, revered, and feared Captain Amatyn to every intergalactic news source worth a damn that Utozex Prime had fallen, but Empress Molina and Princess Kaya had been tragically killed fighting against The Order of the Banshee."

"WHAT?!"

Both royals were outraged. Good. Stay that way.

"Crazy, right? Less crazy and more expected, Prince Megz and Princess Morphea both instantly started laying down claims to the throne, adding even more chaos to the mix. If you're wondering why you haven't been alerted about any of this via com, you can thank Griffin. Or, more specifically, you can thank Marcos and Jellz. Griffin made a call to some of his friends amongst the guards and had them released from your dungeon in response to an explosion within the palace. Where did the explosion come from, you ask? Well, that one was me, but also sorta Kaya. You know Popcorn? The new shipping company who you've been commandeering ships from? Yeah, that was mine. The inheritance I got from Yael was really nice, and Kaya's been buying all sorts of products from it for the last year. I made sure to be manufacturing certain products I knew would interest her myself, so that I could fill them with near undetectable micro explosives for an occasion like this!"

I got a little carried away feeling awesome and took a diagonal sword slash across my stomach and chest because of that.

"You're insane!"

"I mean that's what you're into, isn't it?"

My whole torso was bleeding, but I'd live. A torn shirt would just get in the way though, so I ripped the rest of it off, leaving just my sports bra underneath.

"But yeah, Morphea and Megz naturally instantly blamed each other for the explosions, causing the fighting between their factions to already get physical. But my hackers weren't done, no, no, no. Once they had tablets in hand, I was able to get a message to them, and the universe was at our fingertips to play with. Economies, bank accounts, data storage, security codes, everything! All made easy-peasy with my double agents' inside knowledge, and the way you've centralized so much. I know, I know, this all happened so fast, but that's what a year of prep from two brilliant women gets you!"

I couldn't dodge Molina's next sword swing, so I went full doggo, claws and fangs coming out, and caught her blade between my hands. The look in her eyes made clear there was no interest in simply beating me and keeping me alive for Kaya; she was going for the kill.

"Everything is going up in flames, Molina. And while I'm here fighting you, and Marcos is continuing to destabilize the digital ecosystem that governs all our lives, I've left P'Ken in charge of all remaining Utozex fleets. They may not be able to win and bring victory to the Authority, but revenge and spite are as good motivators as any!"

Pulling myself up by the sword, I kicked Molina back and sent her stumbling. "Now, you might be wondering: what about Aarif? What could he possibly do from here?"

"You've been upgraded," Molina seethed.

I giggled menacingly.

"Close!"

I'd been talking loudly this whole time. That had two effects. One? Dramatic. And two?

It made sure the best girl knew where we were.

The ceiling above Molina was broken through as another me, controlled by Juri, came from above and, on her way down, grabbed Molina's head and smashed it into the floor.

"Mother!"

Kaya charged herself up, but I couldn't let her get in the middle of things. I dived for the Glass Striker, pulling it away from Molina's clutches, and put Kaya in a yellow sphere while she was still screaming at me to stop this.

"Dammit, Layla! I wanted things to change, but not like this!"

While I leaped away from Molina, Juri walked right up to the entrapped Kaya. Kaya looked back into her eyes.

"Juri?"

Juri smiled back at her. "Hello, Princess. You gave me treats and belly rubs. Please stay safe."

"No," Kaya said, as Molina, bleeding all over her face and more pissed than ever, stood up. "No, you don't understand! You're spoiling everything! Kaybell is still in the palace! She should be taking charge! She is the emperor! She—"

"Kaybell is dead!"

Time froze as I uttered that truth. It was a truth I'd learned with Yael before we parted ways. Kaya's alternate reality prison had been set under two conditions. First, that she'd returned from Cykeb after the attack on Utozex Prime. And second, that she be confronted by her healthy mother, with the likely expectation that she'd lash out and kill her. And once Yael knew what had been warped, she'd been able to figure out what was reality.

"Kaya, your mother has been dead since your birthday. I'm so sorry."

"No. No! That isn't true! Mother, tell me that isn't true!"

What little actual emotion Molina was still capable of mixed in with her rage as she panted. "I apologize for the deception, my love. But with how she hurt us both, I believed you would enjoy looking forward to killing her together after we'd—"

Kaya shrieked. I had never met Kaybell, the real Kaybell, but I could still feel her pain.

Molina looked behind her at Juri, then back to me. Killing me was no longer just her intention. It was the only thing on her mind.

"I wanted to protect us all. But if you're all just traitors... then you can die with everyone else!"

Molina dashed at me, faster than I could process, and body checked me, smashing her shoulder into chin and knocking me through three different walls. That one wasn't so easy to just walk off.

"I do not understand you, Layla," Molina said as she approached me. "What are you even seeking? It cannot be to make the universe a better place. If the scope of what you're describing is what you claim it to be, then society is done for! There will be no structure, no security. People will eat each other alive!"

"Yeah. Yeah they might." Barely able to stand, I pushed myself up. "Or maybe they'll come together! Build something better! Different people will do different things, but starting from scratch, maybe, just maybe, we can build equal and free societies. For once."

Molina arrived in front of me.

"The 'distractions' you write off? They're what make us who we are. They're what make life worth living. And everyone deserves the chance to live their life however they dream. I'm giving them that chance."

Molina looked me up and down. "You're out of fight, aren't you? Without your weapon, without your power, you're nothing but an obsolete cyborg. Like all things from the past, you no longer have a use. And once I have disposed of you, I will clean up your mess. I will rebuild my empire, but this time, in my own image, exactly how I wish it to be. Those who cling to stories, cling to dreams, will be purged!"

I bent over and coughed up blood. "Honestly. How do you say all of that and not realize you're the bad guy?"

"Countless people have no doubt already died because of your immature arrogance. You're hardly the good guy."

"Of course I'm not. We were never the good guys. I'm no hero." I grinned. "But I could be."

Molina charged me again. Absorbing Juri back into me and getting access to the upgrades Aarif gave my other self, I could react to her this time. I raised my pipe, brought it to my mouth, and performed my final—!

"Guh."

The Glass Striker fell from my hand and hit the floor. I hadn't been fast enough. Looking down, Molina had driven her sword straight through me.

"All you have done is delay the inevitable," Molina said. "Once I have watched you die, I will come for the rest. I will kill each and every one of you traitors, myself. I will build a new family, one loyal to me and me alone. And the empire we rule over will last forever!"

Two more blades were driven through me. But they went through Molina on the way. "Kaya…"

Tears in her eyes, Kaya had broken free from her sphere. "You… lied to me."

Kaya ripped out her katars, and both Molina and I fell over onto our sides. Kaya dropped to her knees. None of us said anything. I was going to die. And so was she. But I'd done what I had to do. And Kaya would have everyone else to look after her.

"Yael?" Molina broke the silence. "Yael, is it really you?"

"What are you talking about?" Kaya asked.

She crawled to me. "What is she talking about?"

I coughed up way too much blood. "I dunno. But I think it's a good thing."

Rather, I was sure it had to be whatever Yael had been talking about.

"Yes. Yes I have. But all for you. For us. No. No, no. Damn you." Molina broke down crying, tears mixing with her blood. "I hate you. No. I don't. I can't. Yes. I do. Yes. I still love you."

Molina focused her uneasy eyes on me. "Why… didn't you tell me?"

Those were her last words. Molina Langstone died in front of us. Maybe. At this point, it was hard to tell.

Kaya clung onto me, sobbing.

"No. No! Not again. Layla, do not die. I didn't mean this! Please!

I'm sorry! I'm sorry I'm like this!"

She screamed. With the little energy I still had in me, I grabbed her wrist. "Then be... who you want to be."

I was ready to go. I really was. I'd known it was likely this could happen. And even if I didn't get to live all my dreams, I had to believe things would turn out okay.

"Layla!"

I grinned. Living really was better, though.

P'Ken, Aarif, and Griffin arrived, with the former immediately moving to put pressure on me, barking at the others to treat my wounds.

"Princess, I know there's a lot happening, but do you want to save her, or do you want to kill us all? If it's the latter, I implore you to please just get it over with."

Kaya looked at my friends, then at me, then back. "How can I help?"

## CHAPTER 22: KAYA

"Go fetch!"

The day was starting to wind down, so I gave Juri a break and only tossed the stick 1000 yards away. Making the most of her recently obtained, beautiful, brown-furred body, she dashed away to try and catch it before it even touched down on the ground.

None of us were too sure if she was still as sentient as she was when she'd been inside Layla. Juri had always been a smart doggo, and she couldn't talk, so it was hard to tell. We didn't know which one of them Yael was in now, if either. Layla really needed to figure out more about The True Adventurer faster so we could figure out exactly what happened to Yael and Molina.

I'd considered hunting down a Banshee and torturing her for information… but I was trying to not do that kind of thing anymore.

'Kaya, get over here! Food's almost done!"

"Coming!"

In perfect timing, Juri returned with the stick and handed it to me. "Good girl, such a good girl," I said, scratching her head.

I ran along the rocky white surface underneath the hot pink sky,

Juri following behind me, toward the campfire where Layla, P'Ken, and Aarif were cooking a whole duck. It smelled delicious.

While we could all only hope Layla's gamble had been well placed and it would pass, populated planets weren't safe right now. Civilian riots were happening everywhere, Megz and Morphea were still clinging to the past and attempting desperately to fight a war against one another, and Cykebian nobles and high-ranking Utozins alike were all trying to build their own bases of power in this new status quo.

Toss in that all of these parties had a vested interest in me being dead, and the fact that if anyone ever found out Layla was behind what had happened, she'd be the most hated woman in the stars, and we'd decided hiding out on their old home of MCV-2 was our best bet until things blew over and the new normal was established.

Sitting down on a log by the fire, right outside the castle that had once been a school, I made myself comfortable. Layla sat cross-legged in a super pretty tie-dye dress, feeling her biceps. Like the first time I'd nearly killed my big sis, she'd needed cybernetics to stay alive. This time, I'd been happy to offer up my own. Even with Juri's robot parts removed from Layla along with her consciousness, she was still a cyborg. I still had some of my weapons and my enhanced strength, but I was over 90% organic now. Being as strong as she was now must have felt amazing; I'd know.

Aarif, working on our dinner, still refused to dress well, wearing a white tanktop and jeans. He'd also had the tattoos that covered his entire body removed. A decision that had landed him and P'Ken in their only scrape in the last two weeks. He claimed it to have been worth it, though. The universe was starting fresh, and he was ready to dream again. He needed a fresh canvas.

P'Ken, monitoring the status of our late arrivals on her tablet, wore one of her native Benkinian dresses. While the rest of us had fled Madame N'gwa's estate together, she'd had a stop to make on her own; she was the only one of us who still had someone outside the group she was worried about, apart from Layla's college friends, who she was pretty sure would want nothing to do with her. She'd flown to Benkin, picked up her mother Lulu which, shockingly, hadn't required any force, and brought her here for safety. That meant that with all of us out here, the castle was currently occupied by her and...

Shun. Even now, I still wanted her dead for all she'd put me through. But if she really wasn't in the body laid out inside the castle, and she could never hurt me again, then it wasn't worth hurting myself to finish her off.

"Mmm," Aarif hummed, tasting the duck. "That's the stuff. How much do you want, Princess?"

"Not too much," I said. "And I told you. Stop calling me Princess."

I couldn't believe I was saying that, but if there was no empire, then I wasn't royalty. And I didn't need to be a princess to be awesome. I didn't know what I wanted to be instead, but I'd figure it out. For now, I got to enjoy some duck in my EZ Street t-shirt, red leather pants, and high-heeled ankle boots.

Layla stopped feeling her muscles for two seconds and picked up the Glass Striker. "Colors?"

"Blue."

"Black."

"Yellow."

Layla did as we asked and blew glass plates for each of us in our requested colors, along with a pink one for herself. Apparently, she'd never gotten the chance to use the Glass Striker's most powerful attack. I still wanted to see it one day, but for now, I'd settle for it being handy around the house.

"Thank you," I said. "Hey, do you wanna spar after dinner?"

Okay. Maybe I wasn't so patient. But it wasn't like there was a whole lot to do around here!

"Do I want to fight you after we've just finally finished fighting for real, and my belly is full?" Layla giggled. "Maybe in the morning."

While Aarif served the rest of us our dinner, Layla pulled her own from a lunchbox, consisting of celery sticks and hummus. If I ever thought I was getting chubby, following Layla's diet was probably the easiest solution.

A cruiser descended from the sky, landing mere meters away from us. The others were here. As we all cheered and applauded, the people who'd made victory possible stepped out… and also Griffin was there.

The plan had been Layla's, and she'd received a ton of assistance from Yael and P'Ken, but none of it would have mattered if she didn't have the two greatest computer geniuses in the stars on her side.

Jellz took a deep breath in and out. "Ahhh, freedom!"

"Yes, freedom which I'm sure you'll use to go camp out on some far less hospitable world in isolation when we're done here," Marcos said, rolling in their chair, holding Griffin's hand. "Idiot."

"Who are you calling an idiot?! I saw your code. It. Was. Sloppy!"

"Sloppy?! How can you call mine sloppy when yours barely functions?!"

"It gets the job done."

Griffin sighed. "They were like this the whole ride here. Big piece of duck, green plate, please."

Layla and Aarif got their plates and food together as the men and Marcos sat down. It really shouldn't have taken so long to get the hackers here from Cykeb, but with how turbulent things were, I could hardly accuse Griffin of dallying.

"Welcome back, guys," Layla said.

Marcos snorted. "I leave you alone for twelve months and you put me in a position where I have to destroy society. You're something else."

"Missed you too, buddy."

Marcos grinned, squeezing Griffin's hand.

Had those two... nah? No way. I guess doing everything Griffin had for them was pretty romantic but...

No. No, I hoped they were fucking. I shipped it.

"Well you won't catch me complaining," Jellz said. "You just made the stars a playground for thieves! I'm half-tempted to get back in the game!"

"Sounds cool so long as you don't work with any Banshees," Aarif said, passing around beers to everyone but me.

"Pfft. Of course not. They're way below the level of my clientele."

I smiled into the fire. A nice home. Good food. Family. Was this all I needed? No. No, absolutely not, I needed lots more. But it was a really nice start.

"So," I said, everyone turning their eyes to me. "Um, first, sorry for torturing you, Marcos."

"Fuck you too. Continue."

I rolled my eyes. "What are we all doing next?"

The fire crackled as everyone waited for someone to be the first to answer.

"Well, I don't know about the rest of you, but I've had an idea you may be interested in," P'Ken said. No one butted in, everyone waiting for her to elaborate. She gestured with her head to the castle.

"While we all may believe that sweet Layla's vision for the future will pan out, it seems inevitable that making an honest living for the foreseeable future will be a difficult feat for many to accomplish. As Jellz said, thieves are going to live well. We made this mess. Let's teach anyone who wants to learn how to survive it."

"Awww," I cooed, pressing my hands against my chest. "That's sweet."

"I like it too," Layla echoed. "Smart thinking."

"Of course it is." P'Ken held her arms out. "Would anyone like to join me?" She narrowed her eyes and smirked at Aarif.

Aarif snickered as Juri ran over to him to lick him and get pets from her still-favorite human.

"Yeah. Yeah, that sounds nice. I can teach engineering and basic life skills, and you can teach them how to pretend to be evil and lie to your friends for a year."

"You joke, but long-term infiltration could absolutely be a class. But we'll need more teachers for that wide a curriculum."

Another pause. This time, it was broken by Jellz's laughter. "Know what? This sounds more fun than being a manager again."

"I don't believe myself to be ready to teach, but if you could help me complete my studies, I'd be more than happy to," Griffin followed.

P'Ken nodded, pleased. "Ladies? Marcos? Please don't leave me with nothing but men."

BARK!

"Apologies. Men and Juri."

I looked at Layla, who didn't seem to be paying attention anymore, just crunching her celery. I was going to cut my own path, but I couldn't do it alone. Wherever Layla went, I'd follow her.

"I'm never working for anyone again," Marcos said. "I learned enough to build my own operation." They smirked. "But it's not like I need to physically be anywhere else to do that. So I guess I may as well live here."

Griffin kissed their cheek. "Yes. You may as well."

"Hate you," Marcos cringed, trying desperately, and failing, to hide how much they loved him. OTP!

Now it wasn't just me. Everyone was looking at Layla. She noticed and wiped her mouth. "I'm happy that you'll all be sticking together, but—"

Everyone else groaned.

"Hey, hear me out! It's great that you'll be helping people survive this bold new world, but I never wanted to be a thief, and that hasn't changed."

"Then what will you do, dear?" P'Ken asked. "Returning to college isn't exactly an option."

"Yeah, things finished messier than I'd hoped." She smiled up at the sky. "I don't know." She looked at me. "What about you, Kaya? Any ideas?"

"M-me?"

"Yeah! If we could go do anything after we said goodbye in a few weeks, what would you want to do? Just the first thing that comes to mind."

Anything. I could pick anything. And I did. The first thing my heart told me to do.

"I want a funeral." Our smiles faded as I hung my head. "I know you already had a small service for Yael and that she's still living on inside... one of you... but her body is buried underneath the school, right? Uncle Megz had Kaybell's body buried and held a private funeral for her, but Molina hasn't gotten anything. I know it's stupid, but even after everything she did to the universe, and to me, I still want to give her this."

I didn't know if Molina really had loved me, if I'd just been her weapon, or if she'd only sought to manipulate me to hurt me. But I did know she wasn't always the type of woman who could want to hurt me like that. I'd killed her. Just like I'd killed Yael. If they really were together again, maybe Yael could help Molina find the woman she used to be.

Layla smiled at me from across the campfire, while also using The True Adventurer to hug me from behind.

"I think that's a great idea. It's what Yael would have wanted. That one I'm sure of."

I beamed back at her, some of the others smiling as well, while others made clear they wouldn't be attending. Whatever. A family didn't need to do everything together.

I wished I could have attended Kaybell's funeral. It was my fault she'd been killed. If I hadn't let Molina turn me against her, things could have been different. I couldn't live for her. That isn't what she would have wanted. I had to do what felt right. I'd broken my chains. Now I had to decide what freedom meant.

"Thank you. And, once that's done… I had another idea?"

Layla giggled. "I'm all ears."

I leaned my head against Layla's. "Let's find a bunch of boy bands, help them if they need help, and organize a big show with all of them!"

"Kaya, that is the silliest, wildest, most childish thing you could have said. Let's do it."

Milton Keynes UK
Ingram Content Group UK Ltd.
UKHW040256291024
450401UK00006B/75